Like a
CHILD'S
New TOY

Jermain L. Reeves

Magical Thinker

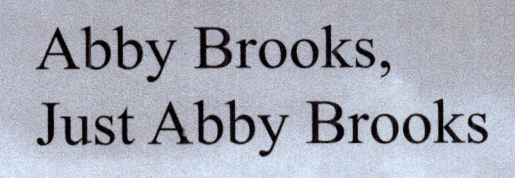

PART I:

Abby Brooks,
Just Abby Brooks

1

There are two things you should know about Abigail Brooks Worthington: she was cold-blooded and insecure. Though she could fake confidence in a crowded room, when alone she sometimes saw an image that had frightened her for years. But then again, a ghost would frighten anyone—no matter how young it was, no matter how adorable its attire, no matter how brief and infrequent its visits. Before long, you'll also know Abby was a bruised and lonely woman who couldn't deal with the past.

The problem was that Abby, at thirty-five years old, was too consumed with her appearance to take time for introspection. This explained why she was wearing a pair of pumps, an animal-print skirt, a black silk blouse, and a pair of oversized sunglasses. Abby had a small frame—short and thin by anyone's standards—but that didn't stop her from looking in the mirror and seeing an overweight woman staring back at her. Her face was as smooth and bright as her porcelain teeth, which looked even brighter against the crimson lipstick she had bought in France the previous summer. She boasted a narrow face with cheeks that were partially covered with brown hair that stopped just beneath the back of her neck. Her hazel eyes were set underneath arched eyebrows, just above her thin nose.

Abby was prone to walk through a restaurant without acknowledging anyone's existence, except those who required a small degree of attention, like a cashier or a valet. And she always made it a point not to associate with blue-collar workers. Consorting with them, in her mind, would reveal one thing about her that she wanted no one to know: that she herself was from a blue-collar family. In fact, she had lived in a trailer with cinder blocks substituting for a front staircase. But anyone who saw the way she was walking in this café would never guess the poor environment she had grown up in.

Abby had been to the Dough House Café enough times not to notice the sugary smell of baking bread or the aroma of brewing coffee. Her only concern was whether or not the other patrons could smell her designer perfume, which was part of the reason she skipped five people to get to the front of the line. A smirk stole over her face when imagining what the people behind her must be thinking. Though she cared little for the taste of French vanilla, she ordered it merely for the way the phrase rolled off her tongue when she spoke to the young male cashier.

The twenty-three-year-old man behind the counter was amply built—tall and muscular—with dark skin and deep eyes set just above a well-defined jawline. He had a bald head and a face free of facial hair, revealing a countenance that showed his discontent with his job. His ears were adorned by a pair of fake diamond earrings that sparkled despite their lack of authenticity. Wearing a white T-shirt, his shoulders were broad enough to make Abby forget he was wearing an apron. *He looks sexual,* Abby thought, *like fresh human cargo from sub-Saharan Africa.*

When the register showed the price, Abby removed her right glove and fumbled around in her purse for her American Express charge card, despite having cash. The young man took the card, swiped it, and said, "Here you go, ma'am," before returning the card along with Abby's purchase.

"Thank you," Abby responded, glancing up from her purse at the man, struck by the whiteness of his teeth.

The cashier—temporarily ignoring the next customer—smiled and stared at this overdressed woman as she exited the café holding a pastry and a cup of coffee. Abby didn't necessarily want these items but had bought them because the small indulgence made her feel upscale and sophisticated. After walking outside, Abby wiped her face with her re-gloved hand when a flurry fell from the sky and hastily melted on her nose. Having lived in Boston for years, the weather in South Carolina didn't bother her. But her instant attraction to the cashier weighed on her mind. Somehow he had had a wealthy New England smile that reminded Abby of her old home.

With a cup of coffee in her lap, Abby drove, turning and stopping slowly to avoid spilling the beverage on her garments. During the short drive to her new South Carolina home, the image of his white teeth resonated with her as the salty wind blew through the slightly open window and thumped against her left ear. Though the cashier's image stuck with her, Abby attempted to shrug it off as a childish fantasy.

The South Carolina coast didn't offer her the solace once found in the fast-paced crevices of Boston. Life down here was slower in every way it could be. These people walked down the street as if the wind pushed upon their bosoms. They spoke like molasses, as if it pained them to finish talking. "Fine-n-you?" was one word to them, and "How you?" was a verb-free sentence conveying all of the trappings of sentiment typifying Hilton Head, a small tourist city.

By the time she turned into the driveway, her coffee had disappeared, and all that was left of her Danish were a few crumbs left in the white bag. Abby lived on a road full of remodeled mansions with lawns that had replaced an antebellum cotton field with green grass, dogwood trees, lavenders, and lily-white gazebos. Abby's home was the original plantation house. Though it was the oldest home in the area, it fit right into this neighborhood, save for the beautiful roses growing neatly up the front of the house. Owning the most historic home in miles was Abby's way of upstaging her neighbors, whom she mocked for never having had to work for anything. She envied their natural look of aristocracy, which she tried so hard to imitate. To maintain her carefully crafted façade, Abby Worthington never told them her story.

Abby looked forward to sitting in the morning room and writing until noon. This ritual started as a catharsis that would hopefully help her deal with her two-year-old divorce and the loneliness of this low-country island. But writing became an addictive passion that changed her life by giving her meaning she once thought could only be found in Boston. She originally decided to write because she loved the thought of becoming a published author, but eventually she began to write to heal. It gave her an escape from the way her life had turned out.

She wrote to channel the negative emotions that were brought on by her divorce. Her husband had rejected her, which made the rejection letters from several New York publishers even more hurtful. After getting those letters, she lost her confidence. Abby, accustomed to writing longhand, was upset that she had spent so much time transferring her writings from her notebooks to her computer, only to be met with rejection. She had assumed a collection of semi-autobiographical short stories would appeal to the masses, but her assumption turned out to be as flawed as her marriage.

Fortunately, Abby did not *need* to be a professional writer and could write off and on without selling a single book because her divorce settlement would keep her financially secure for the rest of her life. She could afford to take breaks from writing, though her heart could not afford the painful rejection of her manuscripts by editors at major publishing companies.

The thought of not being accepted consumed her as she looked at old pictures from her childhood days. Life was so much easier when she had been a poor and abused little girl in Tennessee, for there had been no accountability then. Abby yearned for the time when her hands had been too small to operate a gas pump or when she could sleep in the backseat while her dad changed a flat tire. Abby wept as she looked at those pictures—the ones she hadn't burned.

Burning objects—pictures, old clothes, her marriage license—relieved stress. Abby adored the finality of fire, beautiful sadness withering into ashy relief that could be brushed from a table like sand, without abrasion to the cherry finish. She relished the control of playing God, returning with fire and destroying Her world, just as it says in Revelation. Everything was at Her mercy, especially revision of the very past that provoked her to burn.

But Abby never burned her writings, because she could control the fictional world she had created in them, and characters were hers to use as she saw fit—to murder with a sledgehammer, to have sex with, to belittle—all to make her life seem normal. Abby's writings were the only authenticity she'd ever put forth, so she guarded them the way a tigress protects her only cub. But her heirlooms hadn't been so fortunate, and most had become ash over the years.

Sitting, she held a photo of her and her ex-husband, Teddy, by its top corner and clutched a lighter with her other hand, smiling while thumbing the switch to draw a flame. As the fire hit the corner, the picture darkened and curled up like a serpent, its composition changing into the ashy relief that she could wipe away from the table without harming the cherry finish.

"Fuck you, you son of a bitch," said Abby as she watched Teddy's and her waistlines turn to soot. When the flame hit the opposite corner and burned her fingers, Abby laughed despite the pain. "Who's in control now, you piece of shit? Answer me, you bastard," said Abby, her words muddled with laughter.

The constant look back at her past created renewed anguish. She thought of the Boston condo she missed so much. Her former home was just a stone's throw away from the Charles River Esplanade.

Her infatuation with the cashier at the Dough House Café—a mere stone's throw away from her new home—distracted her from her past. Meeting him had given her a sudden burst of creativity. For months Abby hadn't been able to figure out how to bring her latest manuscript to a close, but by nightfall she had finished the first draft of *The Silver Brooch* and put the spiral notebook in the drawer. Then the telephone rang.

"Hello."

"Abby, how you?"

"I'm doing just fine, Mother. And yourself?"

"I'm all right, I reckon. Just maintaining the best I can."

"I see," said Abby, rolling her eyes and choosing not to comment on the grittiness in her mother's voice. Abby had no desire to hear the story behind the rasp.

"So, how have you been, sweetie?" asked Abby's mom.

"Things have been going great. I've just finished redecorating the house and everything, and I love what Kathy has done with the place. Every room is just magnificent."

"Kathy who?"

"Oh, silly me. My interior decorator," Abby said.

"Well, I was just calling to see how you've been doing, since I haven't heard from you in a while. I know it must get pretty lonely down there all by yourself."

"Well, I'm actually dating someone, so I'm not as lonely as you might think," Abby said, before producing a laugh.

"So, what's this fellow's name?" her mother asked.

"Trevor."

"Trevor? Tell me about him."

"Maybe later, Mother. I have some ideas for this book, and I just have to get them down on paper. Heaven knows I don't want to forget them."

"I understand, sweetie. Just call me when you can, all right?"

"All right, Mother."

"I love you, Abby."

"Bye."

Abby hung up the phone and pulled her notebook back out of the drawer. She whispered, *"The Silver Brooch* by Abigail Worthington."* When she was married, Teddy had given her a silver brooch that had her name engraved on it. She had kept it in the same drawer in which she stored her notebooks. Though her marriage had failed and her love for Teddy had waned, she still wore the silver brooch on special occasions because it represented the perfect image she'd once had. The years had caused its clasp to loosen, so she was always afraid of losing it after fastening it to her designer blouses. Not wanting to toy with the integrity of the brooch, she had never gotten the clasp repaired.

"Damn you, Teddy," she said, slowly rising from the table like a woman twice her age. She looked around her morning room in the same slow manner. It boasted only a table and a chair, both wooden and white. The only important things in the room were her Boston College diploma and a crystal paperweight bearing the words *Collegium Bostoniense* underneath a coat of arms. On the other side of the crystal cube was a maroon eagle design that made her think about the moment she had met Teddy on the yard. It also made her recall the time when he decided to turn down a Rhodes Scholarship and pursue a Harvard MBA, just so he could be closer to her.

But that was way back then, when they were in love. No longer did they have those feelings for one another. Thinking she would never have anything to look forward to, Abby stood in a room filled with memories and a diploma that hung crooked on an otherwise empty wall.

∽∾∽

When the sun dismissed the moon and sunlight brightened her bedroom walls, Abby was up again, but unlike the days before, there was something, rather someone, to look forward to. She had gone to sleep the previous night accompanied only by sadness. As usual, when the sleepiness tugged at her eyes, Abby had turned off the television and rested her head on her pillow, pretending it was the chest of a man. She even turned the pillow lengthwise to make it seem real. But something troubled her about her fantasy this time. Her pillow had reminded her of the man behind the Dough House Café counter. Never before did her pillow have a clear face.

And this particular morning brought the same face to her mind. Abby pulled her finest pantsuit from the closet. Before showering and getting dressed, she exercised. An extra fifteen minutes on the elliptical did wonders to get rid of whatever insecurities she had about her body image.

By the time she pulled into the parking space at the Dough House Café, Abby couldn't understand why her heart had started to race. After all, it was just a café, and he was just a cashier. *Silly me*, she thought, *silly*. Nevertheless, she took a moment and bowed her head to pray—though she hardly did that in her life—and stared at the door of the café.

"God, please don't let me make a fool of myself," she said, before making her way to the entrance.

It was almost a quarter of eleven when Abby walked through the door, so the usual morning crowd had dwindled down to a lone redhead who ordered a lemon bar and a cup of cocoa.

"Here you go, ma'am," said the cashier.

"Thank you," said the redhead, before turning and leaving the cafe.

As Abby walked to the counter, she couldn't have cared less about the redhead or anyone else, aside from the dark-skinned man who worked there. She already knew what to order but pretended to study the pastries on display. Though her eyes were fixed on the glass, she paid no attention to the pastries. All Abby saw was her faint reflection, forcing her to smooth out a wrinkle in her cream-colored suit, though she knew full well there hadn't been a wrinkle there in the first place.

"May I help you, ma'am?"

"Just a minute." Abby once again pretended to decide. "I'm ready."

"Okay, what would you like?"

"A cheese Danish and a medium cup of coffee."

"French vanilla, right?"

"Why, yes," said Abby, wanting to smile.

"It'll be just a minute, ma'am."

She made sure to pay with her charge card, so he could see her name. He swiped it but didn't seem to notice.

"I'm Abby Worthington, by the way."

"I'm Spencer Gibson. It's nice to meet you."

"And you as well," said Abby, with a smile.

"Okay, ma'am. Here you go."

"Thank you."

"You have a nice day," Spencer said.

"I think I'll be eating in here today. I have a little work to do. Is that all right?"

"Course, ma'am. Sit anywhere you like."

Abby picked a table as far away from the cash register as possible, so she could monitor Spencer. Then she pulled her laptop from her dark-brown leather bag and pretended to work, even going as far as opening up a blank document and typing her grocery list, something she had already done the night before. Abby finally got a good look at Spencer as he walked across the room toward her, prompting her to hastily open up a document she had transferred from her spiral notebook the previous week.

"Can I get you a refill?" Spencer asked.

"Yes, please."

For the first time, Abby noticed how incredibly dark Spencer's skin was, giving it the leathery look of her computer case. And he had a walk and a swagger that suggested self-assurance. She couldn't figure out why he dipped down when his right foot hit the hardwood floor.

Before he returned, Abby had rubbed out another nonexistent wrinkle in her blouse.

"Here you go, ma'am." Spencer poured the coffee slowly.

"Thank you." Abby also noticed how dark his hands were, with knuckles that were even darker than the rest of his fingers. His nails were dirty and jagged, but that was appropriate, she thought, given his dark face and his menial job.

"What are you writing?" Spencer asked.

"A novel," Abby answered.

"About what?"

"Well…about…it's a love story." Abby sat upright and asked, "Do you read?"

Spencer laughed.

"I'm sorry…I didn't mean it like that. What I meant was…"

"I know what you meant. I read sometimes," Spencer said.

"What kinds of books?" she asked.

Spencer set the coffeepot down on the table, wiped his hands on his apron, and sat down. "I don't really have any particular taste," he said.

"You should try Faulkner or Fitzgerald. I love them a lot," Abby said, while turning her computer screen away from his sight.

"I'm not much of a reader. When I do read, it's usually books about crime and shit like…stuff like that. Sorry."

"It's okay."

Spencer lowered his voice. "I've never been into Faulkner and

Fitzgerald. I remember reading those books in high school, at least the days I went to school."

"Well, it's never too late to go back."

"Go back to do what?"

"Get your diploma or a GED," Abby said.

"I never said I didn't graduate. I already have a high school diploma, Ms. Worthington."

The only response Abby could muster was "I see," as her cheeks reddened out of embarrassment. Abby had imagined a sexualized creature that possessed no knowledge of anything but intercourse in the form of wild, animalistic thrusts. So when Spencer spoke of graduating, Abby could picture his penis getting smaller and his skin becoming civilized.

"So how old are you?" asked Abby.

"Twenty-three."

"Oh, I see."

"And you?" he asked with a smile.

"It's impolite to ask someone their age."

"But you just asked me," said Spencer.

Abby laughed and said, "It's impolite for a man to ask a *woman* her age."

"Really? So how old are you?"

"Men don't listen," said Abby, who shook her head and said, "Thirty-five. I'm thirty-five."

"See, that wasn't too hard," Spencer said.

Abby laughed and detected he was flirting, and knowing his age made her enjoy it something fierce.

The door to the café swung open, and Spencer said, "Well, I have to get back to work."

"Okay. Well, it was nice talking to you, Spencer," Abby said.

Spencer noticed her eyeing his chest.

"Nice talking to you, too," he replied.

"Don't forget the coffeepot," said Abby, before taking a sip from her cup.

⟨⟨⟨⟩⟩⟩

Later that night, Abby sat down in her morning room to write again, deciding to begin a screenplay about a woman in her mid-thirties who falls in love with a young cashier at a café. Wanting to cash in on this new surge of creative energy, she decided making a few minor changes to *The Silver Brooch* would just have to wait. The conversation with Spencer had given Abby the most inspiration she'd received since moving to South Carolina. Having written for only twenty minutes, she couldn't wait to cuddle with her pillow and pretend like it was Spencer, so despite the urge to take advantage of this newfound artistic fervor, she welcomed the opportunity to slumber. Loneliness and lust for attention once again trumped her artistic desires.

Days passed with Abby's usual stops by the café to order the same two items. And like clockwork, Spencer would begin preparing her order as soon as he caught a glimpse of her. Though Abby always had a pressing desire to stay in the Dough House Café, she would take her coffee and Danish and walk swiftly to her car. She did everything in her power to look uninterested in the dark man behind the counter. But the monotony was broken one morning when Spencer casually told Abby the worst news she'd heard in a long time. Abby had decided to find a table and write inside the café, since she was tired of being home, and when the crowd died down, Spencer approached her to deliver the news.

"Well, ma'am, today is my last day working here. I signed on with the Marines a while back, and they're finally shipping me off."

"Well, good. Not that you're leaving, but that…"

He laughed and said, "I know what you mean. I guess this is the last time I'll see you in here. Too bad we never really got to finish our conversation."

"What conversation?" asked Abby.

"About books."

"Right."

"Maybe you could send me a draft of that book you're writing. It'll give me something to do on my downtime at the base," Spencer said.

Abby sensed he was interested in more than her manuscript, but like a seasoned New England bridge player, she handled her cards carefully by saying, "It would be good to get some feedback. I'll tell you up front it needs a lot of work. I need to develop a few more characters, and the ending needs a little work too."

Spencer laughed and said, "I understand."

Abby's cheeks reddened the same way they had before, and she asked, "Do you have an address where I can contact you?"

"Don't know yet. I'll know in a few. You know, when they give me specifics."

"I understand," said Abby.

Spencer took a pen from his apron pocket and scribbled onto a sheet of paper. "Here you go."

"SBlack1982?" asked Abby.

"My screen name on Magic Message," said Spencer.

"Thank you," said Abby, who wanted to laugh at the youthful nature of this conversation, wondering what had happened to the conventional exchange of phone numbers. But she took a pen from her purse, tore a sheet from her stationery, and wrote down her screen name—WorthiPrincess—and said "Here" as she handed the paper to him. "I have a Magic Message account too. Who doesn't these days?"

"Thank you," Spencer said, looking at the paper and appearing to suppress a chuckle.

The door swung open, and he said, "Well, got to go. You take care. Hopefully I'll be chatting with you soon."

"Okay," Abby replied.

"Later," said Spencer.

"Bye," Abby said, wondering about the significance of the numbers in his screen name. *This is obviously not the year he was born,* she thought.

Deciding not to ask, Abby simply watched him walk away. This was the slowest she had ever eaten a cheese Danish, and the coffee had cooled before she took the last sip. After taking a fifty-dollar bill from her purse and leaving it on the table, the lonely woman exited. That would be Abby's last appearance at the Dough House Café for a long time.

It would take her a long time to write again, too. Her inclination to form even one sentence had eluded her. To make matters worse, despite logging in to her Magic Message account almost every day, she hadn't seen Spencer's screen name active online. Abby even went as far as buying new pillows and throwing the old ones away, since they reminded her of Spencer. No longer would she turn her pillow to make it feel like his muscular chest while envisioning his dark face.

2

The phone rang early Sunday morning when Abby was on the elliptical, and she answered it to get her mind off of Spencer.

"Hello."

"Abby," said her sister in a muffled voice.

"What's wrong, Sue? Why are you crying?"

"Abby, Momma is dead."

"What?" Abby asked.

"Momma is dead."

"What are you talking about, Susie? That can't be."

"She's gone, Abby…gone."

"Calm down. I can barely understand you," Abby said, as a tear that felt as warm as coffee escaped her left eye.

"She's been in and out of the hospital ever since the aneurysm last year."

"I can't believe this," said Abby, whose eyes brewed more coffee.

"She had her ups and downs, but it finally got the best of her. I just don't know what to do with myself."

"Just calm down. You'll—we'll—be fine. Why didn't I hear about this sooner? I would've come up to take care of her," Abby said.

"I called you to tell you."

"When?" asked Abby.

"When it first happened. But you don't never pick up your phone when I call. I left like 20 messages."

"I'm sorry. I'm so, so sorry," said Abby, remembering she deleted the messages without listening to them.

"Momma tried to call you, too. You know, after she got a little bit better. She told me she called, and you sounded real busy. Didn't want to interrupt you, I reckon."

"Interrupt?"

"She said you were excited about decorating your house or something, and she didn't want to make you all sad and stuff. She said it was the happiest she ever heard you talk in a long, long time."

"Shut up, Sue. Please shut up."

"Why are you mad at *me*?"

"I'm not mad at you," Abby said.

"We got to plan this funeral. I can't do it by myself," Susie said.

"I'll be on the first plane to Memphis."

"And we need to…"

"Susie, just…we can talk once I get there, okay?"

"Okay. See you in a little while, sis. Bye," Susie said.

"Bye."

When hanging up the phone, Abby's devastation weighed heavily upon her heart as she recalled the last conversation she'd had with her mother. Each remembered word almost killed her. She thought her life couldn't be emptier as she fell to the carpeted floor of her workout room and wept like an injured child calling out for her mommy. Even the cold-blooded cried sometimes.

Abby wondered if the sadness was really about losing her mother, the woman who'd meant so little to her just five minutes before. Her own tears frightened her—not because they were warm, but because they existed at all. That woman's primitive nature had upset Abby since she had been old enough to know what *primitive* meant. Something about her mother's old-fashioned ways had puzzled Abby as a child and had disgusted her as an adult. Because of her judgments about her mother, their relationship had incinerated, leaving ash and the odor of the dead.

But memories were still alive and well. There were the small things, like the time when her mother gave her a mixture of whiskey, honey, and lemon juice to treat the flu. Her mother blamed such things on a lack of money, and Abby had believed it until she was old enough to realize that whiskey was more expensive than cough syrup. And there were the big things, like her mother's constant blind eye, the one she used not to see how her husband's alcoholism and violence affected Abby.

Now, after hearing the news of her mother's death, Abby wished she could pour whiskey in her mother's dead, blind eye, minus the honey and lemon juice. Even still, hearing about her mother's death was like hearing a news bulletin: you shake your head at the thought of an innocent shop owner being gunned down, but it doesn't ruin your day.

"It serves the bitch right," said Abby, as she walked away from the telephone.

That's when it happened again: the wind started to howl until it faded into a whistle that filled the room.

"Not again," said Abby, as she ran to her bedroom and covered herself up to her neck with sheets. "Not again."

The howl of wind made its way up the staircase and into the bedroom, and, just as it had downstairs, faded into a whistle.

"Leave me alone. Just leave me alone," Abby said, as a breeze pushed her hair from her face.

Then she heard the scariest sound she'd ever heard: the sound of a little girl laughing repeatedly. After the laughter subsided, Abby heard the little girl sing her usual song: "A warm flow of the waters may never be. A warm flow of the waters may never be. A warm flow of the waters may never be."

"Leave me alone," Abby said, covering her ears.

The singing and whistling stopped. Knowing what would happen next, Abby cried.

Through foggy eyes, she then saw a red bow—perfectly tied, with ribbons that dangled to the floor—appear next to her bed. Then she saw the hem of a pink dress on the floor that materialized upward, with white lace outlining the hem, neck, and sleeves. Then came little white gloves that floated around where hands should have been. Abby looked at the girl who had no face, no arms, nor feet and said, "Get away from here! Leave me alone!"

"I'm not here to hurt you," said the girl, whose name was Muriel.

"What?" asked Abby, who in seven years had never heard the girl speak to her. All she'd ever heard was the little girl singing that same song lyric: "A warm flow of the waters may never be."

"I'm here to help you," said Muriel.

"Leave me alone. What do you want from me?" Abby said to the girl, whose name she still didn't know.

"I'm not here to hurt you. I'm here to help you…help you…help you. I'm not here to hurt you. I'm here to help you…help you." The little girl's voice echoed, punctuated by giggles.

Abby asked, "Who are you? What are you doing here?"

"Making a dollhouse," the ghost girl said, her gloves holding up something Abby couldn't see.

"What?"

"Making a dollhouse…dollhouse…dollhouse…dollhouse," Muriel said again before giggling.

"Leave me alone."

"I'm here to help you. And you're the only one who can help me. You can help me build my dollhouse, so I can be free, so I can see my mommy and daddy again. Because the floor will be gone, and God will make me leave." The echo of the girl's voice disappeared as she approached Abby.

"What floor? What are you talking about?" Abby rubbed her hands through her hair.

"The floor in my house. I'm making dollhouses out of the floor. And when I'm all done, God can send me away because I can't live in a house without a floor," said the ghost girl, who giggled again before singing her usual song: "A warm flow of the waters may never be. A warm flow of the waters may never be. A warm flow of the waters may never be."

"Go away," Abby said.

The little girl took Abby's orders this time, now crying instead of giggling. The gloves disappeared. The pink dress with white lace followed suit. Then the red bow turned around and floated toward the door, disappearing before it crossed the threshold.

And that was why Abby Worthington was so afraid of the little ghost girl. An apparition was the one thing she couldn't burn away.

So Abby pulled the sheets over her face and, like a little girl herself, began to cry.

Abby didn't move until she no longer heard the sound of the little girl laughing. Then she removed the sheets from her body and fell asleep, fully dressed—shoes and all.

⟣⟢

Abby wore those same high-heeled shoes the next day when going back to Tennessee to make arrangements for her mother's funeral. People looked at her shoes as she walked through the airport, and Abby took satisfaction in their stares while pretending not to see them.

The taxi ride from the airport to her childhood home was among the longest Abby had ever taken. She stared at the back of the strange man's head and mustered generic conversation. Then, put off by the driver's poor grammar, she decided to stop talking altogether.

The sound of the worn rubber tires hitting gravel awoke her from her trance. Abby never forgot this noise. The people in her old neighborhood seemed content as they huddled together and talked and laughed and watched their children jump rope and play freeze tag.

This place hasn't changed one bit, Abby thought.

And for the most part, neither had she.

"Right here, sir," said Abby.

The taxi pulled to a stop, and Abby gave the driver twice the necessary cash.

"All right, ma'am. You're home," the driver said.

"This is not my home, sweetie. I'm just visiting. I live in Hilton Head."

"Hilton Head? Swank."

Abby offered a tight-lipped, toothless smile. She was glad to see he believed her. Why wouldn't he? She had made it a point to adorn her neck with a string of pearls, which she had clutched immediately after hearing the familiar sound of gravel underneath the tires. She was stunning in her pink suit accented with fur around the neck and wrists. Her liberal New England bridge buddies would have disowned her for not wearing faux fur, but Abby cared more about style than preserving the wildlife.

After walking up three cinder blocks and stepping foot into the doublewide trailer, she was both depressed and pleased. As with most homes in the neighborhood, the front door had been left unlocked. The pungency in the room evoked memories of her parents' drunken stupors. Abby couldn't control her urge to look around for empty bottles of whiskey, even though her mother had been sober for over nine years.

When sitting down in a lawn chair in the kitchen, Abby recalled how her father waved at her before getting into his El Camino and driving out of their lives forever. Abby had been eleven years old, smiling and waving back at him for the last time. Despite his perma-nent departure, life had gone on. No one had missed him except his Princess Abby, who had longed for masculine love ever since.

Now Abby felt accomplished and sophisticated. At home in Hilton Head, there were straight-backed English dining chairs sur-rounding a glossy table with a cherry finish. At home in Memphis, mismatched lawn chairs surrounded a metal card table with a rust finish.

"I've come a long way," Abby said to herself—one of the big-gest lies she'd told in a long while.

An hour later, Abby was still alone, sitting in the lawn chair, because her sister had not yet arrived. The window just over her shoulder was open slightly, so she got out of the chair to close it. This act took several straining attempts, the last of which killed the annoying draft, which itself had been a figment of her imagination.

"What happened to the blinds?" Abby said to herself, looking up at the top of the window where her sister had torn the blinds down over twenty years before. It had never really bothered her mother, since most people in this neighborhood didn't have blinds or shades or curtains. No one had anything to hide, because dysfunction was the norm.

Abby looked out the window and remembered being a little girl growing up in the trailer.

Abby.
What Susie?
Look at that cloud up there. It looks like a troll.
I see it. Looks like one of the disciples.
You're right. It looks like John.
No, it's not. It's Peter.
It's John.
No, it's not.

Yes, it is.

No, it's not.

Yes, it is.

Mommy, come here and look at this cloud.

Lookie, Mommy, lookie.

Susie says it's John. But I think it's Peter.

How can y'all be so silly? It's neither one of them. It's James.

You're right, Mommy.

Me and Abby were wrong. It's James.

It looks like James to me, too.

Well, I got to finish making dinner. Just promise me one thing.

What, Mommy? Anything...me and Susie will promise you anything.

Promise me you'll come and get me when you see Jesus.

I promise, Mommy.

What about you, Abby?

I promise.

And why would you promise anything to little ol' me?

Because you're my mommy, and I love you.

I love you, too, Mommy.

And I love you girls more than you'll ever know.

After looking through the window to her past, Abby cried. Unlike the fast pace of greater Boston or the unfamiliarity of Hilton Head, there was no need for a façade or the suppression of her emotions, because here at home there was no need for studied show.

Susie entered the trailer and saw Abby sitting there. "Abby, give me a hug," she said.

Abby rose from the chair and gave her older sister a pressureless, cursory hug without closing her eyes. Susie—taller and bigger than Abby—stood there with her curly brunette hair tied into a ponytail with a rubber band. Her outfit, a long T-shirt that covered her cutoff denim shorts, revealed her fishnet stockings. Her shoes were black, like her stockings, with a gold clasp resting on top of each.

Abby shook her head from side to side and said, "You look like a whore."

"Fuck you," said Susie.

Abby laughed and hugged her sister again, with a little more pressure this time.

"I haven't laughed since you called me yesterday," Abby said.

"I haven't either. I figured she would die soon, but it still seemed so sudden."

"I know, just wish I could've…"

"It's okay. Momma understood," Susie interrupted.

Abby's countenance reddened at the cheeks, guilt and embarrassment cloaking it like a veil, forcing her to put her hands to the sides of her face to lift the imaginary garment.

"You ate?" asked Susie.

"No," said Abby.

"Get in the car. We can grab a bite to eat at Bubba's."

"Okay," said Abby, who wasn't in the mood to go to a country diner whose sign featured a horse and a bale of hay. "Bubba's sounds fine," she added. If her voice had been a hug, it would have lacked pressure.

3

By week's end, Abby was as cold as ever, sitting in the back of the limousine wearing a black dress with pumps to match. After planning her mother's funeral and taking numerous trips down memory lane, she was exhausted by the time Emma Sue, her mom's best friend, gave a heartfelt eulogy. And when a few strangers lowered the casket into the ground, Abby looked around the graveyard and saw tombstones that rested above decaying flesh and skeletons. She thought something only a depressed person would have thought: *This is a pretty graveyard.*

The corpse was already rotting away underneath Abby when a rush of cool air made her hug herself for comfort, since her mother was too dead to ever embrace her again. Her mother had always been too dead to hug her pretentious child, and before the true death took her away, she had willed this lack of emotion to her youngest daughter. So instead of looking within herself, clad in black and clutching a new purse, Abby looked around at the wonders of the graveyard. The terrain was flat, replete with tombstones engraved with names of the dead—names that were already forgotten, as evidenced by unkempt, flowerless sites. Even still, she saw the beauty in this bone-filled paradise because the grass was greener on *this* side.

That thought made Abby turn toward the casket, though it had already been lowered into invisibility—closing a sad chapter in her own empty life. Abby felt the permanence of it all with whatever warmth was left in her heart. Susie cried, wanting to jump into the hole with her mother's remains; Abby cried, thanking a God she barely believed in for this blessing called closure. Abby didn't realize that the blessing had not come, so her tears—if they were cleverer—would have trailed back upward into her eyes to be used for a more authentic mourning on a more peaceful afternoon.

⚬➳➳➳⚬

It was another type of morning when Abby packed her belongings to take the trip away from the Tennessee memories that caused her Carolina depression. Having stayed at her childhood home for almost a week, and having endured the most desolate funeral she'd ever attended, the South Carolina coast called her name. For reasons beyond her comprehension, Abby vacuumed the entire trailer and washed the dishes. She even took the time to spray cleaning solution on the kitchen window, though she failed to do a thorough job of wiping it clean.

A car horn blew. Abby stood in the doorway and said, "Just a minute. I'll be right out." The man was the same person who had driven her there.

Before leaving the house, Abby pulled out a pen and her checkbook and wrote her sister a check for $20,000. Then she retrieved a sheet of paper from her purse and wrote a quick note:

Susie,

Sorry I've been so distant for all these years. I'll be a lot better from now on. I promise. I left you a check. Call me if you need more.

Abby

Leaving the front door to the house unlocked, she stepped down the cinder blocks, leather luggage in tow.

"I love you, Mommy," Abby lied in a whisper, while looking up at the clouds and wondering if her mommy was up there taking whiskey shots with Jesus.

"You headed back to the airport, ma'am?"

"Yes."

"Okay. I'll get you there as fast as I can."

"Take your time. I'm in no hurry. I didn't get your name the last time we met."

"My government name is Joseph Jamison. But everybody calls me Bubba."

Abby wanted to laugh but instead just said, "I'm Abby."

Mr. Jamison was seventy-four years old. He had owned one of the largest investment companies in the South and had sold it five years before. Boredom had convinced him to become a cab driver. Some of Abby's assets were managed by the firm he used to own. Based on his unkempt facial hair and cheap shirt, Abby had thought him unworthy of her time. He may have recognized her disposition, because he laughed when she gave him a twenty-dollar tip.

"I know it's more than the tips you usually receive, but I'm in a generous mood today," Abby said as she handed him the bill without making eye contact.

"Thank you, ma'am," Mr. Jamison responded. "You'd be surprised how this bill can make someone's life a little better," he said to Abby as he handed the luggage to her and watched her disappear in the crowd.

"That poor woman," Mr. Jamison said as he put the car in drive and eased it forward.

Despite the relative shortness of the plane ride, the trip home was exhausting. The quietness almost killed Abby because it allowed for intense self-reflection. The first part of the trip was fine, but after the layover in Georgia, sad thoughts began. The desolation reached a crescendo when the plane left Hartsfield-Jackson Atlanta International Airport and leveled above the clouds.

Abby feared introspection the same way she feared the little ghost girl who had been haunting her. On the plane she had nothing to distract her from holding a mirror to herself and illuminating all of her flaws. Three packs of peanuts into the flight, she realized the one thing a lot of her friends had already known: she wasn't happy.

When entering her house, the crispness of the air unnerved Abby. Arriving well into nightfall was the best thing that could have happened to her, because she wouldn't have to stay awake and battle depressing thoughts of the past. The balance of chemicals in her brain caused more turbulence than the jet she had just traveled in, and going upstairs to sleep would have to be her antidepressant until she could make it to the pharmacist to get the real thing.

Abby turned on the television to get her mind off of her mind. She watched a cable news story about a man named Simon Blanc, an arsonist who was setting homes on fire throughout Massachusetts. According to the police, he had already burned down eight homes, killing six people, and he was still on the loose. Abby, a burner herself, laughed at the story because she understood the high you get from burning things, and when the laughter subsided, an evil thought entered her mind—the infancy stage of a scheme she hoped would relieve her of one of her biggest failures.

"I hope he burns down Teddy's house," said Abby with a laugh. "Because the son of a bitch deserves it." Abby turned off the television before finding out that all of Blanc's victims had been Hispanic.

She then booted up her computer and checked her e-mail. When opening her inbox—just like when first entering her physical home—she found nothing of substance. After deleting junk mail, she stepped away from the computer to unpack and change into her loungewear, a silk nightgown that, from a distance, looked like something you would wear to a ball.

Blip.

The noise sent Abby rushing back to her computer because the sound signaled an instant message.

SBlack1982: what's up?

WorthiPrincess: just putting a few things in order clothes and whatnot

SBlack1982: so, ur busy?

WorthiPrincess: no it's nothing important it can wait

SBlack1982: u know who this is, right?

WorthiPrincess: yes, Spencer from the cafe

SBlack1982: okay thought u forgot about me

WorthiPrincess: how could I forget

SBlack1982: i'll take that as a compliment

WorthiPrincess: lol I'm surprised to hear from u it's been almost three months

SBlack1982: i know hadn't had much of a chance 2 get on the net much

WorthiPrincess: ic

SBlack1982: did u miss me?

WorthiPrincess: not really lol

SBlack1982: real funny

WorthiPrincess: r u back home?

SBlack1982: yes finally spent time in Iraq and was discharged the first week there

WorthiPrincess: i dare ask why?

SBlack1982: don't feel like getting into it right now

WorthiPrincess: i understand

SBlack1982: i'd rather explain in person

WorthiPrincess: in person?

SBlack1982: yes i'll tell u about everything…boot camp, deployment, my discharge, the whole 9

WorthiPrincess: sounds fine

SBlack1982: what r u doing tomorrow?

WorthiPrincess: i don't have any plans

SBlack1982: would u like 2 meet for coffee?

WorthiPrincess: yes where and when?

SBlack1982: 8 at the Dough House of course ☺

WorthiPrincess: okay i'll be there

SBlack1982: we can finally finish talking about lit

WorthiPrincess: that would be lovely

SBlack1982: i look forward 2 it i'll see you tomorrow

WorthiPrincess: okay

SBlack1982: one more thing

WorthiPrincess: yes?

SBlack1982: the French vanilla and cheese danishes r on me?

WorthiPrincess: you bet

SBlack1982: later

WorthiPrincess: bye

Abby closed the dialogue box, shut down her computer, and went to the closet to pick out something to wear the next day. That didn't take her long at all. Just a pair of tennis shoes, jeans, and a plain blouse. No jewelry. There was no need to dress up anymore, because she was Abby Brooks, just Abby Brooks. She could shed the last name that had been given to her by her ex-husband. Though she had embraced the Worthington name, because it sounded moneyed and aristocratic, she would be a Brooks again, if only briefly. And that was fine with her.

Abby looked at the window and saw that the blinds were wide open, but that didn't bother her one bit. This night would be different from all the rest because the window would not be filled with disheartening memories she had brought from Memphis or depressing glances toward New England. Rather than go to bed, Abby sat at her desk and pulled out a spiral notebook and a fountain pen. It would be hours before the sleepiness would tug at her eyes. There was no reason for Abby to slumber because, for the first time in almost three months, she had some writing to do. It was also the first night in a long while that she wasn't worried about the little ghost girl.

Before writing, she took a moment to look back at the funeral of the woman who had never hugged her, choosing only in passing to think about the appeal of the graveyard while ignoring the ugliness of the casket. Abby remembered what she'd thought of the cemetery and laughed. Truth be told, it *was* a pretty graveyard, but Abigail Worthington had been the only one to notice.

PART II

Elijah Redwater and His Wishful Thinking

4

There are two things you should know about Elijah Redwater: he was depressed and insecure. Elijah knew sadness was ingrained in him and had tried to conquer it, to no avail. His depression had haunted him since childhood, and today, when moving into his dorm, that ghost still haunted him. But you wouldn't be able to tell by the manner in which he walked through the lobby of one of the worst residence halls on campus. He was confident about who he was on the inside but unconfident about what he looked like on the outside, which fueled his insecurity. He often exuded self-assurance about his sexuality and made few attempts to hide it, especially from strangers. But his fronts didn't change the fact that he was a sad, self-doubting young man. Before long, you'll also know him as a bruised and lonely whore who couldn't deal with the past.

Elijah had a small frame, with little hands and feet. Puberty had been stingy when giving his shoulders broadness, so—at eighteen—he had a prepubescent frame. Below those permanently underdeveloped shoulders was a chest bearing a visible rib cage, just above a thin waist. His hips curved outward and gently curved inward to meet his thighs in a way that made women envious while making men suddenly aware of their own penises. This—and his thighs—made him walk with a switch. He spoke in a soft, almost alto voice that sonically complemented his hips and thighs, which, like the rest of his body, were the color of chocolate.

Minutes before, Elijah's godfather Clyde, a friend of his father, had simply dropped him off on the curb in front of the dorm and drove away, not saying anything but "Good luck; I'm proud of you." But Elijah didn't mind, because his godfather had been there for him in the absence of a biological father, who had died years before. Elijah had watched Clyde's Dodge turn the corner and go down the hill and disappear into an influx of automobiles whose emissions gave a stench to the air.

When walking through the lobby, Elijah had his face down, eyes fixed on the steps he took. From the way his hands trembled when shaking the resident assistant Tommy Cason's hand, it was apparent that Elijah's self-esteem was lacking. He was instantly attracted to Tommy, and when putting his bags down, Elijah looked at the bulge in Tommy's soccer shorts.

"How are you doing?" asked Tommy.

"I'm doing cute. And yourself?"

"I'm good," Tommy said, with a laugh. "What's your name?"

"Elijah Redwater."

"Nice to meet you, Elijah. I'm Tommy."

They shook hands before Tommy found Elijah's room key. "Here you go," said Tommy, who wore a prominent rainbow bracelet.

"Thank you, sugar."

Tommy offered a wide smile and said, "You're welcome. Do you need help with your bags?"

"No. I'm okay, sugar." Elijah wanted to make sure Tommy was aware of his sexual orientation.

Tommy had known who Elijah was at first glance. Tommy winked and said, "Okay. Welcome to the residence hall."

"Thank you."

Elijah put his key in his pocket and dragged his belongings to the elevator. While ascending, Elijah thought, *Tommy is sexy. I want to give him some of my cat.*

All that really concerned him was meeting his roommate, a

North Carolinian named Grayson Sinclair Dobson. Reading that name made Elijah feel underprivileged. Though he was poor, he didn't want to feel like it and thus made up his mind to do everything in his power to hide his economic status. Though he knew nothing about Grayson, Elijah thought all people who had first names that sounded like last names were from money. In this case, his theory would prove true.

The odor in Elijah's room made him frown as he walked through the doorway. Thanking God his roommate wasn't there, Elijah dragged his possessions into the room: shower shoes, a laundry basket filled with garments and linens, and the clothes on his back. And two pillows. That was all he'd brought from home. Given how utterly depressed the room made him, he should've brought something to cover up the spots on the walls, which were made of large exposed bricks that had been painted an off-white color that had become yellow over the years.

The sun had begun to tuck itself into the horizon when Grayson finally returned and saw Elijah sitting on the floor, leaning against the bed, fast asleep.

"Wake up, dude."

"What?"

Elijah quickly rose from the floor as Grayson laughed.

"Are you all right, dude?" Grayson asked.

"Yeah, I'm good," Elijah replied.

For a moment they just stood there, as if about to engage in a duel. Elijah looked at this tall guy who wore a pair of soccer shorts and a plain white T-shirt. Grayson's legs were big and long, with hair that went from his lower thighs down to his feet. He had on flip-flops that seemed more appropriate for a walk on the beach. But Elijah liked the look on him and suppressed a smile. Grayson's hair hadn't been combed or saturated in product. He hardly ever groomed his dirty blond hair. He wore three earrings—one at the bottom of each ear and the third a hoop placed near the top of his right ear.

Grayson, the son of two CEOs, made it a point to look like he didn't care about material things, unlike his father, who had founded one of the largest tech companies based in North Carolina. His mom was equally impressive, going from a Yale MBA to work her way up the advertising ladder. She eventually started an agency of her own. All the while, Grayson was raised by a nanny. He was an only child, so his social skills had been stunted until he discovered he could serve a tennis ball with lightning speed. Tennis had given him his own identity, but even that had gone nowhere once he realized he wasn't good enough to be a professional. The same was true about his stint as a soccer player.

As for his academics, math and science were his strong suits. He had never taken a liking to any other subjects, though he excelled at them nonetheless. College, Grayson thought, would give him the opportunity to explore his scientific prowess and even become a little more himself. The last part would be much easier to do, since he wouldn't have his mother around to tell him to tuck his shirt in, nor would his father be there to complain about selecting a tie that was too busy for a cocktail party. Their son was never the high-maintenance type. Grayson loved to walk around in minimal attire, often with no underwear, so he could sit with his legs open and let people glance through his shorts to see his enormous semen dispenser.

"Nice to meet you," Grayson said, walking toward Elijah and extending a hand.

"Nice to meet you, too." Elijah smiled from ear to ear.

They shook hands and stared at each other. Grayson was masculine as he stood there and invaded Elijah's personal space. He grabbed the sides of Elijah's face as if he were about to kiss him and said, "You look uncomfortable. Am I scaring you?"

"No," said Elijah.

"I don't believe you."

Elijah laughed.

"You have a pretty smile," said Grayson, who was still holding the sides of Elijah's face.

"Thank you, sugar."

Grayson offered a huge grin before removing his T-shirt to reveal a muscular chest and chiseled arms. His stomach was defined, with a navel that was partially hidden underneath dirty blond hair.

"So you're a country boy from South Carolina?" asked Grayson, who sat down on his bed and put his hand down his shorts. "I'm just teasing you, dude. I'm really not such an asshole once you get to know me."

Elijah smiled.

Grayson stood up and began unpacking his belongings. "Have you eaten yet?"

"No," Elijah replied.

"I'll order us a pizza."

"I'll chip in."

"Don't worry, Little Guy. I got it," responded Grayson.

"What did you call me?"

"Little Guy."

Elijah smiled. That was Grayson's cue to call him "Little Guy" many more times.

❧

By the time the pizza arrived, Elijah had become comfortable with Grayson as they told stories of their respective childhoods.

"My family went to church every Sunday, and I hated it," said Grayson.

"Really?"

"Yeah. I'm not a religious person. It all seems like bullshit to me," Grayson said.

"What do you mean?"

"All of it." Grayson put his right hand down his shorts and adjusted himself before inadvertently smelling the same hand. "You seem offended. What—are you a Christian?"

"Yeah."

"So you believe all the nonsense about Jesus being crucified?"

"It's not nonsense," Elijah answered.

"Whatever you say," said Grayson with a laugh. "You really believe God sent his son to be murdered by an angry mob of Romans?"

"An angry mob of Jews," Elijah said.

"They were Romans."

"No, they were Jews."

"Jews would be offended by that statement."

"They always get offended," Elijah said.

"Whatever," responded Grayson, with a shrug. "Then Jesus supposedly died on the cross. They buried him. And three days later, he kicks his way out of a stone tomb and flies up through the ozone layer." Grayson laughed and said, "If you believe that, you're on some serious drugs."

Grayson saw the frown on Elijah's face and walked over to the other side of the room. "Didn't mean to offend you," he said.

"It's okay."

"I'm just not a religious person anymore," Grayson said, his voice taking on a serious tone. "There was a point in my life when I was. Because my parents were. So I had to go to church with them every Sunday and listen to what I've always known was bullshit."

"What do you mean?"

"Well, I guess I shouldn't say bullshit. But there's something wrong with religious people. They seem to think they know it all. How could they possibly know there's a God?"

"Do you believe in God?" Elijah asked.

"I don't know."

"You don't know?" asked Elijah.

"No, I don't know. How could I? There's no way of knowing if there's a God. It's just a bunch of guesswork."

"That's not true. The Bible says there's a God."

"The Bible is a bunch of nonsense, invented stories to answer questions that can't possibly be answered. No one knows this stuff."

"You're really crazy," said Elijah.

"You're the one who's crazy." Grayson smiled. "Can I ask you something?"

"Go ahead."

"Let's say you're dying from a gunshot wound, and there are two doctors available to save your life. You're in pain, but you're still conscious and able to choose which doctor."

"Okay," said Elijah.

"And one doctor comes up to you and tells you he thinks the world is round. Then the other doctor comes up to you and tells you he thinks the world is flat. Which doctor would you trust with your life?"

"The one who thinks the world is round. That was a stupid question."

"Why was it a stupid question?" asked Grayson.

"You would have to be a moron to believe the world is flat, so I would never trust a doctor stupid enough to think that."

"That's what I thought you would say."

"Yeah, so what's your point?" Elijah asked.

"My point is, the people who wrote the Bible thought the world was flat."

That embarrassed Elijah.

Grayson then asked a question but used a declarative tone. "Why would you trust morons like that to tell you how to live your life?"

"I don't."

"Yes, you do."

"You can't be mad at me for believing in God," said Elijah.

"I'm not mad at you. I just think you don't understand. Nobody understands."

"Understands what?"

"Whether or not God even exists," said Grayson.

"He does exist."

"How could you possibly know such a thing? There's no way for someone to be able to answer that question. It's an impossible question to answer."

Elijah was scared, because he began to understand Grayson's point and even began agreeing with it. But he lied and said, "I disagree."

"There's not anything to disagree with. You've been indoctrinated, is all. Scared into believing something that—if you really thought about it—you wouldn't agree with. Most people are like that—afraid to challenge the things that have been instilled in them as kids. Religion is such a part of childhood that people believe it's fact, even when they reach adulthood. Because they're too scared to question anything. Because when they start asking themselves questions, they realize we humans aren't sophisticated enough to answer such questions."

"Questions like what?" asked Elijah.

"Well, for starters, if God created the universe, who created God? How did he get here?"

Elijah became even more scared, realizing that Grayson was even smarter than the theologians he'd come to view as geniuses.

Grayson rubbed his right hand through his hair. "No one can answer that question right now. And people don't like to admit they don't know the answer, so they come up with foolish stories and call it the Book of Genesis. They come up with bullshit about 'let there be light' because, at the time, they were not advanced enough to figure out how the sun was formed. But we know how it was formed, so we know the Book of Genesis is full of shit."

Elijah grabbed his chest as Grayson continued, "Then they say God created the Earth in six days and rested on the seventh. That doesn't make any sense, because a day is determined by the amount of time it takes the Earth to spin around one time. So if the Earth hadn't been created yet, there was no such thing as a day—much less six days. They didn't know about the Big Bang Theory when the Bible was written. And the Big Bang Theory might turn out to be wrong—but at least it's based on science and not fairy tales. The Bible is the greatest work of fiction of all time. It's so well written and so creative people are forced to believe it's true when, in fact, it's total bullshit."

"Well, I believe it," said Elijah.

Grayson snickered.

"Stop laughing," said Elijah, who realized it was the first order he had given his new roommate. "Well, the Bible says that's how it happened, and that's how life was created. So I believe it."

"What about evolution?"

"I don't believe in evolution."

Grayson laughed and replied, "So you think man just popped up in the world and began to rule the entire animal kingdom?"

Elijah wanted to laugh but instead said, "I don't want to talk about this anymore."

This discussion overloaded Elijah's indoctrinated mind. Grayson understood as he walked across the room and hugged Elijah, who stopped being offended as he took in Grayson's scent. To Elijah, it was the best smell in the world. He felt a connection to this man.

When they finished hugging, Elijah beamed. And for the brief time they would live together, Grayson would never tire of seeing Elijah's smile. They continued talking and told each other about their academic interests.

5

Elijah had decided to be a double major in creative writing and French. By mid-November he'd given up on his dreams of becoming a lawyer, because he didn't really want to be one anyway. He couldn't see himself working fifteen-hour days for years and years...all for what? Just to please a mother who didn't approve of him. French was a language that was easy to him, so it seemed to be a good enough subject to get a degree in. And letters had developed into his passion, so creative writing would be perfect for him as well. This satisfied his urge to be able to tell people he was a double major, thinking it made him sound academic. And thanks to Grayson, his transition into college life had been relatively easy. They had already become close friends whose pillow talk always preceded a peaceful sleep, and they both looked forward to waking up and getting ready for the day together, sharing toothpaste and spitting in the sink at the same time.

They liked looking at each other in the mirror as each got his hair in order. Elijah always took the longest, since all Grayson did was throw a little water on the palm of his hand and rub it in his hair, topping it off with two uneven strokes of a comb. Elijah dipped his index and middle fingers into a plastic jar and rubbed grease into the palm of his hands. Then he rubbed his greasy hands across his hair, back to front. Elijah felt uncomfortable with himself when looking in the mirror, because he didn't like his wide nose, thick lips, and hair. He wished his hair were long and blond like the guy who was standing next to him, watching Elijah train—as it were—his nappy hair. Grayson stared every time until another guy from the hall entered the bathroom or he thought someone was looking at them. Soon there would be five young men standing in their underwear brushing their teeth and rubbing sleep from the corners of their impressionable eyes.

Elijah and Grayson lived on South Campus, and all the classes were on North. So it took them ten, sometimes fifteen, minutes to walk to class, but that bothered them little, since they enjoyed each other's company. And they talked about the same things over and over again each day, but each topic seemed new.

"See you later," Grayson would say, when their paths split. "Okay," Elijah would respond. Then Grayson would go off into a world of Bunsen burners and flasks, and Elijah would dive headfirst into a world of literature. And later they would meet in the cafeteria to discuss the boredom of structured academia.

One morning, well before the time Elijah would usually awaken, the phone rang.

"Hello," he answered.

"Hey, Elijah. How you doing?"

"All right, Momma."

"Did I wake you?"

"Not really," said Elijah.

"You not telling the truth," his mother said.

Elijah said nothing and looked at Grayson to make sure he was asleep.

The huskiness in her voice became more pronounced as she said, "I'm just calling to check up on you since I ain't heard from you in a month of Sundays."

"Everything's good, Momma."

"How about class? How's that going?"

"Good," Elijah said.

"Just good?"

"Yes. My grades are fine. It's the math class that's killing me, but I think I'll get away with a B." Elijah coughed.

"What's wrong?"

"I've been a little sick. Yesterday it hurt a little bit when I swallowed," said Elijah.

"Do you have a sore thoke?"

"No, my throat is not sore anymore."

"You better take something for that sore thoke. It might turn into that there pleurisy."

"I said my throat is not sore anymore."

"Oh, well that's good," his mother said. "Any girls up there you like?"

"There're a lot of girls here, Momma. This is a coed school, you know."

"Don't get smart with me. I said, 'Are there any girls up there *you like*?'"

"I don't have time to talk right now, Momma. I need to get some sleep."

"Okay, I'll talk to you later."

"All right," Elijah said.

"Bye."

"Bye," he said.

Elijah's mother was a woman who was afraid of any place that didn't look like home, and she mistrusted anyone who didn't favor someone from the town where she grew up. Men in suits scared her, unless they were white, in which case she thought such attire was expected. As for women—she looked down on those who wore dresses cut above the knees and thought even less of the ones who didn't go to church. As for women who wore accessories that weren't earrings or rings—she chalked them up as snobs, though she preferred to call them "seditty women." *Seditty* was a word Elijah had heard her say but could never find in the dictionary. So when she had called this morning, he wanted to hang up the phone, having grown tired of her backward values—like her belief that *lie* was a cuss word or how she considered women who wore red dresses to be whores.

Elijah still had about two and a half hours before it would be time to wake up. The bed felt good as he climbed onto the mattress, careful not to make it squeak too much. It did make a noise, but it didn't wake Grayson, who lay in his bed shirtless in a pair of boxer briefs. Elijah stared at him and watched his hairy stomach move up and down with each sleeping breath. He gazed at his roommate for ten minutes before falling into the best slumber he could in two hours and thirty minutes' time, not eager to awake and take his final exams.

∽≈≈≈9

By the time finals were over, both Elijah and Grayson were confident about what their grades would be, and they were ready to put the semester behind them and take a break. Elijah had to make arrangements to get home. Grayson had invited him home to his family's estate and received the decline he expected, having noticed the first day they had met that Elijah was too proud to accept any offer from him.

"Do you want me to wait for your godfather to come?" asked Grayson.

"No, you don't have to do that. I'll be all right."

"What time is he coming to pick you up?"

"In about two hours," said Elijah.

"Okay." Grayson just stared at Elijah as if he should've responded.

"What?" Elijah asked.

"Nothing." He folded his arms. "I told you it's okay if you

come home with me? You sure you don't want to?" Grayson's voice showed optimism—his face, pessimism.

"Yeah, I'm sure. My folks are expecting me to spend time with them. Plus my ride is already on the way. Too late to change plans now." Elijah answered, proving that Grayson's face had better instincts than his voice.

"I see." He stared at Elijah again.

"What?"

"Do you want to go grab a bite to eat before I leave?" asked Grayson

"Yeah, sure."

"I'll take you anywhere you want to go."

"Greekos," said Elijah.

"Of all the places to choose from, you pick a lousy burger joint. I'll go get my car and pull it around."

"All right."

"Look for me out the window. I'll be back in about five minutes. My car is in the lot across the street," said Grayson.

"Okay."

The door swung open, and Grayson left. Elijah watched him leave and then lay down on the bed and looked up at the ceiling.

Minutes later, the door swung open.

"You were supposed to look for me out the window," Grayson said with a smile.

"Sorry," Elijah said, smiling back.

"So, dude, are you ready?" asked Grayson.

"Yeah."

"Okay, let's go."

Sometime between going down the flight of stairs and getting to the first floor, they decided to walk to Greekos instead of driving Grayson's car. They both felt that walking would be the perfect way to prolong their time together. It wasn't that cold out, and even if it were, they would've decided to walk anyway. The unusual warmth of this December day prompted Grayson to wear the same soccer shorts he'd worn on move-in day. And he put on a pair of tennis shoes with no socks and a white T-shirt. Elijah wore a taupe shirt, a pair of khakis, dark brown shoes, and a belt to match.

They didn't talk much over their meal of cheeseburgers and fries. For the first time, they seemed to exhaust all conversation. Grayson and Elijah had no more classes to talk about, and they'd gone over their family histories several times, usually just before going to sleep. And this was the first time Elijah didn't argue when Grayson pulled out his bank card and paid the check. Without speaking or glancing across the table, they left Greekos, where they had eaten the last meal of their first semester in college.

"How long before your godfather comes?" asked Grayson.

"Should be here in a half hour or so. At least I hope so," Elijah replied.

"Well, I'll go ahead and get going once I get back to my car You can lock up the room and everything."

"All right," Elijah said.

They walked in silence through the quad, where some students lay out in the sun with books in their hands, waiting for their parents to come. The campus seemed a little odd this time of year, when it was on the verge of becoming a ghost town. It wasn't there yet, though, as evidenced by the faces of the sleep-deprived students who still had finals to be stressed out about. Elijah and Grayson felt strange walking with no books or papers in their hands. By the time they were just yards away from their residence hall, Grayson broke the silence as they stood on the brick walkway leading to their dorm, which for the first time didn't look like a bad place to stay.

"Make sure you call me when you get home," Grayson said.

Elijah realized that Grayson hadn't wanted to say that but, as usual, played along with him.

"I will," Elijah said.

"I'll call you from time to time to see how things are going in South Carolina."

"All right."

"Later, dude," said Grayson.

"Bye, sugar."

They both offered a nervous laugh before going in different directions.

"Elijah," Grayson yelled.

"What?"

"Come here for a second."

Elijah walked briskly to his roommate and realized that Grayson had on the same shorts he was wearing on move-in day.

"If I do something crazy, you promise you won't freak out?" Grayson asked.

"Yeah, I promise."

Then Grayson did what he'd wanted to do since the first time they'd met. He leaned down and forward, until his face was right in front of Elijah. Some students began to stare. Elijah and Grayson didn't notice. And when they kissed, those thick gray clouds that covered the sky burst open, and rain fell down upon the onlookers. But it missed Elijah and Grayson, who stood dry in the downpour as everyone else placed things over their heads and ran underneath porticos for cover. Elijah and Grayson continued, and as they put their arms around each other, the rain suddenly stopped as a spectrum of light formed in the sky. It was an arc with lines of color…red, orange, yellow, green, blue, violet. It was a rainbow that landed beneath their feet. They held hands and were lifted from the ground as they began to rise up to that part of the sky where gray clouds used to be.

Elijah giggled like a girl as he looked down at the campus, which seemed so small to him, and the people all looked like ants that scattered about underneath the rainbow.

"It's nice up here, Grayson."

"Yeah, it is, isn't it? Come on, let's go. Take my hand."

Elijah did, and Grayson led him to the other side of the campus, the two stepping foot on each color of the rainbow. Elijah reached down to touch the arc and scooped up sugar crystals. He and Grayson put the crystals on their tongues to taste the sweetness while they danced above the town. As they moved, the earth spun faster and the sun was gone, replaced by the darkest night with the brightest stars. But somehow the arc survived—a rainbow in the midnight sky!

"This is awesome, Grayson."

"Yeah. I wish I'd taken you here sooner. But I was scared."

"Of what?"

"That you wouldn't want to come up here with me."

"I'll come up here with you anytime you want."

"Look over there."

"What?"

"It's the moon."

"Wow."

Elijah tried to reach out and touch it, but the moon ran away.

"You might be able to touch him next time. He's shy around new people. We'll see him again soon enough. Take my hand."

"Okay."

Grayson led Elijah back to the other side of the campus across the colorful, sparkling bridge. Elijah tried to keep his foot on the color yellow, but orange and green kept getting in the way. The earth spun in the other direction, the sun came back up, and just like that, the night was gone. Pieces of the rainbow turned into sugar underneath their feet and fell, disappearing before hitting the ground. Elijah and Grayson descended, too, holding hands—coming down slowly in a back-and-forth motion like feathers. Elijah giggled.

"Well, I have to get going. I'll call you tonight," Grayson said.

"You promise?"

"Yeah, Elijah, I promise."

Grayson walked to his car, and Elijah went back to the dorm to wait for his godfather who, because of a car accident that had backed up traffic, wouldn't be there for another two hours. But Elijah didn't mind one bit. He just lay there on his bed and looked at the ceiling, replaying the semester over and over again, not regretting one decision he'd made. For the first time in a long time, he didn't care at all what his relatives thought and wished this bliss wouldn't evade him like it always did. But, upon getting into his godfather's car, the euphoria was gone. It would be a while before he would again be able to reach down into a rainbow and taste the sweet crystals in his little hands.

6

There was nothing sweet about the blue, rectangular road sign that read, WELCOME TO SOUTH CAROLINA. It startled Elijah in a way it never had before as he and his godfather Clyde rode down the interstate on their way home. Elijah felt so far removed from this place, even though he'd just been back the previous month for Thanksgiving. So much about him had changed, and so much about this place had stayed the same. Nevertheless, it was home, or at least it was the place where he'd grown up, where he'd learned to be antisocial and insular, where he'd learned that writing gave him an escape from loneliness and suicidal thoughts, where the world seemed to be against who he was. It would take him years to realize that all of this wasn't South Carolina's fault.

When he opened the front door, Elijah could smell the familiarity of his childhood. Had he the money, he would have bought a plane ticket to San Francisco and stayed in a hotel until the following semester to escape the vivid memories of being bullied by neighbors and being taunted and slighted by those closest to him.

"All right, Elijah, I'll see you later," Clyde yelled out the window of his car and then sped off as if he'd just robbed a bank. Elijah simply waved his hand and closed the front door of the house as Clyde drove away. Elijah left his belongings in the foyer and headed upstairs. He fell asleep for hours and awoke to the sound of his mother slamming the front door.

"Elijah, you done left all your shit in the way! Come down here and get it!"

Elijah heard her but was still in that stage of sleep in which he was unable to give a cohesive response.

"Elijah!" his mother yelled again.

He was awake then.

"Come down here and get your shit out the doorway!"

"Okay, Momma," Elijah replied with a sigh, shaking his head from side to side.

Then he walked to the foyer and dragged his belongings to his room, which took two trips.

"I'm about to get to cooking. So be down here time the food is ready, hear?"

"All right," Elijah replied.

The doorbell rang, and soon Elijah heard his two older brothers enter the house.

"Hey, boys, how y'all doing? Give me a hug."

"Hey, Momma," said Terrence and Mike.

Terrence was two years older than Elijah, and Mike was three years older. They both went to college in Florida, so they came home together to save money on gas. Terrence and Mike had cars, apartments, and girlfriends.

"I'm going to take my stuff up to my room," Terrence said to his mother.

"It's all right. Y'all boys leave your stuff right there at the door. It ain't gonna hurt nothing."

Elijah heard that loud and clear.

"Where's Elijah?" Terrence asked.

"He's upstairs. I think he's taking a nap or something."

"No, Momma, I'm awake." He walked toward his brothers, wondering how his mother could possibly think he had been taking a nap after she'd just yelled at him about his luggage being in the doorway.

"What's up, Elijah?" asked Terrence. "I didn't even hear you come down the stairs."

Elijah nodded his head and walked to the kitchen. He hadn't had a home-cooked meal in what seemed like years. Cooking was the only thing his mother did that didn't upset him. When she talked, he wanted to cry. But when she cooked, he thought back to the few good times he had spent with her.

Mike and Terrence both stood in the kitchen and watched their mother prepare dinner. She took a coffee cup from the counter. In it there was oil that had been drained from bacon she had cooked that morning. She poured the leftover grease into the skillet before rolling the chicken around in flour, making sure each piece was covered completely in white. Then she took one of the chicken-filled bowls to the stove and peered into the skillet, leaning forward while smiling. Elijah picked up a bowl too.

"What are you doing? I don't need no help," his mother said.

"Okay," Elijah said, and then he walked between his two older brothers and went to his room. As he made his way through the doorway, he could hear his mother asking one of his brothers to put the other pieces of chicken in the skillet. He missed his depressing college dorm room more than any other place.

⁂

Elijah was glad four weeks later when his godfather knocked on the door to take him back to his college dorm, so he could once again delve into a world of creative writing and French. When opening the door to his room, he hoped Grayson would be there, ready to take him back to that place up in the sky. After hauling his laundry basket and his book bag into the room, he received the worst news he'd received in years. Grayson's sheets had been removed from the bed, his family pictures were no longer on his desk, and his computer was gone. Elijah opened Grayson's closet and found nothing, not even clothes hangers.

The love of his life was gone.

Although the first thing he'd seen when entering the room was a letter on his bed, Elijah couldn't stand the thought of reading it, because opening it would confirm what he already knew. When nightfall came, he eventually read the letter:

Elijah,

I know this might come as a shock to you. But I've decided to do something a little more meaningful with my life. I love school, but in the end it's not for me. It's a little too easy for a rich brat like me to go to college, especially since I got accepted because my dad donated a ton of money. So I decided to join the Army. You know, to bring a little purpose to my life. But I'll be thinking about you wherever they send me. Looks like I'll probably be writing you from the Middle East. Just so you know, I think about that kiss every day. And it means a lot to me. I'll write you as soon as I have some free time. I promise.

I love you, Little Guy,
Grayson

After reading the letter, Elijah fell into a deep sleep. That semester became a depressed blur to Elijah. His family life didn't change much: his mother still managed to insult him in ways that varied from subtle to blatant, and he lost most contact with his two brothers. At least his grades didn't suffer. He would have had a perfect grade-point average if it hadn't been for the math and science requirements. He received B's in those classes.

Elijah was relieved when summer came. He dreaded the thought of going back home, so he took on an internship with a theater group in Winston-Salem. There he made up his mind that playwriting would be his concentration, encouraged by the fact that he would see one of his plays acted out by the university drama club. *Rainbow Dancer* was the play's working title. It was about a pair of young boys who would say a couple of magic words and would suddenly leap into a parallel universe where everyone danced and everything tasted like candy. The roads were made of peppermint, and the sky rained sugar water. Elijah pitched the idea to the head of the Department of Theater, and it was approved. *Rainbow Dancer* would give Elijah a much-needed escape from the world of academia and the social cliques of college life.

Since reading that letter more than six months earlier, Elijah's lust for life had been gone. Several times a week he would read it, hoping to find something new. He was upset that more letters didn't follow.

He can't be dead. I know he's still alive. Should I call his parents? Elijah thought.

His worries about Grayson weren't enough to prevent him from intimacy. During that semester he finally found someone to tongue kiss him, a frat boy named Rick who was drunk and who claimed he was just experimenting. Despite that, Rick came back for more, and an empty Elijah rarely turned him down. The attraction had nothing to do with Rick's personality, because Rick wasn't an intelligent person at all. Eventually, Elijah tired of him and stopped returning his calls. Rick finally got the hint and stopped calling, and on the occasions when they would see each other on the quad, they would glance at one another and try not to get within speaking distance.

⁂

Elijah had long ago completed his internship in Winston-Salem, and almost halfway through the second semester of his sophomore year, he decided he would leave the comfort of dorm room promiscuity and venture out into the campus to find another organization to join. The *New Age Letter*, the most respected literary magazine on campus, became his favorite pastime. He'd never forget the day he walked into the magazine's headquarters.

He opened the glass doors of the student-run office and saw three handsome guys standing there. Elijah, in his khakis and tucked-in shirt, felt markedly out of place. His hands began to shake and sweat.

"May I help you?" one guy asked. He wore a pair of shorts and flip-flops despite the rain and cool weather. His hair was long, and his face was chiseled underneath a beard.

"I read an ad in the paper saying you were looking for writers," Elijah said.

"Sure."

"Are you still looking?"

"Of course we are. My name's Teddy."

"I'm Elijah."

Teddy casually wiped his hand clean on his shorts, and the two shook hands.

Elijah noticed the bulge in those shorts and immediately knew Teddy was circumcised, because he could see the imprint of the coronal ridge hook. Though he knew that an uncircumcised penis could have a crown that could be visible even in a flaccid state, he correctly determined that Teddy's cock was foreskin-free. Elijah was an expert at analyzing dickature. He also saw something stuffed in the right pocket of Teddy's shorts. It was a container of cocaine that Teddy planned to snort later with some of his future fraternity brothers.

"Have a seat," Teddy said.

The other two guys in the room turned out to be Steve and Mike, both computer science majors who had an interest in letters. They ran the magazine to quell their desire to create characters and play with words. It was a relief from all of the math classes they had to endure. Because calculus was calling them, they packed up their belongings and walked out of the room.

As they left, Elijah looked at Steve, who was about the same size as Elijah—short and small. Though Elijah wasn't physically attracted to men his own size, he enjoyed being with them because they could do a perfect 69. Since they were the same height, their penises would line up perfectly in each other's mouths.

"Did you bring any samples?" Teddy asked.

Elijah produced folded papers from his messenger bag—two short stories laced with ghosts and phantoms and all things paranormal. He hoped it wouldn't be too juvenile for a college publication.

"Come back tomorrow, and I'll let you know," said Teddy, while sniffing and scratching his nose.

"Okay," said Elijah. "What time?"

"Around this time. Is that all right?"

"Yeah," said Elijah as he left.

⸺

The next day, Elijah went back to the office of the *New Age Letter*, but he was not nervous this time. He walked to Teddy's office.

"You're hired."

"What?" asked Elijah.

"You're hired," repeated Teddy. "Dude, your stories just took me on the biggest fucking trip. We really need to put them in our next issue."

"Okay."

The trip that Teddy had experienced had less to do with Elijah's stories and more to do with using the contents of the other bulge that had been in his shorts the previous day.

This was the first time since Grayson that Elijah would forge a lasting friendship. Everyone else on campus seemed so content with having fun and being social. He, too, had wanted to be the fun-loving, social type, but he was afraid of rejection. Teddy would give Elijah the acceptance he thought he wanted.

"Do you want to grab a bite to eat?" Teddy asked.

"Yeah, why not?"

"How's Greekos sound?"

"Fine…it sounds fine," Elijah replied.

"What? Do you not want to go there?"

"No, Greekos is fine."

"Are you sure?" Teddy asked.

"Yeah."

"Okay, let's go."

Elijah hadn't been there in a long time and couldn't resist the urge to glance at the table where he and Grayson had been. Two students sat there—a guy and a girl—laughing and eating and looking out the window at passersby.

They don't realize just how important that table is, Elijah thought.

Being there, smelling the good food, and hearing the inviting music cut like a knife. The need to get out and get some fresher, less reminiscent air pained Elijah.

"Is everything all right?" Teddy asked.

"Yeah, everything's fine, Teddy."

That was the first time Elijah had said Teddy's name out loud.

Teddy seemed to have a good time, and after they sat down to eat, he was largely oblivious to Elijah's discomfort. There was an intellectual attraction there. They had a conversation about obscure novels that could only be found online and in small bookstores. They caressed each other's minds and sense of creativity like never before. Elijah didn't really want to embrace this experience.

Thirty minutes later, they left the restaurant and walked through the maze of students and professors until they reached the office of the *New Age Letter*. Teddy opened the door for Elijah just like he'd done at Greekos.

"Well, I have to go. I have class in fifteen minutes," said Elijah.

"All right, Elijah. It was nice hanging out with you. I'll be in touch with you about your short stories."

"All right."

They hugged for what seemed like a long time—time enough for Teddy to smell Elijah's perfume. And off Elijah went, happy about his new literary group and uneasy about his new relationship with Teddy. The dinner, the shoulder-to-shoulder walk, and the hug made him feel dirty. Though Grayson had been long gone and they were never officially together, Elijah felt like going out to eat with Teddy had been infidelity—as if Grayson had been owed a wait. Elijah knew the relationship with Teddy would develop into something more, unlike his previous flings. His brain told him that going out with Teddy was okay, but his heart told him it was wrong—all this guilt over an impromptu date. It was one of those things that, though technically not wrong, just wasn't right—like masturbating on your grandmother's birthday.

7

After class, Elijah walked slowly back to the dorm, clutching the straps of his book bag at his armpits and avoiding eye contact with anyone who walked near him. Noah Cohen, who himself had seen twenty-five masturbation-filled years, quickly approached Elijah from behind. Elijah flinched.

"Sorry, man. Didn't mean to scare you," Noah said.

"It's okay," said Elijah, glancing at the smiling man next to him.

Elijah stared at the guy's shorts and studied the bulge, which offered proof of circumcision because Elijah could see prominent contours of the coronal ridge hook of this guy's penis. Underneath the polyester-cotton-blend fabric, Noah's semen dispenser flopped around as he walked. Elijah stared long enough to watch it sway four times. Noah, who sometimes purposely wore thin shorts with no underwear to show off his instrument, smiled when he saw Elijah's reaction. Elijah himself had never had qualms about staring so noticeably. It was his way of announcing who he was without speaking. He thought guys who went without underwear wanted the attention.

"I'm Noah," the guy said. "What's your name?"

Elijah responded by saying his full name, which made him feel like an adult.

"Nice to meet you, Elijah," said Noah, while extending his hand.

Elijah reached for it. They had to alter their steps to allow for a handshake. It seemed Noah didn't want to let go of Elijah's hand, which was small and soft to the touch. And Elijah didn't want to let go of Noah's large hand because it made his own feel secure and warm despite the cool breeze.

Noah was tall by anyone's standards and had an athletic frame, but hadn't always been that way. The stubborn chubbiness in his cheeks made that clear. His dark brown hair was wild and curly, but didn't look unkempt because it seemed to go with the rest of his face: the cheeks, the facial hair, and the ears that protruded outward from his head. His eyes were a shade of brown lighter than the hair on his head but slightly darker than the hair on his face, giving him a monochromatic appeal that worked to soften any fear Elijah may have had when meeting him. It made Noah look deliberately put together and thoughtful.

Noah was a PhD student who was working on a degree in political science with the hopes of getting a professorship, hopefully in Boston, which was a city he'd fallen in love with from his visits there as a child. It was also the city where he was born, and he wanted to experience it in his adult life. He had studied political science and art as an undergraduate student in San Francisco, and after graduation, he had decided to go to the South for graduate school, a region that would offer him a change of pace. Going to school in the South was his way of making his own name for himself, his way of distancing himself from his parents, whose names were well known in scholarly circles. Regardless of where he was, Boston had always been his destination.

Despite his love for New England, New York was what he considered home. Noah was raised on Long Island, the place where he realized he had an affinity for both males and females. At that point in his life, Noah was barely old enough to speak, though he was already wise enough to understand he was unlike most boys he knew. And it was his wish to hide his true self from his parents.

Mr. and Mrs. Cohen, both college professors, were educated at

Cornell, where they met and later married. After establishing separate careers as acclaimed scholars, they had Noah. They were affluent, but it didn't show. They drove middle-caliber cars and lived in a ranch house where they took turns cutting the grass every week during spring and summer. No need to get someone else to do a job they could do themselves. All for what? Just so neighbors could talk about how pretentious they were for hiring a gardener? The Cohens never indulged in anything but books, often going to auction houses to bid on rare first editions of novels by their favorite writers. They had a keen interest in foreign travel, which they felt was worth the money because of the worldly experience that shaped their philosophies.

On the side, they owned a fancy boutique specializing in tailor-made suits for men, but Dr. Cohen, never really the fashionable type, bought his suits off the rack. The only things worth spending thousands of dollars on, he thought, were his son's education, books, art, and travel. Other than that, money was to be saved, invested, or given away to causes like scholarships for minorities and, at the behest of his wife, feminist organizations. But they never made a fuss about that, never wanted their name on anything. They always donated money with business checks bearing the name of their boutique for the sake of anonymity. The only personal account they had was a joint one at a credit union. They shunned large commercial banks because of their excessive maintenance fees. Mrs. Cohen, who had the foulest mouth of anyone in Nassau County, cursed out her broker for charging a consultation fee for a five-minute phone call. After hearing her threaten to move her money to a firm down the street, the broker relented. Though that had happened eight years before, he still apologized to her at every opportunity. How could the broker forget the odd combinations of curse words she'd put together, mixing German with New York slang?

Noah, however, was easygoing. Inspired by his father's love of art, Noah was painting at the age of five, and by the time high school came around, he'd sold a few paintings and had become known as an artistic genius by his classmates, though he himself never felt that way. A proud Mr. Cohen designated the basement as Noah's own private space to create art, and it eventually became a showcase for everything Noah had painted and drawn since he was a small child.

By the ninth grade Noah developed a fascination with male nudity and had produced dozens of paintings of naked males that he hid from his parents. Mr. and Mrs. Cohen stumbled upon his homoerotic works and concluded their son was bisexual, but decided not to pressure Noah to tell them. They didn't care what his sexual orientation was, so long as he maintained a humanitarian zeal, loved art, and remained liberal.

But his parents were worried about one aspect of his paintings: the subjects—the boys he painted—looked prepubescent, with soft faces and wide eyes that stared innocently away from the canvas and out at the real world. Even worse—the little boys were naked, with their hairless genitals as the focal point. His parents never spoke a word about it, neither to Noah nor to each other. They hoped the realism in his paintings was the result of Noah's imagination and not the benefit of nude models who had soft faces and wide eyes that stared frighteningly away from stolen innocence and out at the Cohens' only begotten son.

Noah had painted females too, but had never felt the need to hide those paintings. Females didn't interest him quite as much, though he had an urge to be involved with them—an urge that wasn't always characterized by carnal desire. Despite that, there was something about males, slim ones in particular, that enticed him, which explained why the rib cages were so visible in his paintings of boys.

But at the moment, Noah had little concern for his paintings, because now, while walking to a dorm he didn't even live in, he was preoccupied with getting to know Elijah.

"So where are you from, Elijah?"

"South Carolina. You?"

"New York."

Elijah didn't respond, except to glance upward to make eye contact.

"I've seen you around before. I see you walking through the Student Union every day at noon," said Noah, who then recovered by saying, "Don't think I'm, like, stalking you or anything. I'm just very observant."

"Whatever you say," said Elijah, who was not at all disturbed by Noah's admission.

"I have to be observant," Noah said, "because I'm an artist."

"Really?"

"Yeah. I paint. I also sketch a lot, but painting is what I love most. But it's difficult to paint in my crappy little dorm room, so I only paint when I go home."

By then they had reached the residence hall, giving Noah the opportunity to open the door for Elijah. This was the first time Elijah had entered the lobby completely unaware of the desk attendant and the other students who were standing around.

"I noticed something else about you, too," said Noah.

"What?"

"That you drink a lot of sodas. "

"Yeah, this is the third soda I've had today," said Elijah.

"That means you're a drug addict."

Elijah laughed, signaling to Noah that it was okay to continue.

"You'll feel better mentally if you stop with all this soda drinking. The caffeine is making you crazy. Did you know it actually makes depression worse?" asked Noah.

"No," said Elijah, who stood rigidly and focused on Noah's beautiful mouth in an attempt to capture every word.

Noah's voice softened but retained its convincing tone. "Caffeine makes you more anxious, and anxiety compounds depression. It may not give you depression, but it makes it a lot worse. Your anxiety problems will begin to go away if you stop drinking all those sodas."

"How did you know I had anxiety problems?"

"Because I'm an artist, remember? I observe," Noah said. "And you're really fidgety."

Elijah didn't respond.

"It's amazing," Noah began, "how American culture has conditioned us to do things that are killing us—like drinking soda, carbonated depression. At an early age we learn to go to fast-food restaurants and order fatty foods and liquid anxiety to go with it. If you were born in the United States, the first two things you saw were the doctor who delivered you and a vending machine."

Elijah laughed. Then he burped.

"See what I mean?" said Noah, pretending to wave away the carbonation that had just emerged from his new friend's throat.

Elijah burped again.

They laughed.

"Okay, Noah, you win," said Elijah. "Well, it was nice meeting you," he added, while heading for the elevator.

"Nice meeting you, too." Noah walked away before turning around and saying, "Maybe you should look at some of my sketches sometime."

"That would be nice," said Elijah.

"Really?"

"Yeah."

"May I have your phone number?" asked Noah.

"Sure."

Noah handed his cell phone to Elijah, who then stored his number in the phone and handed it back.

"I'll call you later," said Noah.

"Okay, sugar," Elijah responded, while pressing the *UP* button to summon the elevator.

"Well, I'll see you later. I have to meet a study group in a little bit. I guess I'll just wait here in the lobby. That's—this is where we're supposed to meet."

"Okay," said Elijah, who embarrassed Noah with a chuckle.

Noah walked quickly to a chair and sat down, making a valiant effort not to look at Elijah but eventually giving in. When he saw the elevator doors close, Noah rose from the chair, exited the building, and walked to his dorm room. Thankful his roommate wasn't there, Noah took off his clothes and grabbed a bottle of lotion. Then he closed his eyes and pictured Elijah's bottom and the way his hips had switched back and forth when entering the elevator. Elijah was in his own room pleasuring himself while picturing the imprint of Noah's coronal ridge hook against the fabric of those shorts.

There was a wrestler on television Elijah often thought about when masturbating. Even though the wrestling was staged, he watched it—not for entertainment (he had no interest in sports) but for the certain muscular white man who had an enormous build and a very rough, manly face fit for a hard-edged marine. Elijah fantasized about this man a lot, and after wiping the semen away, he was surprised that Noah had temporarily replaced this wrestler in his masturbatory fantasies. Both Elijah and Noah had been pleasuring themselves at the exact same time, and by some orgasmic coincidence, both men had ejaculated simultaneously—a sign of things to cum.

By nightfall, satisfaction from the orgasm had worn off, as had the novelty of having met Noah. Elijah was alone, left with intense sadness. Although this horrible state of mind was always there, it surfaced quite brilliantly when he was alone. The power of this desolation made him think up the most morbid things. Elijah stood in front of the window, picturing himself jumping out and crashing headfirst into the parking lot, blood spilling from his twisted body while people covered their mouths in shock.

He flinched at the thought of the impact but smiled at the idea of

the aftermath. Thoughts of his funeral quickly removed that beautiful smile. *Will anyone show up? Will anyone mourn? Will anyone
care? Will they give this room to another student before my body
gets cold?*

Elijah wanted to cry at his inability to produce answers. All of
his friends, or at least the few he had, were off at their own colleges,
making new friends—getting on with their lives as if they had never
really known him. That thought forced him to open the window to
let the cool air hit his face. He fumbled with the screen but couldn't
remove it. After nearly ten minutes of trying to twist knobs and turn
latches, Elijah gave up.

Then it happened. Pink pixie dust began to float around the
room. The dust then fell to the ground, made a circle, and formed
the outline of a small man the size of a can of soda. The dust then
turned into a fairy with translucent wings. The fairy was a black man
with smooth skin who wore green pants with a yellow jacket.

"I hate this fucking outfit," said Phillip the Fairy.

"You're back."

"Of course I'm back. I had to stop your dumb ass from commit-
ting suicide."

"Is that why you're here?" asked Elijah.

"Who do you think stopped you from prying open the screen?"

"Okay. I get it," said Elijah.

"No, you don't get it. Your life is too valuable to take it. You
don't understand that. Many people would kill to be in your situation. You're smart; you're beautiful."

"And I'm lonely."

"For now," the fairy replied.

"Forever."

"You just have to be patient, and the right guy will come along,"
said Phillip the Fairy.

"The right guy did come along. Now he's gone."

"If he was really the right guy, he wouldn't have left."

"Go away," said Elijah.

"I'm just telling the truth," replied Phillip.

"I'm in love with him."

"That wasn't love. That was infatuation. There's a difference," said Phillip.

"What do you know? You're just a fairy."

"So are you."

Elijah laughed.

"Finally I see a smile," said Phillip. "You were in love with the *idea* of Grayson because he's white."

"What does that have to do with anything?"

"You think if a good-looking white guy like Grayson wants to be with you, then you must be beautiful too."

"That's not true," said Elijah.

"You want white people to validate you."

"Whatever."

"I see you pinching your nose to try to make it look like a white man's nose," said Phillip.

"Shut up," said Elijah.

"You need to hear this," said Phillip. "You've got to stop this self-hate. You've got to stop wanting to be like them and start loving yourself. Look at history. Why would you want to be like those pale-faced bastards? White people are the ones who did all those horrible things? Slavery. The Holocaust. Apartheid. Hell, they murdered Indians and took their land. And white folks had the nerve to make a holiday out of that shit! Motherfucking Thanksgiving! Founding fathers my ass. More like founding crackers. They rewrite history to cover up their dirty ways."

"How do they rewrite history?" asked Elijah.

"They pretend like Columbus discovered America even though Indians were already here. How the fuck can crackers claim they discovered a place that already had motherfuckers in it? Explain that shit to me. That's like if I go to Tennessee and come back next week talking about I discovered Chattanooga. People would look at me like I was crazy." Phillip cleared his throat. "Why the fuck would you want to be like those white devils? You're crazy, Elijah—fucking crazy."

"No, I'm not."

"You have to be crazy to want to be like them," said Phillip the Fairy.

"Imagine that. A racist fairy."

"I'm a fairy who knows history."

"You've got to stop hating white people," said Elijah.

"I don't hate white people. I just can't stand those crackers."

"Then you're a racist," Elijah replied.

"Think what you want about me, but I want you to remember this one thing, even if you don't remember anything else I tell you."

"What?" Elijah asked.

"There is no one more dangerous than a white man who has a sense of entitlement."

"Okay," said Elijah while shrugging his shoulders.

"But white guys are good in bed, especially the Jewish ones," said Phillip.

"There are Jewish fairies?" asked Elijah.

"Of course. I had sex with a Jewish fairy last week. I gave him some of my cat."

"How was it?"

"Amazing," said Phillip. "That white boy sprinkled some pixie dust on his dick and fucked the hell out of me. He loosened my rectum up so much if you put your ear up to my asshole, you can hear the ocean."

Elijah laughed. "Really?"

"Yeah." Phillip grabbed his backside. "My cat is still sore. He fucked me like I owed him some money."

"I need to pour some holy oil on you to get the devil out of you," said Elijah.

"What-the-fuck-ever."

"Holy oil works. I bought some."

"You wasted your money. It's nothing but cooking oil bottled up in a religious package. You can use that shit to fry some motherfucking chicken," said Phillip the Fairy.

"It *is* holy."

"What makes it so holy?" asked Phillip.

"I don't know."

"Good answer. I might need some of that holy oil tonight. If I run out of anal lube, that white boy can pour it in my asshole before he sticks his dick in it."

"Enough," said Elijah.

"I'm serious. Pixie dust is too abrasive. My cat was bleeding."

"You're silly. I'm going to pray for you."

"Not that bullshit again," said Phillip.

"I'm not getting into another debate about religion. I'm tired of debating," said Elijah.

"Okay. Fine."

"Just because you're a fairy doesn't mean you can't accept Jesus into your life. I try to live a good life because God is watching. When I was growing up, the minister would say you have to live your life like Jesus is right beside you," said Elijah.

"Really?" asked Phillip, as he folded his arms.

"The minister was telling the truth," said Elijah. "What would you do if Jesus walked into the room?"

"I would suck his dick."

"That's enough," said Elijah. "It's time for you to go."

"That's the thanks I get for saving your life? Niggas don't appreciate shit."

"Just leave."

"Remember what I said, Elijah. In order to be happy in life, you got to love yourself. Here, take this," said Phillip, as he handed Elijah a container of pixie dust.

"What's this for?" asked Elijah.

"You'll know," said Phillip, as he disappeared into pink dust that floated around before disappearing itself.

෴

Later that day, when the pixie residue was long gone, Elijah decided to try to go to sleep and dream his worries away, but not before checking his e-mail. Getting online before going to bed was a ritual of his. It was his way of linking himself to the outside world without enduring the stresses related to personal contact.

Usually he would be disappointed, but this time the computer gave him what he'd been looking for. He saw a message from Grayson in his inbox. Upon seeing the name, he was suddenly aware of his heartbeat. His hands shook uncontrollably.

But Elijah managed to click on Grayson Dobson:

Dear Elijah,

Life sure knows how to send us twists and turns. And this has been one of them. I never thought I'd be in Iraq fighting insurgencies and dodging snipers and eating rations and pissing in holes and doing everything else I see in the movies. But I am. Though it's nothing like a movie, it feels surreal. Waking up not knowing if you're going to make it. It's like in this short time, I've seen it all. Death. Dismemberment. Babies' fatal wounds. It's all very painful. It makes you appreciate what you have back home. Being able to walk around without worrying about a bullet flying through your head.

There are good things. The camaraderie is amazing. Unlike anything. I've met people from all over. And I love them a lot. Nothing prepared me for this type of friendship. Not sports, not college…nothing prepared me for the love I have for the men beside me every day. I know I said earlier that it's very surreal. Well, that part isn't. The camaraderie is very real. Especially now that two guys I'd come to know died last month in a helo crash. At least that's the story that was told to us. I'd never cried before—I mean really cried—until I found out the two guys who used to sleep next to me every night had died. Luke and Bruce were their names. They slept right beside me, making strange noises with their bodies and talking in their sleep. I miss those things.

I guess that's why I'm writing you. Because you have to hold on to something familiar in times like this. You know, to keep you sane. I haven't known you for that long, but you are very familiar to me.

Well, I have to prepare for another helo ride. I'm scared to death to go up in the sky, but it's a fear that I've had to conquer. Part of me will always be afraid of flying, especially after what happened to Luke and Bruce. The only time I wasn't afraid of being high up in the sky was after that time we ate at Greekos. That was something else, wasn't it? It'll happen again real soon. I promise. I love you, Little Guy.

Sincerely,
Grayson

That was all Elijah needed to stay awake a few more moments. No longer was he worried about the loneliness the night always brought him. That e-mail felt like Grayson. It seemed as though Grayson was with him in that awful dorm room on the bad side of campus. It seemed like he was there—beside him—wearing soccer shorts and a plain white T-shirt. Elijah was confident that he and Grayson would be on the rainbow again, looking down at the town and laughing at the people who dared to judge them. The naysayers didn't matter anymore, at least not right then. Elijah leaned into the computer and put his forehead against the screen, and for a second he thought Grayson would appear. Wishful thinking on his part, to be sure. But for the first time in his life, wishful thinking wasn't bad…wasn't bad at all.

PART III

Red Blouse

8

A red blouse would be appropriate for Abby's date with Spencer. Her late mother thought red was for sluts, a memory that gave Abby pause. But her rebellious stage didn't end with her mother's death. Her pants were black, a slimming color that would compensate for the lack of time spent on the elliptical that morning. It had been three months since she had seen Spencer, but more important in Abby's mind, it had been three months since Spencer had seen *her,* forcing Abby to wonder if the wrinkles of a thirty-something woman had set in. She questioned whether her night cream really lived up to the promise on the box.

Nothing had really changed about her appearance in the past few months. The usual weight gain that stress brought on was nowhere to be found, thanks in no small part to her everyday walks around the neighborhood. That was the only thing in her life she welcomed, since strolling among the stately homes and manicured lawns gave her a sense of calm that couldn't be found inside her house.

"Hi, Dakota. Didn't expect you to be out taking a walk so early," Abby said to her neighbor.

"Had to get my mind off of things."

"What things?" Abby asked.

"A dead husband. Getting old and missing my children. Lovely life, right?"

"If it makes you feel any better, you look good for a forty-year-old hag."

"Go to hell," said Dakota, as she moved her red hair from her forehead.

Abby laughed. "Do you mind if I walk with you?"

"I could use the company. Besides, you're the only one in the whole neighborhood who's not full of shit."

"How have the other neighbors been?" Abby asked.

"Didn't I just tell you they're full of shit?"

"You know what I mean. I barely associate with them, those racist bastards."

"Welcome to the South," said Dakota.

"I've been here a few years now, but I picked up on that the first ten minutes. It's the same in the North too. Trust me, I've lived there. You've been here all of your life."

"Yes, and hating every minute of it. The people here are awful."

"You mean the socialites?" asked Abby.

"Who else? Ever since my husband died, they've shunned me from every affair. I guess I'm not important to them since I'm no longer a congressman's wife. To them, I'm just a sad widow whose husband died in a freak boating accident," said Dakota.

"Well, you're more than that to me. You're the best friend I've got down here, and I've only known you for two years."

"Thanks. That means a lot."

"Anytime," said Abby, who didn't respect much about her friend.

Dakota had dated men for money without having any goals of her own. Abby appreciated Dakota's intellectual abilities, but despised her monetary quest for another man; Abby had always hypocritically looked down on women who dated men to move up the economic ladder. She was no longer concerned with superficial things like how much money a man made or what kind of car he drove. She was only concerned with the more important things a man had to offer, like his body and penis size.

As they walked, the sun seemed more timid than usual, ducking down just underneath a cloud as if it were afraid to show its face. The rain that had fallen the previous night left a slick film over everything, so the grass shone like an oil painting. The wind would've prompted someone else to bundle up, but not Abby. Instead, she unbuttoned the top of her blouse to show off the necklace she'd bought. She quickly buttoned it back up when she remembered that the neck tends to show more age than the rest of the body.

Once they finished their walk, Abby went home to sit alone in her mansion, which she had furnished to capacity with tables and rugs—filling spaces that would've been better left empty. The furniture and accessories were her attempt to reclaim her New England life. But this home was still different, whatever *home* meant.

The people in South Carolina were much less progressive than what Abby had trained herself to be accustomed to. Many of the people in her neighborhood were from New England, yes, but a little too old-fashioned for her taste. She was thankful Spencer was around to give her a distraction. Having cleaned herself up after her walk, Abby was glad to be behind the wheel of her SUV, taking a drive to see him.

Her vehicle seemed to lack the pep it had just the day before, as if it didn't want her to make it to the Dough House Café to meet her date. Could this rendezvous even be called a date? She decided the answer was a resounding yes and would make it a point to tell her sister she was dating someone. And the convenience of telling her Spencer was a real-estate mogul and a Harvard business graduate wouldn't make her feel guilty in the least. Details didn't matter, neither did the truth. As long as he was educated in the bedroom, there was no need to have an Ivy League degree, and besides that, there was a bit of allure about a military man that the polished Wall Street types didn't have.

Spencer had arrived at the Dough House Café before Abby and was sitting at a small table right next to the window. Abby pulled her SUV into the space she'd parked in the first day they met. She was embarrassed to be driving the same car. That had never crossed Spencer's mind, since he drove a used SUV desperately in need of a new transmission. Abby could see his smile through the window, his perfect teeth, which looked even whiter next to his dark skin. She beamed back, wondering if the bleach job had worn off on her teeth. For the entire date, Abby wouldn't give full smiles, out of concern for the way her teeth had dulled since her dentist appointment a mere two months prior.

"Hi, how are you?" asked Abby, as she entered the café.

"Doing good." Spencer's voice was laced with uncertainty.

They hugged, and Abby smelled him, appreciating the scent of his aftershave. Spencer pulled out a chair for Abby before sitting across from her.

"I already got the coffee and Danishes," he said.

"I see," Abby replied with a smile, as she stared at him.

Those few months had been kind to his body, filling him out so that his muscles were bulkier than they'd been when he used to work behind the counter. The cool breeze outside didn't stop him from wearing a sleeveless shirt to show off what the Marines had given him.

"So how was it?" Abby asked, reaching across the table to get her coffee and pastry.

"How was what?" Spencer flashed a cunning smile.

"The military? How was the military?"

"It was all right. Don't feel like talking about it much. Not much to talk about, really. Went to boot camp. Was shipped off. Was discharged for cussing out my superior. Like I said, nothing much to talk about."

Abby laughed. "Well, sounds like there's a lot to talk about. You just don't want to give me details. I'll let you slide this time."

"Okay, good." He took a bite of his Danish. "So what have you been doing the past few months?" Spencer asked.

"Well, my mother passed away. Had complications from an aneurysm." Abby's tone was that of a news anchor. Before Spencer could show sympathy, she continued, "And I finally finished the book. I think I might've told you that."

They sat there long after the food and coffee were gone and talked about everything—except for past love interests.

"I'm amazed at how little I know about you," said Abby.

"What do you want to know?"

"Not sure. Just a little background information. Basic things."

"Well, I was born in a Richland County prison," he said.

Abby leaned forward.

Spencer put his right hand over his left. "My mom gave birth to me while awaiting trial."

"For what?" asked Abby.

"Robbery. She was on trial for robbery. She didn't rob anything. She was just an accessory, since she was driving the getaway car."

"So who committed the actual robbery?"

"My father," said Spencer.

Abby leaned forward a little more, trying to cover the surprise on her face. "So where is she now?"

"Dead."

"Sorry I asked," said Abby.

"It's okay."

"What—what about your father?"

"Dead too. He died during the robbery. From what they tell me, he got out of the car and an officer shot him for no apparent reason. He wasn't resisting arrest or anything. They later found out the police officer used to belong to the KKK. But he wasn't punished for anything—the trigger-happy bastard got away with killing an innocent black man. I guess he wasn't innocent if he was robbing a liquor store, but he still didn't deserve to be gunned down."

"So who raised you?" Abby asked.

"My grandparents on my momma's side."

She was amazed at how open and direct Spencer was when telling her this, so she became comfortable asking him questions. "How did your mother die?"

"The bitch died of a heroin overdose," said Spencer.

Abby's mouth flew open.

Spencer leaned forward like her. "My grandparents were strict and very religious. So it was tough. Plus they didn't have much money, so I had to fend for myself on the block."

"On the block?" asked Abby.

"Selling drugs," said Spencer, before telling her that both his grandparents had died in the same month, leaving him alone at the age of seventeen.

She sure got an earful, and much of what she heard saddened her because it brought back memories of her own troubled childhood, though it illumined the notion that hers wasn't nearly as bad as she'd thought. She wanted to lean across the table and kiss Spencer's thick lips.

"You haven't told me anything about you," he said. "Tell me one thing about yourself. It has to be a secret."

"A secret?"

"Yes," said Spencer.

Abby surprised herself with her candor by answering, "I suffer from chronic depression."

That was the first time Abby had revealed her mental illness to anyone. Immediately, a smile formed inside her because her mind was a little more at peace after this revelation. Hiding it from her friends and family had made it much worse, since living a lie—a life of inauthentic sanity—had made her even more insane.

"I read a lot about depression. Have some military buddies who are going through it."

"I can imagine, considering all the blood and turmoil military people see."

"Yeah, it can make you go crazy if you don't know how to deal with it," said Spencer.

"How did *you* deal with it?"

"Art," said Spencer.

"I guess that's the best way," said Abby, who felt guilty about taking antidepressants that stifled her creativity and sometimes prevented her from writing.

"I'll show you some of my work someday, but let's keep talking about you," said Spencer.

Abby smiled, impressed and falling in love, for a man had never said that to her before. Men had never listened to Abby, choosing instead to penetrate her and use her as a trophy to raise their own profile and solidify what society taught them was masculinity. She had let them use her and had enjoyed it because her own mother had taken self-destructive pleasure in her dealings with men. That learned behavior and a lust for money had motivated her to become a prostitute while in college. The moments of thoughtless sex were enjoyable, to be sure, but the dirty feeling afterward—staring at a stranger who had just entered her—killed Abby emotionally because happiness didn't take the form of reckless intercourse. She hadn't been grounded in that emotion because her secret past was something she tried to get out of her head, and refusing to face her past compounded her depression.

"Sometimes I don't know what to do to treat it," said Abby.

"You could start by stopping with all the caffeine."

"What do you mean?" asked Abby.

"Caffeine makes depression worse, because you begin to crave it like a drug. It actually should be considered a drug."

"What?" Abby wanted to laugh.

"It changes your brain function by making you high and alert in an abnormal way. And you begin to need it every day the way a crackhead needs crack," said Spencer.

Abby didn't want to laugh anymore, thinking he was probably right.

He sensed her resignation. "Someone on drugs, once the high wears off, they feel sadder than they were before they actually took it. So the next day, or maybe that same day, they go back to get more of the drug. In this case, it's caffeine."

"Do you think it'll help me if I stop with my caffeine fix?" asked Abby.

"Yes, almost immediately. You might crave it for a few days or so, but it'll wear off. And your body will start feeling better, and your mind will be more at ease." Spencer looked down at Abby's cup of coffee. "It's not a difficult thing to do, though. You're a strong-minded girl. You can handle it."

Abby smiled.

"I read somewhere that one in ten people suffer from caffein-ism," said Spencer.

"Really?"

"Yeah, which means one in ten people are drug addicts and don't know it."

Abby and Spencer both laughed.

Something strange happened at the table in the café—Spencer got a peek behind the façade of a seemingly poised woman. But Abby was desperate to put up a wall to correct her revelation about her depression. No one had ever truly known her—not even her ex-husband—and that was a distinction she would have to maintain, even if it meant pushing away Spencer, who, despite her doubts, really did have feelings for her. She left a fifty-dollar bill on the table as a tip and glanced at Spencer to gauge his reaction. Exactly the response she expected—his mouth opened slightly and his eyes opened wider. She hadn't revealed too much after all, she thought to herself while walking out of the café, clutching her Gucci handbag as if it were the hand of a hyper toddler.

As they stood outside, Abby stared at Spencer.

"What?" he asked.

"Do you want to come to my house for dinner tonight?" Abby asked.

Spencer nodded. "When?"

"Six."

"Six is good," Spencer said.

"Okay. I'll text you the address. What's your number?"

Spencer grabbed Abby's phone, entered his number, and gave the phone back.

"Good. I'll see you tonight at six," said Abby.

"All right. Looking forward to it."

They hugged before getting in their vehicles and driving away.

⌒※※℘

When Abby entered her home and placed her handbag on a table, her mansion once again felt unfamiliar. So, to bring back a touch of Tennessee, she went upstairs to her bathroom, which was too big for one person, and pulled out her comb. She had been over thirty years old before realizing just how soothing it was to stroke a comb through her hair. The strokes resurfaced memories of her sitting on the floor while her mother combed her hair.

The motions also brought back one of the few good recollections of her father, who had tried to comb her hair once but haphazardly snatched it in a way that pulled out several strands of hair from her nine-year-old scalp. As the comb moved back and forth from scalp to ends, Abby laughed out loud, remembering that she and her father had let out the same raucous cackle and both had fallen to the floor and laughed for minutes on end, faces toward the ceiling.

Now, as Abby stood in front of her mirror, comb in hand, the features on her face did resemble those of her father. The long, slender visage. The set of lips that made everything, even solemnity, look like a smirk. The way her ears were small and uneven—only noticeable when her hair was pulled back, like she held it at this very moment while trying to envision more good times with her father. But she then remembered the time her father had called her fat when she was four years old, even though Abby was small for her age. She had been too young to know what the word really meant, but her ignorance didn't stop her from understanding the sting of his voice—the tone he would take when belittling the helpless.

Who am I?

Abby Brooks, Just Abby Brooks, was the answer, but the Worthington in her placed the comb back on the granite counter and walked into the bedroom to sit down on the velvet-padded chair in front of her vanity.

Maybe this mirror will reveal something, Abby thought.

It did. The lights didn't shine nearly as brightly as those in the bathroom, giving her face a gentleness that threw her back to the time she and Susie were looking up at the clouds for disciples. The softness of her countenance hid the years and years of collected expressions that had been placed on her face by Massachusetts and Tennessee.

⌘

Later that day, just after combing her hair again, Abby called a taxi.

"Hello."

"This is Abigail Worthington."

"May I help you, ma'am?"

"Yes, I need a cab."

"Where are you going?"

"To the Cadillac dealership on Parksdale."

"From?"

Then Abby told the dispatcher where she lived, misinterpreting his pause to be one of awe, though he was simply writing down the address.

By the time the cab came, Abby was inappropriately dressed for the occasion: silk blouse, dark blazer, skirt, high-heel shoes, handbag, and teardrop diamond earrings. She said nothing to the taxi driver for the duration of the ride and simply nodded when paying him. The driver shook his head from side to side. Abby smiled, noticing his disapproval as she firmly closed the car door.

While walking away from the taxi, she could see a salesman approaching her.

"I want that one," was the first thing she said to him, as she pointed at the vehicle.

"I'm sorry, ma'am?"

"I said, I want that one." Abby's inflection was that of a grade-school teacher writing a misbehaving student's name on the blackboard.

"The SRX?" asked the car salesman.

"Of course the SRX. What else would I be here to buy?" Abby, earrings sparkling, walked toward the SUV and looked at the price on the window. "Forty-five thousand dollars?" she asked.

"Yes, that's correct, ma'am."

Abby unbuttoned her handbag, removed a bank card, handed it to the salesman, and said, "Now go do the paperwork." Abby shooed him away with her hand.

9

Spencer pulled into the driveway and emerged from his old, used vehicle, which he parked beside Abby's new SUV. Spencer looked around at the exterior of the house while walking to the front door. He was holding a folder, clutching it tightly as if it could run away. Abby, prompted by the noise coming from his vehicle, had scurried to the window to regard his stride, adjusting her blouse and fixing her hair while holding back the curtain just enough to see him. The lighting of the café looked much different on him than the scant rays emanating from a setting sun, relieving the shine of his skin, replacing it with dull, supple warmth that made him look stronger.

Spencer knocked on the door three times despite the doorbell. Abby, after waiting for a few seconds, walked to the foyer, still adjusting her blouse.

"Hi, Spencer."

"Sorry I'm so late." He leaned down and hugged her.

"It's no problem. I just got here," Abby lied.

"This is a nice house." Spencer looked around at various things in the room: the yellow paint on the walls, the curtains adorning the bay window, the marble flooring, the furniture laced in floral designs.

Abby didn't respond except to turn away to hide her smile.

As if he already knew where to go, Spencer walked to the kitchen and sat down on a stool at the granite counter and placed the folder just in front of him. After pouring two glasses of champagne, she joined him on the other side of the counter and looked at him, thinking to herself that he was the only guest, except for Dakota, to come to her house in two years. Aside from workmen—the cable guy, movers, painters, electricians, and the like—no one had ever been to her house. Though the countertop was blocking his view, Abby crossed her legs to make her thighs look thinner.

"So, aside from writing, what kind of work do you do?" Spencer asked, wanting to lean back in the chair, but unable to because it didn't have a back. He planted his elbows on the counter instead.

"Nothing, really, though I'd love to be an editor again. That was what I did back in Boston. Don't know if I told you that already," said Abby, who failed to mention that she lived a lavish lifestyle because of her wealthy ex-husband. She also failed to mention that her divorce settlement made her one of the wealthiest women in the state.

"No, you never told me that," said Spencer.

"Well, that's what I hope to do eventually, but this isn't exactly the area for that. I'll probably lease a condo in New York when I start my job search. That's the ideal place for that type of thing." Abby looked at Spencer above the champagne glass she held to her mouth, hoping to see a reaction. There was none. Then she asked, "And what about yourself? What would you like to do?"

Spencer replied, "Not sure. Hopefully become an artist, but you can't really make a career out of that, you know. Artists don't really make any money until they die."

Abby laughed, placing her hand across the middle of her chest, her shoulders bouncing up and down like pistons. Though that wasn't intended to be a joke, Spencer laughed with her, thinking it was the first bit of genuine mirth he'd heard from her. It was refreshing to hear something he could relate to, something other than vacations in exotic locations and European antiques.

"What kind of artist are you?" Abby asked.

"A painter. That's my passion, but I sketch a lot too. I like to paint all sorts of things, but I especially like religious subjects," Spencer answered.

Luckily the glass was pressed against Abby's lips, so it hid her agape mouth. He'd never come across as a religious man.

Without solicitation, he continued, "One day I want to go to Italy and see the places all my favorite artists lived. And France, too." Spencer rose from his chair as he spoke and walked around looking at the artwork on the walls.

Abby marveled at how his face lit up when speaking the names of impressionist painters she'd studied but forgotten about. For the first time, Spencer wasn't just a dark creature with something swinging between his legs, nor was he her way of cheating on someone she'd divorced years ago.

"Look at the brushstrokes on this one. He must've been sad. You can tell by the strokes what mood a person was in. I know when I'm feeling down, I paint like this." Spencer picked up a pen from the counter and made a motion that resembled the sway of a conductor's baton. He continued, "But I never really get to paint much now. My apartment isn't big enough. One day I'll get one of those big warehouse apartments with a big open room where I can just paint all day long." Spencer spread his arms wide as if he were attempting to fly and said, "Maybe one day."

There was a period of silence during which they both noticed the sound of air coming from the vent overhead. The hush wasn't the least bit awkward for either of them. Like a pupil unable to grasp a concept, Abby put her hand under her chin and squinted. It was as if Spencer were a blur she wanted to make clearer. She hoped he would continue speaking in a manner that was antithetical to his appearance.

"What are you looking at?" asked Spencer, who looked down at his body.

"Nothing."

"Nothing?" he asked.

"Okay, I admit it. I was looking at your muscles," Abby said.

"I knew it," Spencer said with a smile.

Another pause made the sound of air coming out of the vent more noticeable until Spencer broke the silence. "When I was in the military, I missed painting more than anything. Didn't really have much family to miss, so I guess I had to miss something. I took a pencil and some notebooks with me."

Spencer continued to look at the painting as he spoke. "In Baghdad, I sketched in my spare time because it was so hard to get some sleep sometimes. Baghdad is where I was stationed, you know; after boot camp, that's where they sent me. It was an experience I'll never forget."

Spencer paused and looked at more brushstrokes, wanting to touch the canvas but deciding against it, out of respect for the artist. "At night all I had was a flashlight, and I would use it for light while I drew stuff. The landscape, my comrades, interpretations of Jesus—I drew everything. I filled notebook after notebook with sketches. It's like when I have free time, I start thinking about all the bad shit that happened to me, so I paint and draw to get my mind off of things."

"That is so sweet." Abby didn't realize she had spoken.

"I got some of my sketches here if you want to take a look at them," Spencer said, sliding the folder across the table as if he were making a deal.

She opened it.

"These are nice," Abby said.

"Thanks."

Abby stopped on a sketch of a soldier who was wearing only a pair of shorts. He was lying on what looked like a jacket that had been folded up. His face was chiseled, and his hair looked as light as it could be with the meticulous shading of a piece of graphite.

His eyes were closed, but Abby knew they had to be beautiful when opened.

"Who is this?" she asked.

Spencer didn't answer, so Abby turned the page and looked at other sketches before pausing to view a drawing of a dark man with curly black hair, a mustache, and a goatee.

"Who is this?"

"Who?" asked Spencer.

"This African man here. He's so beautiful."

"It's Jesus," said Spencer.

Abby squinted—eyes fixed on the picture. "Not the Jesus I'm accustomed to seeing," she said.

"What do you mean? You mean you're not used to seeing a black Jesus?"

"Yes, that's what I mean."

"Well, he was black. You do know that, don't you?" asked Spencer.

"If you say so, sweetie." Abby chuckled with the word *sweetie*, then took a sip of champagne, not even bothering to look at Spencer.

"I can tell you're being sarcastic, but I'm going to let it slide this time." Spencer leaned toward Abby, his dog tags dangling from his neck.

"But none of that really matters," said Abby, with a shrug of the shoulders and a shake of her head.

"Why not?"

"Because I'm not really into religion," she said.

"It's okay. You at least believe in God, don't you?" asked Spencer.

"No, I don't."

"You'll believe in God when you go to hell," said Spencer.

Abby laughed.

"You'll be praying for the Lord to get that piece of brimstone out your ass," Spencer said.

"Forgive me for not believing the bullshit in the Bible."

"What bullshit?"

"The bullshit that's from beginning to end. It starts with this foolish story about Adam and Eve."

"I know that already," said Spencer. "And what's wrong with the story about Adam and Eve?"

"Everything," said Abby, as she took another drink from her glass. "If you and your girlfriend were walking through a garden and a snake started speaking to you in ancient Hebrew, what would you do?"

Spencer smiled.

Then Abby said, "After that, the snake tells you to eat an apple. So not only is the snake fluent in your native language, it also has the dietary knowledge to suggest cuisine."

They both laughed.

Spencer interrupted Abby's reflections when he stood up, leaned across the counter, and kissed her slowly, softly, and gently while shifting his body so as not to knock over her glass.

His lips felt smooth, and they covered her entire mouth, painting her lips like an empty canvas—making her want to cry tears of joy from the tenderness of his gesture. And his tongue was just as smooth, like the sweetest wine trickling down her throat on a Sunday morning, just as pure as communion. Religious.

"Do you want to go upstairs and get comfortable?" Abby asked.

"Yes," Spencer replied.

"Come on," said Abby, with a smile, motioning for him to follow her.

He walked behind her up the staircase. When he made it to Abby's bedroom, he stopped and looked around.

"This is the biggest bedroom I've ever seen," Spencer said.

Abby had left the curtains open. Moonlight poured into the room, giving them sparse visibility, just enough to see the path to the bed that was raised high from the ground on four wooden posts that had a cherry finish. The sheets were red, though they looked burgundy in the moonlight. The room somehow had gotten smaller and smaller every time Abby had entered, probably because it seemed a little stuffier alone in the room.

But with an artist sitting on her bed, a man who was fascinated with the queen's expensive things, the room opened up a bit. The walls didn't cave in on Abby like they had a few nights before, when Spencer was thought to be a part of her past.

He removed his sneakers like a toddler, not bothering to touch them with his hands—rather, sliding the opposite shoe off at the heel with his toes. Abby thought it cute and laughed a little, and Spencer laughed too, wondering what was so funny.

By the time they were lying atop the red-turned-burgundy sheets, both seemed a little nervous about what to say or do. They hadn't choreographed what would happen next, since neither had thought it would go this far. They could feel each other breathing and could hear cars going down the road outside.

"So what next?" Abby asked, hoping it didn't sound too forward.

Spencer, shirtless by now, answered by rolling on top of her and kissing her slowly. She closed her eyes as those thick lips kissed her forehead, reminding her of something, but he didn't give her time to remember. Each of his kisses closed her eyes. And each of his stares opened them.

Finally Spencer did something no man, not even Teddy, had ever done to Abby. He moved her hair away from her face slowly, the way she herself did when the wind blew—but his hands were rough. Then they undressed each other. Their movements seemed like a number that had been rehearsed over and over again. The way his lips felt exploring Abby made her feel ashamed of not having known him all of her adult life. Abby breathed as his lips resurfaced to touch hers. She cried tears of pleasure from the slip of his tongue and the way he nibbled on her bottom lip.

Spencer was so heavy, but the pressure warmed Abby. She didn't welcome the cool air she felt when he lifted his body away from her, though she liked the way he looked down at her with his hands propping himself up and his silver dog tags dangling from his neck, tapping her face. She bit down on the chain, holding it between her lips to brace the shock as he entered her, but there was no pain, just heat…much better than the warmth of his body when it was pressed again her.

She had never been filled this way before, but it didn't hurt. So there was no need to bite down on the chain anymore. Abby was not embarrassed by the noises she made while clutching Spencer's back. Nor was she ashamed of the weakness she felt with every thrust of Spencer's body, because he protected her with his methodical stroke, moving around in circular motions like an artist with a brush, drawing the moon. No, the circles were larger, so it must have been the sun.

The circles made Abby remember how to cry. She let the tears form slowly, like ice melting in the corners of her eyes, and let them roll down the sides of her face. But Spencer didn't let the tears get far. He wiped them away before they hit the pillow, and the motion—the wipe of his dark thumbs across the sides of her face—made more ice melt and trickle down, only to be wiped away again and again with every circular stroke. Abby heard herself trying to say something, but her mouth was closed so she moaned instead. And with every moan, Spencer made deeper, wider circles. Abby could feel the Spirit moving her, and with each of Spencer's back-and-forth caresses, she was becoming closer and closer to God. Spencer Gibson was using his penis to thrust religion back into Abby's soul.

He lay down on top of her body, and the warmth of him inside her sent her away. Her eyes were closed, but she could still see him, could still feel his strokes. Spencer made smaller circles, but the heat of his chest against her and the tongue in her ear made the circles seem bigger. Abby couldn't moan anymore, so she let out a noise. Spencer made a sound of his own—a deep, layered one.

When the spotlight darkened and the curtains were drawn, he didn't remove himself from Abby, choosing instead to stay inside her…deep, deep inside her. And she was thankful for that. Abby felt honored to have him within her, to still have him there, to have experienced real pleasure for the first time in her life.

Abby wept like the mother of Jesus, for she—Abigail Brooks Worthington—had been saved by a black man's penis and was now born again. Abby understood that there would be a lot less evil if people had a man like Spencer. If everyone could experience sex with this man, the world would be a much better place, for one stroke of his penis could bring peace to the Middle East.

Jesus must really be black, Abby thought to herself.

When Spencer finally pulled out, Abby found that her soul was as empty as her vagina.

Who was Spencer, besides a man with a remarkable phallus?

The red bow was answering that question as it floated across the threshold, its ribbons dangling without the usual benefit of an indoor breeze. Abby had given up on expelling the ghost, thinking that even an act of carnal passion couldn't prevent the little ghost girl from entering her mind or her sights.

Not wanting to scream in front of Spencer, Abby cried and shivered instead, her face against his chest. Though he felt the tears, he didn't utter a word, because her tears were ice cold. He himself shivered violently as the arctic water fell upon his dark body. He knew then that Abby wasn't worth enduring frostbite, especially on the part of his chest that was above his heart.

Abby, too, felt the distance between them, the ocean that separated two entities. But she attempted to swim across this vast body of salt water by touching Spencer, resting her head on his strong body, only to drown before reaching the lighthouse, moments after experiencing the joy of moist sand on her bare feet.

"You comfortable?" asked Spencer.

"Yes," said Abby, as she touched his body. It felt like plastic, a mannequin that was beautiful at a glance but heartless upon closer inspection.

The red bow Abby thought she saw wasn't Muriel at all. The little ghost girl had been crying in the lightkeeper's room, watching Abby drown slowly in the Atlantic. The cold was killing Muriel, not the water. But Abby wondered why the ghost girl continued her singsong even when the currents were freezing the life out of her: "A warm flow of the waters may never be."

Muriel continued singing because she knew her savior would never truly love Spencer. Abby knew as much too, and tears glossed over her eyes to blur her sight. But stubborn still, Abby blinked her vision back to see this dark mannequin and vainly held onto it to keep afloat.

At that moment Abby had the sudden urge to burn Spencer's things, beginning with the crotch of his pants, and then the sketches he had left on the counter downstairs—starting with the picture of the black Jesus—all to erase this toy she had met in a café. There was nothing between them, and Abby knew full well that it was impossible to burn away nothingness.

So she put one hand on his chest to gain some degree of comfort. She wasn't content with mundane actions—like turning the pillow over while half-asleep so she could rest her head on the cooler side of the pillow. Abby was more concerned about the sheets than the bed itself, more worried about the shutters on the house than the plumbing. Inner workings had never mattered to her, because no one could see the bolts that kept the bed upright or the pipe work that brought water, life's necessity, to the house.

Abby had liked Spencer more when he was just a muscular man with a seductive walk. But his artwork had turned her off, as had his conversation, because with every sketch she saw and word she heard, Spencer Gibson became more than a man she wanted to thrust away her depression. He became well rounded and deep, too good for her, because she herself was none of those things. So now, as she lay there using Spencer as a pillow, Abby desperately wanted to burn something because she didn't have the power to manipulate this situation.

Despite how little Abby cared for Spencer, she clutched this black cure for loneliness and rested her head on his chest, shifting to find a comfortable spot. Spencer sighed when this happened, and before his breath could fade away into the rest of the room, Abby knew deep down that desperation had brought this moment. She felt loneliness prying her ear and his chest apart. And it found a comfortable space in the hollow and would stay tucked beside her eardrum until the moon made its unhurried ascent to the top of the once-blue sky.

10

Two days after Spencer had visited her home, and after the pseudo-validation of being touched by a man had set in, Abby gave him his first real diamonds, earrings she had bought from the mall a few days before. Spencer pretended not to want them, took them, and drove away. Abby watched him pull out of the driveway, and she smiled at the man she had just bought. Though she had no deep feelings for him, she'd given him the diamonds to make sure he continued to fuck her. But he didn't call her for a week after that; during those days sadness came over her. By the weekend she had left thirteen messages on his voice mail, ranging from anger to sadness to desperation.

Despite that, Abby didn't cry. Crying was for a child whose doll was broken. She believed herself not to be Muriel, a lonely girl making dollhouses out of planks in the floor of a lighthouse that wasn't really a home. Abby seemed to forget that she had wept a few times in the past few months.

Instead of calling Spencer and leaving another message, Abby picked up the telephone and called her ex-husband, Teddy, in a spontaneous move that surprised even her. They hadn't spoken to one another in over two years.

"Hello," he answered.

"Hi, Teddy. How are you?"

"I'm doing just fine. I'm at the beach house getting a little rest." Teddy's voice was laced with more delight than surprise. "How are you doing?"

"All right. Better than all right. Very good, actually." Abby poured a glass of champagne and took a sip before drinking the entire contents of the glass in seconds.

"That's good. What have you been up to?" asked Teddy.

"Writing," Abby said, pretending to drink from the empty glass, holding her pinky out as if he could see it through the phone.

This was the first time since they'd known each other that an awkward pause had insinuated itself into their conversation. Never had there been nothing to say. The two-year estrangement brought civility to their relationship, matched only by the gauche nature of their banter. The tones of their voices were congenial, as if they were old friends who hadn't spoken for a while because of busy schedules, not because of a messy divorce. It was something how their voices would always be familiar to one another. When he had said "Hello," it sounded just like the Teddy she'd always known.

Abby poured another glass of champagne and drank it before breaking the silence. "So what've you been up to?"

"A hell of a lot, really. Sold the company."

"What?" Abby asked. Thanks to the way her mouth was so close to the phone, the happiness in her voice was too muffled for Teddy to detect.

The effects of the alcohol hadn't set in yet, but unreasonable thoughts already formed in Abby's mind. Like the one telling her Teddy sold the company because it wasn't the same without her, though she never really had anything to do with it. While they lived together in Boston, she had shown no interest in his business, except to use the company credit card from time to time to buy things that were strikingly similar to the decorations in her plantation house.

"Well, I just got burned out, so I sold it. Next to divorcing you, it was the best decision I ever made," Teddy said.

They both chuckled.

"And a lot less expensive," Abby added.

They laughed at this for what seemed like a long time, and for a minute Abby thought about the moments they were on the yard at Boston College, walking with each other and ignoring everything else in the world. Now, hearing him speak seemed like visiting the neighborhood she grew up in, finding charm in it but glad she had gotten out of there in good time.

"Well, didn't want to hold you up from anything, Teddy. Just wanted to see how you were doing. It was good talking to you."

Just then Abby heard a woman's voice in the background and identified it as Rebecca Smith, her childhood best friend.

"Good to hear from you too," said Teddy, with a shaky voice that told Abby everything she wanted to know.

Before she could respond, the sound of the dial tone made tears fall from her face. And finally Teddy's ex-wife cried like a child at the thought of how her best friend could steal her doll. Just a few days before, there hadn't been a reason for her to believe that such a feeling would overcome her. By the time noon came around, Abby was too drunk—passed out on the floor from a combination of intoxication and despondency—to pick up the phone when Spencer finally called back.

⚸

The nighttime renewed her sense of creativity and resulted in unpolished pages of her next book. And Spencer's love (or her own delusion?) also prompted her, even with a slight hangover, to call a few old friends to see how they were doing. Phone call after phone call, she told them about how fabulous her life was in Hilton Head. There wasn't much need to embellish anything, save for Spencer's profession. But the core of her conversations was true: she'd moved to a nice neighborhood, renovated a plantation house, wrote a novel, began another one, and fell in lust with Spencer.

Then she thought of hearing Rebecca's voice when she had called Teddy. The thought brought on intense rage. Abby would make her ex-husband pay for this indiscretion. Exactly what the indiscretion was, she couldn't articulate. It wasn't cheating, since they weren't married anymore, and he wasn't really having sex with a friend, since she and Rebecca had grown apart. Abby wouldn't think about those minor details until after letting them know they couldn't get away with betraying her. No one betrayed Abby. No one—except for Abby herself.

Beach house? He's at the beach house? Too bad he never got the locks changed after the divorce. Too bad for him, and too bad for that wench who used to be my best friend, Abby thought as she waited for morning to come.

11

Before the morning had arrived, Abby was already on the interstate on the way to her former beach house in Cape Cod. Abby hadn't remembered going to the grocery store, nor did she remember even getting onto I-95. But there was no stopping her. With every mile of road that passed underneath her car, memories resurfaced. Like the time her father had spit on her for not cleaning up her room. She *had* cleaned the room, but as always, her father had to find fault. So he used a bit of mildew on the windowsill as an excuse to spit on and cuss out his nine-year-old daughter. After that, Abby's mother angered her by attempting to explain away his actions. So her mother, too, pretended to complain about the mildew on the windowsill. And her mom knew full well a nine-year-old couldn't possibly reach way up there to clean it.

And years later, when Abby's father waved good-bye to his daughter and never came back, the home became a little bit cooler. The rooms in the house, especially the living area, seemed a little more spacious. And her mom seemed to be a little more mommy than mother. But by then it was too late, because Muriel was being born. There was no way Abby could change the past; she could only influence what lie ahead on her quest to seek revenge against her ex-husband and ex-best friend.

By the time Abby arrived at the beach house, darkness had already cloaked the sky. The house looked exactly like she remembered it—gorgeous atop a hill, with large windows that made it

seem like you were always standing outside. The beach house offered more than the stuffy feeling of the trailer where she'd grown
up, which was why she had liked this waterfront property so much
when they picked it out. It was bright and open and on high ground,
which meant they could literally look down on people walking on
the beach below them.

Approaching the house, Abby saw Rebecca and Teddy standing at the doorway, kissing and hugging. She had already reached
the conclusion that they were an item, but she hadn't expected to
get confirmation so soon. What was she to feel? Sadness? Anger?
Betrayal? The answer was all of the above, though it was anger that
had made her stop at a store in South Carolina to buy one ingredient
for her plan and another store in North Carolina to obtain something
else. And to stop in Virginia to purchase the last component. Buying
it all at the same location would've been a little too obvious.

Abby knew the best place to hide. Every summer she and Teddy
had taken a trip to Cape Cod to relax in this house for weeks at a
time, taking walks outside and stopping at nice eateries, or sometimes just sitting on the sand and talking. So it was easy to find a
place to hide her SUV and watch what Teddy and Rebecca were doing. Abby saw them standing in front of the bedroom window on the
second floor, though from a distance they were merely two shadows
in a lighted room. But the one on the left had to be Teddy, because
of the broad shoulders. The one on the right just had to be Rebecca,
because of the long hair. The two shadows came together as one big
shadow then separated, then did it again and again for the next few
minutes. Finally, the lights in the home went out, prompting Abby
to make a move. Since there were no streetlights, the stars and the
moon kindly lit her way. But she was much too smart to rush into
anything. Rebecca and Teddy needed time to fall into a deep sleep.

During the two hours Abby sat in the SUV, some of the past
crept into her mind again. This time she remembered sitting at the

table in the kitchen as her father stumbled into the room, cussing at the air until finding a better target: his daughter.

"What the fuck are you looking at?"

Young Abby didn't respond, deciding instead to ignore the monster, hoping it would go away. But it didn't.

"I said what the fuck are you looking at?"

The monster hurled a bottle at the wall. The glass shattered, and a shard cut Abby's arm.

"You know we didn't even mean to have you, right? You do know that, don't you? We were doing just fine until you were born. You know that, don't you? We were too fucking broke to pay for the abortion," her father continued.

As if to add emphasis to his words, another bottle flew across the room, this time soaring over Abby's head and hitting the wall behind her. She covered her ears. That was when she took notice of the blood running down her little arm. The redness. The consistency. The trickle of it prompted her to cry and run outside. Later her mom found her sitting on the dirt road in her school clothes, still crying from her painful wound, a piece of glass embedded in her innocent little arm.

The times he slung the bottles and slapped her across the face one summer were the only instances physical harm had been brought to her. A hand to the face felt like a baseball bat to a five-year-old. And just as bad was her mother saying "Abby, it's time to go to bed," as if nothing had really happened, failing to acknowledge the terror. Her mother's standing there (but not being there) pained Abby almost as much as the baseball bat. Most kids were afraid of the dark or scared of ghosts, but as a little girl Abby had been afraid to wake up.

But that was a long time ago. She was never interested in the past, which was why she hated being alone and bored, with nothing to do but travel down Memory Lane. Once she stopped thinking about long-ago, Abby remembered she had brought the silver brooch that Teddy had given her years before. She pulled it out of the wooden box and stared at it, proud that it still glistened in the night. After slowly fastening the brooch to the top of her dress, she got out of the vehicle and approached the house. It didn't surprise her that her key still worked. This beach house—*her* beach house—felt welcoming. The clean smell. The freshness of the air. And even more inviting was her ability to move around in the darkness since nothing had changed; not one bit of furniture she'd picked out years before had been moved. Abby carried all three containers of gasoline she had bought on the way to Cape Cod, so she wouldn't have to take more than one trip from her SUV to the beach house. She quietly doused the gasoline about the house, tiptoeing and containing her laughter so as not to wake Teddy and Rebecca. There was only one staircase, and Abby made sure to empty a full container on the stairs to prevent Teddy and Rebecca from escaping.

Then Abby stood in the doorway and finally snickered aloud while striking a match and hurling it into the house. It landed on the antique sofa, which looked even more beautiful when the flames engulfed it, giving it a glow. The blaze ate the fabric and spread throughout the house, devouring all in its path. The fire burned with a crackling and tearing sound that had a strikingly appropriate harmony.

Abby turned, lifted up her dress just a little so as not to trip over the hem, and ran like hell from the house, laughing hysterically. By the time Teddy and Rebecca awoke to the crackling noises and the beeps of the smoke detectors, the fire had come through the floor, and it had run up the stairs, giving them nowhere to go.

As Abby ran, she heard a familiar voice.

"Wait!" said Muriel. "Wait!"

"Not now. This can't be happening now. Go away." Abby said as she continued to flee.

"Wait! You have to go back." Muriel tugged at Abby's dress.

"Let me go! You can't do this, not now!"

Abby made it to her vehicle and ignored Muriel's pleas, and she drove swiftly from the scene. No one saw Abby there. No one saw a woman running with the sides of her dress bunched up in her hands. No one heard the laughter that escaped her mouth. No one saw her drive away. No one saw a thing. No one except the little ghost girl.

When the firemen silenced the flames and entered the house, two charred bodies were on the staircase. It looked like Teddy and Rebecca had died reaching for something, just the way Abby had imagined. What she hadn't pictured was nearly running her car off of the road when seeing a red bow floating on the interstate while driving home. She drove through it, cursing herself, the car, and the vision all at once.

Why now? Abby thought, exiting the interstate. *Why now?* She pulled into an empty parking lot and began to weep, hoping not to see another floating bow. She had no problem being a cold-blooded killer, but seeing hallucinations upset her because it was symptomatic of a feeble mind.

By the time Abby made it back to Hilton Head, the sun had come back up again. When she opened the door and entered her home, it was refreshing, especially the cool air hitting her tired face and the orderly look about the foyer: the rugs lining up parallel to the wall, no paintings tilted, all of the fake flowers still radiant. The paint on the walls had a majestic shine that made each room seem a little brighter.

Upstairs was the same. Comfortable. Roomy enough for her to stretch out her legs on the bed to relieve the stiffness of being cramped under the steering wheel for hours on end. Abby immediately closed the blinds after entering her bedroom, thinking someone could look through her window and see guilt on her face. But the only inkling of remorse had left her before the match had land-ed on the antique sofa back in Cape Cod. Despite the red bow, the drive home had been full of laughter. *That's what they get*, Abby had thought as she passed the mile markers on the interstate. Could anyone have blamed her? One of the people who had caused her the most dismay was gone.

Even still, lying down on the bed gave her relief, a sense of much-needed solitude to not reflect on her past and to instead replay the flames that engulfed the beach house and laugh—yes, laugh—at the thought of Teddy and Rebecca waking up to die in that house. After taking a shower, Abby put on a nightgown, as if the sun were not hanging in the sky. She then checked her phone messages.

"Hey, Abby. This is Spencer. Just wanted to call you to see how you were doing. Sorry I didn't get the chance to call you sooner. Had to go out of town. I'll explain later. Didn't want you to think I was the type of guy who would run away. Later."

Abby cried as she walked downstairs to get away from her emp-ty bedroom.

If she'd gotten that message two days before, she might not have been an arsonist and a murderer—not because Spencer had that strong of a hold on her, but because he would have been a dis-traction. But knowing Abby, no diversion could have stopped her psychotic determination. Teddy deserved it anyway…and so did Re-becca. At least that was the last thing Abby thought before falling into a deep sleep on the living room sofa.

The telephone woke her hours later.

"Hello," she answered.

"Abby, I got some awful news." Susie's voice was trembling, causing Abby to sit up in her bed.

"What is it, Susie?"

"I don't know how to tell you this."

"Just say it. Go on and say it."

"Teddy and Rebecca died in a fire. The investigators said the arsonist used gasoline," Susie said.

"They're dead. What? Arsonist? Susie, you can't be serious. That can't be true."

"No, Abby, it's true. They're dead, and it was arson."

"I can't believe this. I just can't believe it."

"It's okay, Abby. It's going to be okay."

"I can't believe it." Abby covered the phone so her sister couldn't hear her laughing and then asked, "Who told you this? And why were they together?"

"Teddy's mom. Says she would've called you, but she didn't have your number. She was so shaken up by all of this. I didn't know what to tell her." Susie ignored Abby's second question.

"This is just too much for me to handle right now. You know, he meant so much to me. Even after the divorce and after all we've been through, he meant so much. What am I going to do?" Abby was doubled over on the floor trying to contain her laughter as she continued, "I just need some time to think."

"Okay. I'll call you in a few. You really don't need to be alone right now." Susie's voice had come down to a whisper.

"I know. Just call back later. I need to get out and get some fresh air or something."

"Okay."

"I love you, Susie."

"I love you too."

Abby managed to hang up the phone; then she checked it and rechecked and checked again to make sure it was hung up. After she was satisfied it was, she laughed until she cried, and after recovering, she laughed some more. But her amusement stopped when a gust of wind blew through the house, accompanied by a faint whisper and followed by giggles.

"No, not again. You can't come in here," said Abby, moving her hand back and forth.

Then the bow appeared, as it always did, floating gently in the air.

Again, Abby ran up the stairs, clutching the sides of her night-gown. Seconds later, she was covered up to her neck in bed sheets.

The gust of wind flew through her room, this time with increased fervor. The curtains swayed back and forth while the sheets fluttered. Abby cried, "Go away! Please go away!"

The red bow crossed the threshold and came as close to the bed as it ever had before. Then the pink dress appeared, trimmed in white lace with white gloves to match.

"You did a bad thing," said the ghost with a giggle. "A bad, bad thing."

"Get away from here…whoever you are…whatever your name is!" Abby cried.

"Muriel. My name is Muriel."

Abby pulled the covers down from her neck. "What did you say?"

"My name is Muriel…Muriel…Muriel."

Abby pulled the covers completely from her body and asked, "W—What are you doing here?"

"I'm here to help you. And you can help me."

"Help you do what?" asked Abby.

"Be with my mommy and daddy."

"I don't understand."

The ghost sat down on the end of the bed. Abby then pulled the sheets up to her neck.

Muriel spoke again, asking, "Do you feel bad about what you did?"

"What? What are you talking about?"

"What you did."

"No—no, I don't," said Abby.

Again, the curtains started to sway while the sheets fluttered.

"Stop it. Right now. Go away," said Abby.

Muriel then sang, "A warm flow of the waters may never be. A warm flow of the waters may never be. A warm flow of the waters may never be."

Then the ghost's garments slowly faded away. But Abby still heard the little girl's whimpers, which became fainter and fainter until they, too, faded into nothingness. Abby had never mentioned the ghost and its floating garments to anyone. But she hoped Spencer would use his penis to get her mind off of the little girl.

A few days went by, during which Abby and Spencer met and had sex again. Susie came to look after her, and Abby's mind inexplicably turned to her failed marriage with Teddy. The day she and Teddy had gotten married both had fantasies of growing old together and retiring somewhere on the tip of Florida and occasionally flying back and forth to Boston on holidays to visit their grandkids and old friends. Maybe even going to Europe from time to time, or maybe taking an exotic trip to South Africa. Or Sri Lanka. That was the way they both had envisioned their lives ending up. They thought they would grow old together, without the messiness of divorce and the estrangement that came with it.

That would have been a good life, but they were never really in love. And they never desired the same things in life. Both wanted successful careers, measured by the amount of profits made in stock, and in Abby's case, the amount of books sold. They never really wanted to cuddle at night or sit by the fireplace and talk about childhood memories or adult desires. Teddy died without knowing his ex-wife loved to watch figure skating and had dreamed as a child of doing a triple Lutz in front of a crowd of people. He died without telling Abby about his hopes of being a schoolteacher and how he wanted to work at an urban school and teach young minorities the skills needed to survive. Those things would have made their relationship real. They would've called each other in the middle of the workday to meet for sandwiches and coffee, and they would've held hands when they walked down the street.

But now Abby was with Spencer, who had just removed himself from her. As the sun was beginning to rise, they whispered plans to meet at a restaurant for dinner that night. He then put on his clothes and quietly left the house, so Susie wouldn't see him.

∞

Later that morning, while her sister was downstairs scrambling eggs and mixing pancake batter, Abby sat in the little nook in the windowsill of the morning room and looked out at cars passing by. She wondered what each driver's life was like. Were they as lonely as she? Had they been victimized for most of their childhood? Did they know about Muriel, the little ghost girl who was trapped in the lighthouse, trying to move on with her death? If they knew, could they coax her into coming downstairs? Could they convince her to leave the dollhouses behind?

With each passing car came a new question. What was the point of having a mansion only to rot away in it alone? The perfection of the house, the expensive paintings, the way the fabric on the furniture had to be the exact shade as the dominant color of the rug. A half-shade off would send Abby into an angry fit, darkening her mood and setting the tone for the rest of the day, sometimes the remainder of the week. Why was it necessary to decorate her home to perfection?

Poor Muriel would just have to wait.

The little ghost girl accompanied Abby all the time, though she remained invisible on most occasions. And this evening was no different. While sitting at the restaurant with Spencer, Abby couldn't see the ghost who sat quietly in the chair next to her.

"I thought about you every moment I was gone," Spencer said, while grinning and looking at Abby across the table.

"Really?" Abby asked, reaching for a cocktail napkin.

"So what did you do while I was gone?" Spencer asked.

"Not much."

"Did you think about me?" asked Spencer.

"Not really." The corners of Abby's mouth turned up slightly.

"I don't believe you," said Spencer.

"I don't believe myself." Abby laughed and quickly quieted down when she looked around and remembered there were others in the room.

"You seem different," said Spencer.

"Really? How?"

"Relaxed. You seem relaxed."

"Well, I am," said Abby.

"Did I fuck you that good?"

"Oh, please."

"Yeah, I did. That's why you're not as uptight as you usually are."

"Uptight?" asked Abby.

"You know. Walking around all dressed up, saying 'whom' and shit like that."

"Whatever," Abby said, picturing a cigarette in her hand, though she never smoked.

Spencer looked at her for a few seconds. "Well, I'm glad to meet the real you."

"And I'm glad to introduce myself to you." Abby forked a piece of the lobster tail out of the shell and put it in her mouth. "So what really happened to you this weekend? You never told me." She had just spoken with her mouth full for the first time in years.

Spencer had spent the weekend going to strip clubs and picking up prostitutes in Myrtle Beach. When he tired of that, marijuana kept him company. But smoking and picking up hookers didn't last long. The military showed him the world was more than running the streets, gossiping about life, and planning ways to get in trouble.

Though he had only been deployed for a few weeks, seeing people die from insurgents and friendly fire had toned him down just a little, save for the occasional fling.

"I just rode around with friends and showed off the earrings you bought me," Spencer said.

"But you didn't tell them I bought them for you, did you?"

"No, of course not," said Spencer.

"I figured as much. Too embarrassed?" Abby smiled when seeing his white teeth and then said, "Your maniacal grin says it all." She pictured herself pulling the cigarette from her mouth and tipping the vestiges into an ashtray.

Spencer was right. Abby hadn't been relaxed since the day she and her sister argued about which disciples the clouds were. Now her shoes were off just a little, and her feet were crossed at the ankles, much more comfortable than positioning her legs the usual way.

The rain tittered against the ground outside, working up to something much more ferocious, no doubt, but she and Spencer just looked out the restaurant window without speaking. Occasionally they glanced at one another, wondering whether or not this date would end with more sun or moonlike strokes. Abby then thought of what Susie's reaction to Spencer might entail, but she wasn't yet ready to let her sister in on this part of her life.

After their mom had passed away, Abby and Susie kept in close contact. They talked about everything from love interests to work goals to travel plans. But Abby didn't disclose all aspects of her love life, choosing not to reveal who Spencer really was. She glossed over her vulnerabilities in conversations about her objectives that ranged from going back to work as an editor to adding another room to the house. Susie, more observant than she appeared—unkempt hair and all—may have understood why her sister was private. Because Abby's biggest fear was showing her true self.

During this time, Susie had found time to do what her passion was. Cooking and waiting tables, for reasons Abby didn't understand, brought pleasure to Susie, who had dreamed of owning the restaurant where she'd been working for the past fifteen years. She didn't need to go to college to learn how to run Bubba's Grill, since she'd been managing the joint since Bubba himself decided to stop coming to his own restaurant, opting to travel to racecar events or hunt. In fact, the best present Susie ever received was the restaurant. The owner had died about a year before and left his prized possession to Susie Brooks, the best employee he ever had. Bubba's Grill was one of the most popular restaurants in Memphis. Susie was a millionaire on paper, and she held enough cash reserves to retire. Despite that, she still lived in the same dilapidated trailer and still drove her used car.

"So, Abby, what are you doing tomorrow?" Spencer leaned forward and put his elbows on the table in the restaurant that was much more elegant than the one Susie owned. "Do you want to meet at the café tomorrow morning?"

"No," Abby replied.

"No?" Spencer asked.

"I won't be here tomorrow. Going out of town," said Abby.

"To where?"

"Boston," Abby said.

"Visiting some friends?"

"There'll be some friends there, I'm sure," she said.

Just as Abby gave her answer, the waiter came to refill their glasses.

"So what's the occasion?" asked Spencer.

"A funeral."

"Who died?"

"My ex-husband and my best friend burned to death in a fire. Check please."

PART IV

Rainbow Dancer

12

Elijah had spent over a year and a half writing *Rainbow Dancer*, and the next day would be the day he'd see his work performed by the university drama club. The marketing billed it as "one of the most groundbreaking plays you'll ever see on campus." Flyer after flyer relayed that message. Poster after poster had those words on them. In the Student Union, in the cafeteria, in academic buildings…the flyers littered the campus.

Elijah wanted the opening night to bring validation for all of his hard work. On paper it was brilliant. At least one of his creative writing professors thought so and had given him high marks on it. *But what about the university drama club?* Elijah wondered. *Will they interpret it faithfully? Can they act? How will they handle the elaborate special effects?*

At the suggestion of a professor, he had e-mailed a copy of his play to a theater company. Weeks later, the company agreed to finance the project and give Elijah a sizable cut of the profits. He accepted the offer on two conditions: that he retain ownership of the play and that members of the university drama club put on the show. The theater company agreed but insisted that some of their associates supervise the project. Elijah felt accomplished when they gave him a signing bonus. It was barely enough money to cover his books for a semester, but he was still proud of his achievement. He didn't know his college professor sat on the theater company's board and had orchestrated the deal.

All of his life, Elijah had wanted some type of acceptance, and this would hopefully give it to him. His mother was coming up to see it, along with his brothers. And his boyfriend, Teddy, would be there too. He and Teddy had finally come to terms with themselves and their emotional baggage, and they had accepted each other as boyfriend and boyfriend. But that wouldn't stop Elijah from introducing him as just the editor of the literary magazine. He wasn't ready to let his family in on that part of his life, though he was sure they already knew. Underneath the gay-pride T-shirts and the lavender polos and the rainbow buttons on his book bag, he was holding on to shame.

But Noah, the artist Elijah had met on the way back to his residence hall, was beginning to heal Elijah through art and intense conversation. He had finally gotten the chance to see Noah's sketches. Noah had called him the previous day and invited himself to Elijah's room. Noah was hoping they would have a connection. That hope weighed heavily on him while walking across the parking lot of Elijah's dorm. Noah looked up at the building as if he hadn't seen it before, and he stared at the air-conditioning units that jutted outside of the windows, thinking they were an eyesore.

Elijah, too, hated the look of the metal A/C units that shot cold air to the inside of the rooms and solicited cold stares from outside. The only time he appreciated his unit was when there was a downpour, and the patter of raindrops against the metal would act as a lullaby during lonely nights. Even during the daytime, the lullaby was a pleasant reminder that life wasn't so bad after all, even if rain accompanied it.

But that was of little concern to Elijah, who—knowing Noah would stop by—had taken a quick shower, put on an outfit that was usually reserved for a nightclub, and sprayed on some women's perfume. Upon his arrival, Noah smelled the fragrance when leaning down to hug Elijah. Noah was wearing a plain white T-shirt and a pair of distressed jeans that were frayed at the bottom. He was sporting the same pair of flip-flops he'd worn when he first met Elijah, except this time Elijah paid attention to Noah's feet. They were long and wide and paler than the rest of his body. And Elijah could see the tan line that happened to be at the same place where the hair on Noah's ankles began to fade. Reverently, he stared at Noah's feet.

"Hope I'm not imposing," said Noah, breaking the silence

"No, it's okay," Elijah whispered. Seeing Noah in the room and looking at his handsome face made Elijah regret having dressed up for the occasion. He quickly untucked his shirt and took off his shoes.

"I'm not keeping you from anything, am I?" asked Noah.

"No. I just got back from a party and didn't get a chance to undress." Elijah hoped the lie was believable.

"Go ahead. Undress now," said Noah, who recovered with, "I'm just kidding."

"I know," said Elijah, who unbuttoned his shirt in front of the mirror, revealing a T-shirt.

"Brought some sketches for you to look at. You said you wanted to see them," Noah said.

"I remember."

Noah sat down on the floor, leaned against the bed, and patted the space beside him. Elijah sat down. Noah positioned part of the sketchbook on his left thigh and the other part on Elijah's right thigh. Then Noah opened it to reveal drawings that depicted places of worship.

"I like this one," Elijah said.

"Thanks. It's a place in Boston where I've always wanted to attend. I was born in Boston but raised in New York. I think I might have told you that already," said Noah, who looked down and studied Elijah's face.

Elijah looked at the architecture of a place that was shaped like a cube, except it had more length than width. There were two domes on each side of the building. Though the sketch was simple graphite, he imagined that the domes were gold in color.

"This is a beautiful church," said Elijah. "I'm guessing you're Catholic, since you have roots in New England. I've never really understood Catholicism. I was raised Baptist myself. But it doesn't matter what your denomination is. As long as you believe Jesus Christ is your Lord and Savior, you're all right with me."

Noah quickly turned to another sketch, then rubbed his hand through his hair as he sighed.

"What's wrong?" Elijah asked.

"I-I need to use the bathroom."

"Okay. I won't turn a page until you get back."

Noah didn't respond, except to walk swiftly to the restroom. As he made his way down the hall, he looked back and saw a guy going past Elijah's room. The guy didn't turn around to speak, so Noah thought nothing else of him and entered the bathroom. He clutched the sides of the sink and looked downward, though there was nothing there that really interested him, just pure white ceramic and a drain that resembled a utensil better reserved to grate cheese. He turned on the faucet, cupped water into his hands, and splashed it on his face. The cool water temporarily took his mind off of the warmth in the dorm.

When Noah reentered the room, Elijah asked, "Are you all right?"

"Yeah, I'm all right," responded Noah, without making eye contact.

"Was anyone in there?"

"No," said Noah.

"Good. I saw Luke pass by the doorway. Thought he might've been coming from the bathroom. You should be glad you didn't meet him."

"Why?"

"Because of his breath," Elijah said.

"He has bad breath?"

"Bad isn't the word. It's much worse than bad," Elijah said.

Noah laughed and asked, "Really?"

"Yeah. It smells like somebody shitted in his mouth."

Noah chuckled and sat beside Elijah as he had before, on the floor with the notebook resting on both of them. Elijah took this as a sign to turn the page, flipping through several sketches of places of worship, most of which looked architecturally similar. Out of a need to fill the silence, he would occasionally say, "I like this one."

"Who is this?" asked Elijah, looking at a sketch.

"Just a guy."

"Just a guy? The only color sketch in the whole album is of just a guy?" asked Elijah. He looked at Noah before persisting, "So who is he?"

"Just a guy I happen to like a lot," responded Noah.

The sketch was a depiction of Elijah, similar in skin tone and facial features, but not so exact as to look just like him. Noah had created the piece the day they met. Elijah had a feeling it was a drawing of him but didn't want to press the issue further because it would be embarrassing if Noah said it wasn't.

After Elijah finished flipping through the sketches, he and Noah sat there and talked. It was dark before they finished, and they had both told their entire life stories to each other in detail, except that Elijah omitted references to his father. By the time the sun had fallen and the room had darkened, they were best friends. Elijah hadn't expected that to happen, previously thinking Teddy would be the man whom he'd come to know on this level.

"Well, I guess I need to get going," said Noah.

"Okay. I had a really good time," Elijah said, staring at Noah's feet.

"Me too."

"'Me too' what?" asked Elijah.

"I had a good time too."

"Oh, right." Elijah was a little embarrassed. He tried to brush it off with an unconvincing chuckle. Then he turned on the desk light, which was bright enough for them to see their steps but dark enough that they didn't have to squint.

The falling water and the A/C unit began another lullaby.

"I think it's raining," said Elijah, who walked to the window. Then he said, "It *is* raining. Bad, too."

"I know this might seem a little forward, but…but do you mind if…"

"No, I don't mind at all," Elijah interrupted.

"Okay."

Elijah fumbled around in a drawer and produced a pair of pajama bottoms. "Would you turn around, please?"

"Sure," said Noah, who laughed.

Elijah changed into the pajama bottoms and took off his socks and button-down shirt but remained in his T-shirt. Noah took off his shirt slowly, studying Elijah's face. Noah was wearing a silver chain with a Star of David attached to it. Elijah walked to him and reached out to hold the star between his thumb and index finger.

"Are you still okay with me?" asked Noah.

"Of course I am. At least now I know you're circumcised," Elijah responded.

Noah let out a loud laugh.

Then Elijah locked the front door and turned off the desk light. "Let's get some sleep, Noah…"

"Cohen. My last name is Cohen."

"If I had known your name before, I never would've made that Jesus comment. Sorry."

"It's okay. We're used to it."

They got in bed. Noah first, then Elijah. Both men were accustomed to getting in bed with men they barely knew, so the shyness went away when Noah had closed his sketchbook. His art was a deeply personal possession that he rarely shared with anyone, but something about Elijah made him open up and show his craft. So he had no inhibitions about getting undressed and lying next to a boy he barely knew but seemed to know so well. They both thought of the drawing of Elijah. Getting in bed was Noah's way of saying, "Yes, it was a sketch of you." And letting Noah lie down with him was Elijah's way of saying, "I figured as much." This was the first time they appreciated the small beds in a college dorm room, as Noah pulled Elijah close. The little guy closed his eyes as the side of his face rested against Noah's chest.

When Noah put his arms around him, Elijah opened his eyes and said, "Good night, sugar."

Noah smiled and said "Good night" as the lullaby carried on.

⚬ ⚬ ⚬

When morning came, they were still in the same position. Noah awoke first, then Elijah, who felt like he was in a house. He imagined Noah taking a shower, getting dressed, kissing him good-bye, and going off to work. Elijah couldn't help but look at the space just above the elastic in Noah's boxer briefs because it revealed Noah's pubic hair, and Elijah loved men who had bushy pubes. Noah pulled his boxer briefs down a little to reveal more.

While Noah was getting dressed, Elijah waited in bed to give his erection time to go down. When it finally did, he asked Noah to turn around. Then he got dressed. After that, Elijah took a piece of paper from his desk drawer—on it, a poem he had written—folded it up, and put it in his pocket, patting it to make sure it was secure.

"You want to go to the cafeteria for breakfast?" Noah asked.

"Yeah."

Elijah had walked this route many times before through varying degrees of bad weather. The sky was overcast, with a gray cloud hovering so low it seemed as though he could've reached up to grab a piece of it. He couldn't grasp why everything seemed different, in a good way. The light hit his eyes in a manner that made the leaves on the trees seem a vibrant green, whereas the other day the leaves were a dark gray that looked painted with a piece of charcoal, no doubt the strokes of a dreary artist.

Now, the only artist he was concerned about was Noah, as they eventually made their way to the cafeteria and ate together for the first time. Pancakes, sausage, eggs, and orange juice made up the meal of choice. Noah smiled as he watched Elijah put a link of sausage in his mouth. They ate their food in silence, for the most part, except to say things like, "The food is good" or "I'm going to get some more juice." During the end of their meal, they finally discussed *Rainbow Dancer.*

"So are you nervous about the play?" Noah asked.

"Very."

"It'll be okay. Everything'll be just fine."

"You think so?" asked Elijah.

"Yeah," said Noah, who really didn't have any idea about the play. Until the previous night, when Elijah mentioned he wrote it, Noah hadn't considered going. Now that he was in love with the author, he had no choice but to attend. He thought of it as his first way of showing support for Elijah. Realizing he would have to buy a ticket, Noah continued to eat his breakfast as he quickly looked at Elijah who, in turn, was glancing at him.

"What are you staring at?" asked Noah, with a smile as he gazed down at his own attire.

"Nothing. I-I like your shirt."

"It's just a T-shirt."

"I know, but I like it," said Elijah.

"Thanks." Noah smiled. "Are you okay?"

"Yeah. I've been doing a lot more writing, to get my mind off things," said Elijah.

"Really?"

"I wrote this poem yesterday." Elijah pulled the piece of paper from his pocket. "Do you want to hear it?"

"Of course I do," Noah said, as he put his fork down and rested both elbows on the table, putting his fists against the sides of his face as if he were posing for a picture.

"Okay," said Elijah, "here it is." Then he read the poem aloud, hoping no one else in the cafeteria could hear him. Afterward he asked, "So what do you think?"

"It was beautiful."

"Really?" asked Elijah, as his eyebrows reached for his forehead and the corners of his mouth moved toward his ears.

"Yeah, really." Noah smiled too.

They finished eating, put up their trays, and exited the building.

"I'll see you later," said Noah. "Maybe we could meet later."

"I probably won't have time. You know, because of the play and everything."

"Right. I'll definitely be there," said Noah.

"You will?"

"Of course."

"Okay, call me later," said Elijah.

"I will."

Noah initiated a hug. Elijah wrapped his arms around Noah's neck. Noah had to stoop down to reach around Elijah's waist. That was when he kissed Elijah, who didn't resist. The kiss was quick but intimate because their eyes remained closed for a few seconds after their lips stopped touching. The brief show of affection would linger on in both of their minds for the remainder of the day.

"I'll see you later," said Noah, after opening his eyes.

"Okay," was all Elijah could say in return. He was surprised at himself for kissing in public. It was only the second time he had done that.

They hugged again before going in opposite directions. When they had kissed, Elijah never once thought that people might have been looking at them, nor did that feeling of dirtiness insinuate itself into Elijah's mood as he walked back to his room.

He didn't take the time to realize Teddy was just his way of dealing with loneliness, while his relationship with Noah was something much more profound. Despite their differences, they had connected in a way that made them seem the same. Noah and Elijah were like two things that made the same sound despite being completely different... like a tornado and a freight train. Because of Noah, loneliness would not find a comfortable space in the hollow part of Elijah's heart.

Elijah realized he had seen himself differently when passing by the mirror in his room. His nose fit his face now, and the fullness in his lips looked normal. And his hair, as usual, wasn't straight—which didn't bother him, since neither was he. The glimpse in the looking glass felt so good, but he didn't want to risk taking another look because it might result in a quick pinch of the nose and pressing of the lips. And it was too early in the day to try to sleep away the ugliness a Child of Israel had made him forget.

Before Elijah could fully appreciate what had happened with Noah, the phone rang, an intense sound that brought nervousness back to his bones.

"Hello."

"May I speak to Elijah?"

"Speaking."

"Hey, this is Will from the drama club."

"Hey, how's everything?" asked Elijah, as beads of sweat began to form on his forehead. "Is everything okay?"

"Okay? Better than okay. We sold the last ticket today. Just thought you'd want to know." Will had the voice of someone who had achieved something, though he had nothing to do with the marketing and would only speak two lines to the sold-out crowd.

"Are you serious?" Elijah hadn't even considered the venue would be filled to capacity. "That's great." He hoped he didn't sound too excited. The sweat stopped pouring from his forehead.

"Well, remember to be a little early, so we can get you and your guests seated. You guys have seats reserved in the front." Will's voice had the same inflection of the bit character he would later play on stage.

"Okay. I'll be there about a half hour early."

"Great. See you then," said Will.

"Later."

"Later, dude."

Elijah had already known that seats were reserved for him, but hearing it again made him feel special, thinking himself to be a movie star going to his big premier. But his nerves, for good or bad, softened his delusions of grandeur. And his mother and brothers would sense his apprehension but would do nothing to comfort him, nor would they congratulate him after it was over. They would just leave the auditorium in disgust—embarrassed, angered, and ashamed. Even if they thought the play was good, they would never tell him.

⁂

In an effort to calm his partner's nerves, Teddy took Elijah out to eat. It was the first romantic date they'd been on since becoming an item. The Palace was the assuming name of the restaurant where they went, and the prices were astounding for two men who were on college budgets. Elijah knew he had money coming from the ticket sales of his play; the largest cut went to him. And Teddy had had several jobs before finding a relatively good one. He had a position as a courier at a law firm before working as a receptionist at a dental office one summer. Then there was a brief stint at a copy shop. He finally received a job hit after posting his résumé on the Internet. A faceless person sent him an e-mail inviting him to write as a columnist for an online magazine. Teddy produced a column every week, and the money was good, considering what his previous work history had been. So he and Elijah weren't really on college budgets anymore. They enjoyed standards of living surpassing most students, who thought having spending money only existed in the real world, and if they did have extra pocket change, it would go toward college necessities like snacks, detergent, and beer.

Although it was a lunchtime date, both Elijah and Teddy had dressed to the nines, and people stared as the two young men got out of the car and walked to the Palace. Elijah was always conscious of the omnipresent gaze of others. He had a habit of staring at strangers because he thought they were looking at him, sizing him up for judgment. Around others, he would try to walk with a pseudo-confident swagger. People judged him for his pretenses, not for his true self.

Teddy, however, didn't let fear consume him, so he walked without a hand in his pocket, and he never stared. Part of the reason he wanted to be with Elijah was to protect him, or at least make him feel safe. Teddy believed that was his role in their relationship—a role that was good for him but one that wasn't always welcomed.

"After you." Teddy opened the door for Elijah, who traipsed through and stood in front of a handsome young man in a suit, waiting to assist them.

"May I help you?" the man asked.

Elijah stood behind Teddy, who said, "We have reservations under Fitzpatrick."

"I see. Come with me, gentlemen."

Teddy held Elijah's hand as they walked behind the restaurant worker. Elijah's nerves got the best of him again, as his heart began to race and sweat formed on his forehead, only to drip down to sting his eyes. At least *Rainbow Dancer* wasn't on his mind.

13

Midway through their lunch, as Elijah wiped his mouth with a cocktail napkin, he felt Teddy staring at him as if he were a stranger.

"What's wrong, Teddy?" he asked.

"Nothing. Watching you eat is all."

"Well, I hate when people watch me eat. You know that," Elijah said.

"No, actually I didn't." Teddy's words hurt both of their feelings.

"You *did* know that."

"No, Elijah, I didn't."

"Oh."

"You want dessert?" asked Teddy.

"Yeah, I'll probably have cheesecake, if they have it." Elijah reached for the dessert menu.

Teddy smiled at Elijah's little hands and at how his fingernails glistened in the dim light.

"Do you polish your nails?" Teddy asked.

"Yeah, I use the clear polish."

"It's cute. You should keep doing it."

"I've always done it," said Elijah.

"You have?" Teddy asked. That question hurt both of their feelings too.

"Yeah. You knew that." Elijah studied the dessert menu as if he were looking for a biography of the man sitting at the table with him. He looked up, saw Teddy staring at him, and asked, "What?"

"Nothing," Teddy responded in the lowest voice he'd used in weeks.

They were glad to see the waiter come.

"I'd like a piece of cheesecake," said Elijah.

"Excellent choice. Anything for you, sir?" the waiter asked Teddy.

"I'll have the same."

Elijah and Teddy spoke in sparse conversation, and for the first time during the date, Elijah thought about *Rainbow Dancer* and worried about how it would be received.

If Grayson were here I wouldn't be so worried, Elijah thought.

"What are you thinking about?" Teddy looked at the dessert menu, despite having already ordered.

"Nothing."

"Are you worried about tonight?"

"Terrified. Just glad to have something to take my mind off it," said Elijah.

"When is your family coming?"

"At five. But knowing them, they'll be a little early," said Elijah, though his family members never did anything early.

"I know we still have plenty of time, but we better get going. Can we hang out in your room for a few?"

Elijah nodded his head and asked, "Should we get a doggie bag for the cheesecake?"

"Yeah, let's do that," Teddy replied.

"Okay," Elijah responded, with a shaky voice before saying, "Excuse me. I'll be right back."

Elijah went to the bathroom and stood in front of the mirror. Then he checked to see if anyone else was in there with him, inspecting each stall like a janitor. He found no one. That same nervous sweat formed on his forehead. He reached for a paper towel with trembling hands, not comprehending what was happening to him but understanding he'd be embarrassed if someone walked in, especially Teddy. Then, just like that, his forehead was dry, his stomach settled, and his hands stilled like mosquito-infested water. Someone entered; Elijah pretended to wash his hands and walked out.

By then the waiter had placed the cheesecake on the table in little white boxes, and a tip was just beside them, compliments of Teddy Fitzpatrick. When they left the restaurant, Elijah and his partner didn't hold hands, but Teddy did open the door for him. Elijah needed someone to hold his hand right then, but he also needed the independence of opening the door himself.

They drove down the road, with Teddy at the wheel. Elijah looked at him, admiring his skin.

"Why are you staring at me?" asked Teddy.

"Didn't realize I was staring."

"I can tell you're nervous about tonight."

"Yeah, I am," said Elijah.

"Everything'll be all right."

They didn't say another word until they got back to Elijah's room.

"So how are you preparing?" asked Teddy.

"For what?"

"Tonight," said Teddy, as he turned on the television.

"I don't really need to prepare. I've already written the play. The rest is up to the actors. But I've been writing other things, you know, to get my mind off things."

Teddy didn't respond.

"You want to hear a poem I wrote yesterday? I might need to fix some things here and there, but here it is," Elijah said, as he opened the desk drawer and produced a piece of paper.

Teddy sat down.

"Okay, here it is." Elijah unfolded the paper and began to read aloud:

If the stars were to fall
and blanket the Earth,
what a wonderful place it would be.
No fantasies. No dreams.
Just the wonderment
of the glistening stars.

"What do you think?" asked Elijah, folding up the sheet of paper and putting it back in the drawer.

"I think it was good," Teddy said, as he picked up the remote and started to surf the channels.

Elijah just looked at Teddy, studying his face as if it were a road map to a place he'd never been. Teddy watched television for ten minutes and left.

An hour later, he stumbled into Elijah's dorm room with a smile on his face. Elijah, who had seen that grin before, was sitting on the side of the bed with his feet hanging above the floor as Teddy stood in front of him.

"Are you all right?" asked Elijah, with a laugh.

"Yeah, I'm good," said Teddy. "Why do you ask?"

"Because your eyes are bloodshot red."

"I have allergies," said Teddy.

"Is that why your eyes are so red?"

"Yeah, it's an allergic reaction," said Teddy.

"An allergic reaction to what?"

"Cocaine," said Teddy.

Elijah laughed.

"So you've been snorting?" Elijah asked.

"Yeah, with one of my frat brothers."

"Which one?" asked Elijah.

"Riley. You've never met him. He's sexy as hell," Teddy said.

"Is he gay?"

"No, he's from Utah."

"Oh," responded Elijah.

Then Teddy pulled off Elijah's shoes and pants and pushed him down, so that Elijah lay there on his back with his legs dangling from the side of the bed. Teddy then pulled his own pants down around his hairy thighs and lifted up his shirt, holding the fabric underneath his chin so it wouldn't fall back down to cover his genitals. He pulled a bottle of lube from his pocket and squirted the contents onto Elijah's asshole. He then placed Elijah's legs over his shoulders and guided his semen dispenser into Elijah. Three minutes later Teddy pulled out and ejaculated onto Elijah's shirt and face.

Teddy pulled up his pants, zipped them, and buckled his belt, while Elijah was still in the same position, except his ankles were no longer on Teddy's shoulders. Without looking back at Elijah, Teddy said, "I guess I'll see you later," and left.

"Okay," Elijah said, while wiping the semen from his eyes, but Teddy couldn't hear him because he had already closed the door and had begun making his way down the hall. Teddy had left the room with a sense of pride, because he had achieved what could only be described as a World War II fuck. His dick did to Elijah's asshole what the atomic bomb did to Nagasaki. And Elijah's self-esteem went from being a thriving city to becoming a heap of ashes—a fate put in motion long before the explosion.

A few minutes before, Elijah Redwater had been a virgin. Yes, he had engaged in sexual experiences. But during the encounters with those guys, he and his partners had exchanged blowjobs, but there was no anal penetration. So this was the time Elijah's man-cherry had been popped. Teddy smirked when walking down the hall, knowing he had been Elijah's first. Still lying on his back, Elijah thought about his virginity and said, "The Lord giveth, and the Lord taketh away," and laughed until he cried—with tears and a stoned frat boy's semen dripping down his face.

Then he sat up and looked down at himself. When Teddy had ejaculated onto Elijah's shirt, the drops of semen splashed to make little cum stars on the fabric. Elijah thought of his lost virginity as he sat on the side of the bed in his semen-spangled shirt.

14

Evening came as briskly as ever, revealing a sky that resembled the American flag with stars bunched in one corner and clouds creating stripes across the almost dark backdrop. Not knowing what to wear. Not knowing how to introduce Teddy to his family. Not knowing how the university drama club would interpret his work. Poor Elijah had always been afraid of the unknown. For the first time since he'd conceived the idea of *Rainbow Dancer*, Elijah began to question its quality. Before, he may have questioned the quality of the drama club's interpretation but never the play itself.

Elijah entered the theater with his family and Teddy in tow. He excused himself to the bathroom and went into a stall to do something he hadn't done in months. He took a printed copy of Grayson's e-mail from his coat pocket and read it, twice. He folded the letter into thirds and put it back in his pocket. Elijah felt that much calmer and stronger after reading the words "I love you, Little Guy."

Then he sat down in the reserved section in the center of the first row to hear people say congratulations, though the play hadn't started yet. Teddy put his arm around Elijah, whose mother cut a knowing glance, then looked at her other children, who snickered like grammar-school kids.

I don't care what they think right now. It's not about them. It's about me. For once, it's about me, Elijah thought.

The lights dimmed. The crowd settled and came to silence. The curtains opened to a young man dressed up as a jester, who danced a jig across the stage to laughter and applause.

He said, "I present to you...*Rainbow Dancer*."

The spotlight left him.

Enter two young men, holding hands.

Andy: You're not ever going to leave me, are you?

Seth: Why would I do that? I love you more than anything. anything in the world.

Andy: Really?

Seth: Yeah, Little Guy. I'm for real.

They kissed.

The crowd applauded. Elijah knew then that the rest of the play would be just fine.

The end of the play:

Seth: Andy, let's go.

Andy: Go where?

Seth: Take my hand.

Andy grabbed his hand. A man named Larry was above the stage operating a pulley. He pulled a lever, and Seth and Andy levitated. The tech guy dimmed the lights to hide the ropes attached to the actors' harnesses. The spotlight shone on the two boys as they dangled above the hardwood floor and then exited, stage right. The curtains were drawn. Elijah cried.

The play had officially made his friends and family aware of who he was, and that scared him and delighted him at the same time. And when walking across the stage to give a brief thank-you speech, the spotlight was on him, literally. The glare was so intense the crowd looked like a black screen. If he hadn't heard the cheers and the shuffling of chairs, someone could've convinced him he was the only person in the room. It was better that way, since he couldn't size up the discerning faces of those in the audience, particularly his family. The only face that mattered to him was on the other side of the world, taking a nap in a haphazardly pitched tent.

Elijah gave his speech: "This has been such a dream come true for me, to have my work come to life right before my eyes. To have it produced, performed, and be well-received right before my eyes is just…is just…like I said, it's a dream come true. And hopefully this is the start of something special. I don't know what God has in store for me…but I'm sure writing has something to do with it. Instead of thanking a bunch of people, I'd just like to thank everyone involved in this production and my friends and family and, most of all, God. Thank you."

The crowd cheered as they remained standing.

Then Teddy walked onto the stage with a bouquet of roses in his hand and gave it to Elijah. And, in front of 1,998 people, they kissed, right there with the spotlight on them. And when the roses fell to the stage, they continued their display of affection. The curtains were drawn.

It was by far the second-best moment of Elijah's life.

"I'll let you stay and mingle with the actors and stuff. I'll call you tonight," said Teddy, before giving Elijah a quick kiss.

"All right," Elijah replied.

Teddy left, navigating through intricate stage props and actors taking off colorful costumes with sequins and glitter and rhinestones that sparkled like stars. Teddy just shook his head from side to side as he looked back at his partner, proud and amazed at *Rainbow Dancer* and how it all had come together. Little did he know that when he walked out of the auditorium his relationship with Elijah would change for the worse.

∽∞∾

One minute Elijah was surrounded by dozens of actors and technicians; the next, he was walking down the curvy walkway alone—

on his way back to the solitude of a South Campus dorm room. Ever since Grayson had left, he hadn't had a roommate, opting for a single despite the fact that the housing department charged more for single rooms. A combination of small scholarships and need-based grants covered all of that, so it didn't bother him. Money would matter less and less to him with every check received from *Rainbow Dancer*. There would be six follow-ups to the debut show, and all would be sold to capacity. Every check he deposited into his account would excite him, a temporary fix that would fade away before the funds even posted to his account.

Walking down the winding sidewalk, he was at peace with him-self, bolstered by his newfound status as an acclaimed playwright, though most students wouldn't remember his name in a couple of weeks. It was very dark as the moon dangled in the sky like a stage prop. No one was on the walkway since it was almost midnight; he couldn't believe he'd lingered backstage for that long.

"Hey, Elijah. Congratulations."

"Thanks," he responded to the stray dog that ran across his path.

"Do you want some company?" the Labrador retriever asked.

"Sure."

"I figured you wouldn't want to walk home by yourself this late. It's not real safe around here."

"Yeah, but I don't think much about that kind of thing. I try to walk in well-lit areas," said Elijah.

"This doesn't seem too well-lit to me." The dog looked up at him and laughed, his tongue hanging from his mouth like a loose necktie.

Elijah chuckled too, for the first time all day. He'd been smiling a lot but hadn't laughed until now.

"I needed that," Elijah said, because the novelty of the applause had already worn off, and the roses, destined to wither away in a garbage can behind the theater, were still center stage, waiting for the cleaning crew to sweep them into a plastic box attached to a handle.

"How did the play come out?" the dog asked.

"It was a hit, I guess. The crowd seemed to enjoy it," said Elijah.

"The real question is, how did you like it? You're the only one that matters when it comes to these things, since you're the writer."

"I guess you're right," said Elijah.

"I had no doubt it would be good. I'm glad it was successful. I heard it sold out."

"So I guess you didn't come?" asked Elijah.

"No, they don't allow pets in the auditorium."

"I understand. I didn't think about that. Where's your owner?"

"I don't have one, so technically I'm not anyone's pet."

"I see," Elijah replied, as he and the dog walked down the hill and around a curve without speaking, until the Labrador broke the silence. "Elijah, been meaning to tell you something. You've got to stop worrying so much about what other people think. You'd be surprised at how little their opinions matter. They don't matter much at all."

"They who?" Elijah asked.

"Other people. Don't let fear of judgment guide you. You deserve better than that. Promise me you won't let people's opinions dictate what you do. If you do, you'll become something entirely different than the real you. You'll become what people want you to be. When you walk, walk like you. When you talk, talk like you. And when you write, write what you really want to write, and don't worry about other people. Promise me that."

"I promise." Elijah knelt down and patted the dog's head, then rubbed a little behind his ears. "Well, I'm at the dorm now. Thanks for walking with me."

"Anytime."

"Bye," Elijah said.

The dog barked in response. Elijah assumed the noise meant "good-bye."

He didn't even wonder what the dog's name was as he walked through the lobby and waited for the elevator, looking at the flyers on the bulletin board. The words *Rainbow Dancer* were written on an 8.5x11 sheet of glossy paper, stapled above another flyer. He pulled it gently from the board.

"*Rainbow Dancer*," he whispered to himself.

Monday morning came quickly. The sun rushed itself up into the sky, forcing thousands of students to wake up to alarm clocks. But Elijah didn't need one. He wanted to sleep in and thought about skipping class for the first time since he'd been in college. He heard guys going in and out of the restroom, brushing their teeth and taking showers and exiting the dorm. Outdoors, a garbage truck turned a dumpster on its head and emptied its contents. Cars could be heard driving down the street. And faint traces of human voices drifted in from just outside his window. But Elijah had no desire to go out there and join those eerie voices. He didn't even want to hear anyone speak for that matter, not even Teddy, the only person in the state who really cared about him, save for Noah. But the darkness had hit Elijah too hard for him to realize that much, because even though it was a bright and cloudless day, his little sun wasn't shining.

He wanted to stay locked up in the room until hunger sent him out alive or starvation sent him out dead, but he knew he couldn't do that and decided to leave the dorm. There wasn't a need to miss a day of class over this. What *this* was, he didn't understand. But he overcame the sadness of waking up in an empty bed and a bare room and ventured to the bathroom to prepare for a walk through the yard.

"Dude, I went to your play last night. It was awesome." This was the voice of a Bostonian named Mark who stood in a pair of boxer shorts. When Elijah turned away, the guy lowered his underwear just a little for Elijah, who pretended not to look.

"Thanks."

"Just thought I'd tell you that. Later, dude."

As Mark left the bathroom, he saw Elijah staring at him in the mirror. When the cool breeze of the hallway hit him, Mark pulled his underwear back up where they were supposed to be.

Maybe this won't be a bad day after all, Elijah thought, trying to replay in his head what had just happened.

Other than reading his name in the campus newspaper and hearing the word *congratulations* ad nauseam, the day was the same as the days before. The only difference was that he didn't stop by the Student Union to meet Teddy for lunch. Teddy stood out there for almost an hour waiting for his partner to meet him for cafeteria cuisine but left when chemistry lab called him, seeing this as an omen. He would try to stay with Elijah, but it would take two people to preserve their relationship, and the playwright was unwilling or, more accurately, unable.

In fact, Teddy hadn't crossed Elijah's mind for the first part of the day, nor had his family—until the phone rang and his mother greeted him. That was when the kiss between Teddy and him really hit home, when he suspected that his mother had been in the audience cringing as it happened, with tears of shame filling her eyes. But Elijah couldn't have seen that because the spotlight didn't shine on his mother.

"Hello."

"Elijah, how you?" his mother said.

"All right."

"Just wanted to let you know we got home all right," she said.

"Okay."

"And wanted to let you know I'm praying for you. It'll pass, Elijah. It'll pass."

"What, Momma? What will pass?"

"This phase you're going through."

"What phase?" asked Elijah.

"This…uhh…you know what I'm talking about."

"I understand."

"You got your copy of the Bible?" she asked.

"Yes, Momma, I got it."

"Okay. You need to get to reading it. I'll look for some scriptures to help you therapize this."

"Okay, Momma."

"Well, I just got in the house, so I'm still trying to catch a holt."

"All right," said Elijah.

"Call you later," his mom said.

"All right. Bye," he replied.

"Bye-bye."

He hung up the phone, sat on his bed, and shook his head from side to side. For the first time in his young life, he understood that nothing was wrong with him but everything was wrong with his family. It was like part of him had died and another part of him was born again. He remembered reading something about that in the Bible, but the scriptures would have to wait. Elijah knew this wasn't the moment to try to decipher words that were centuries old. This was the time to live in the now.

Usually when his mother started talking to him about who he should be and what he should do, a knot would form in his stomach and tears would follow. Why he didn't cry this time was beyond him. Sometime between shaking his head from side to side and lying back on the bed, a rainbow had come into his window and landed on the floor. There wasn't a pot of gold, but there was the realization that *Rainbow Dancer* would shape every major decision he'd make for the rest of his life.

The phone rang again.

"Hello."

"Hey, guy. How are you doing?" Teddy asked. "I waited for you today for lunch, but you never showed up."

"Sorry. I forgot."

"It's okay. Is everything all right?" Teddy asked.

"Yeah, everything's fine."

"For real?"

"Yeah, for real," Elijah said.

"So you're not mad at me for kissing you onstage last night?"

"No, why would I be mad at that?" Elijah asked.

"I know how you are."

"What's that supposed to mean?"

"It's just that I figured you would be a little…"

"Teddy, I can't really talk right now. I'm tired. So we'll just talk later, okay?"

"Elijah…"

He hung up the phone, hearing his boyfriend say his name just before the phone hit the receiver. Knowing the tantrum was an over-reaction, he got a little pleasure from hurting Teddy's feelings.

Pleasure?

Was that what it was?

The phone rang again.

Elijah didn't answer and took his laptop and walked out of the room, trying to block out the sound of the ringing phone as he walked down the hall.

Grayson, not Teddy, was on the other end of the line.

Elijah decided to go to the café instead of the library. It was always quieter. There was still a part of him that liked doing things like going to the café, because it seemed like an upscale thing to do. So when he got there, he ordered French vanilla.

"And a cheese Danish," said Elijah.

"Okay, sir. Coming right up."

Elijah placed the money on the counter, deciding not to put it in the cashier's hand. He then took his goodies and his change and went to a table and opened his laptop.

"Elijah?" a young man said.

"Hey, Steve. How're you doing?"

"All right, just finishing up some studying."

"For what class?" Elijah asked.

"Calc. It's killing me."

"Tell me about it. Math has never been my thing either," Elijah said.

"Congratulations, by the way."

"Thank you."

"It took a lot of courage to do what you and your partner did yesterday. And the play was good too," said Steve.

"Thank you," was the only response Elijah could muster, though he'd used that one up already.

"Well, I have to get going," said Steve.

"All right. See you later," said Elijah.

"Later, dude."

Elijah watched Steve walk out of the café and get into a red jeep that had the top down. He focused heavily on Steve's legs. Something about white men's hairy legs enticed him. While taking a sip from the bad coffee and having a bite of the cheese Danish, he couldn't take his eyes off of Steve. Once the computer was booted up and he'd opened up a blank document, he started typing a sequel to *Rainbow Dancer* to help him cope with the sadness that polluted his soul.

His fingers rested across the home row of the keyboard. Elijah closed his eyes and let the story come out without over thinking it, devoid of his usual pretentious words and, above all, lacking the bad aftertaste of French vanilla. And magically his fingers started to type, and the computer screen began to fill with letters that turned into words that formed sentences that became paragraphs that would eventually develop into chapters and then fashion a book. He decided to take on the unusual task of making the sequel to *Rainbow Dancer* a novel, not a play.

Elijah paid no attention to the people outside the vast café window: The students walking here and there, this way and that. The buses stopping to pick up strangers, some who wouldn't seem so strange to each other once the bus ride was over. The homeless asking for loose change, which seemed like a fortune to most college students. People walking in and out of the café, ordering lattés and pastries stuffed into plain white bags.

He closed his eyes and saw none of this, because a story was forming in that mind of his and pouring out of his hands and into the keyboard.

In the wilderness, a child walked through the brush and leaves of a Carolina autumn. He was looking for that intangible place where you start from a wiggling child and grow into a young man or a young woman.

That place is called home. But sometimes home isn't the inviting place you see on the sitcoms. It's more like a place that suppresses you from being you, but you stomach it as best you can until you reach heavenward for independence.

He opened his eyes, saved those unpolished paragraphs, and left the café.

"Elijah," Teddy yelled down the sidewalk.

Elijah turned around and tried to hide the annoyed look on his face.

"We need to talk," Teddy said.

"I know," said Elijah.

"Do you have time now?" asked Teddy.

"Yeah, a little time. But I have some papers that are due, so I'll have to go to the library in a few."

"Do you want to talk over dinner?"

"Just ate," Elijah said.

"Well, I'll walk you to your room."

"Okay."

Teddy wanted to hold Elijah's hand but chose not to.

"What I did yesterday, did it upset you? I know I already asked you that," said Teddy.

"No, the kiss didn't bother me."

"Well then, what is it? You seem a little distant. I don't want to sound overly dramatic," said Teddy, with a laugh.

Elijah laughed instead of answering.

Nothing was funny.

They continued to walk toward Elijah's dorm, both wanting to extend the time in hopes that the conversation would enlighten them by revealing certain idiosyncrasies they didn't know about one another, like the way Elijah dodged cracks in the sidewalk, or the way Teddy would fold his arms in defense from a sudden burst of cool air. Elijah sat down on a short wall and placed his hands over his face. Teddy found a spot beside his boyfriend, put his arm around him, and ignored the rest of the world.

A tear fell from underneath Elijah's hands.

"What's wrong?" asked Teddy.

"Everything." Elijah was crying for Grayson.

"Everything like what?"

"I wish things could be better. I wish people would just be a little different. It's like even when I'm supposed to be happy, I'm not. Even when I think I've done something good, it isn't good enough."

"You mean the play?" asked Teddy.

"That and everything else."

"When was the last time you were happy?"

"Freshman year, right after finals," said Elijah.

"What happened?"

"Everything."

"What do you mean?" asked Teddy.

"Everything just fell into place. And now everything has fallen apart. I'll never be able to…"

"Shhhhhh," Teddy interrupted.

That was the first time since they'd met that Teddy knew he was just a stand-in for someone else. He didn't know for sure, since he'd never heard of Grayson, assuming Elijah had never had a roommate before. *Shhhhhh* was the only way Teddy could keep his self-esteem. But that night Teddy would try to fix this poor little critically acclaimed playwright with the best thing he had: his big penis. At night, while they made love under the sheets, was the only time he had any control over Elijah. As they entered Elijah's dorm, they each felt closure hovering like the dark clouds that hung over the sky, signaling the need for shelter, emotional and physical.

Outside, it rained like pre-ejaculation—a few drips and drops here and there, but the major downpour would not cum until the climax. Inside, there were three guys in the hallway as Teddy and Elijah walked by. The three of them, all soccer players, looked at each other and smirked when Elijah and Teddy passed them. When the two had entered Elijah's room, the soccer players decided to comment, and the acoustics in the hallway allowed Elijah and Teddy to hear.

"Fucking queers," said the goalie, pretending to whisper.

"Wonder what they're about to study. I can just smell the fudge." Guy #2 waved his hand in front of his nose as if shooing away an odor.

"Whatever they're about to do, I don't want to know. It makes me sick to my stomach." That was the voice of Guy #3.

It was the first time Teddy had been in Elijah's room in over a week. The posters hanging on the walls were the same as before but looked new to Teddy. A computer sat on top of a wooden desk. The carpet was hunter green, making the lint a little obvious for Elijah's taste, but *Rainbow Dancer* had kept him from checking out a vacuum cleaner from the office downstairs. A television—small even for a dorm room—sat on a stand. There was only one window, which looked out onto the yard. The blinds were dusty and didn't line up like they were supposed to, so a little dash of light always managed to creep in even when the blinds were closed. There was only one twin-sized bed, which made the room seem a lot larger than the one just next door. The sheets were navy blue or something very close to it. Not nearly what Teddy had remembered, but the unfamiliarity didn't stop their clothes from coming off.

They didn't speak. Teddy just undressed Elijah, who unclothed Teddy. They got under the sheets and pulled the comforter over themselves. After giving gentle kisses to Elijah's body, Teddy finally got the control he'd wanted when he penetrated Elijah. This would be one of their last stage performances together. The orgasms held a sense of finality, for the curtains of their relationship would soon be drawn. Though there were no roses and yells for an encore, the sky congratulated them with camera flashes, warm tears, and thunderous applause. Quite literally, they had fucked up a storm.

"Are you okay? Are you ready to talk now, Little Guy?" asked Teddy.

"What did you call me?"

"Little Guy."

Elijah smiled and kissed him.

"What was that for?" asked Teddy.

"You being you."

"Are you ready to tell me what's wrong?" asked Teddy.

Elijah sighed. "I think we should end this."

"Our relationship?"

"Yes," said Elijah.

Teddy sat up in bed and asked, "Why?"

"Because there's not much love between us. It's just sex."

"It's more than sex," said Teddy.

"Do you love me?" asked Elijah.

Teddy looked away.

"I guess that's my answer," said Elijah.

"I *do* love you," Teddy replied.

"Well, why don't you show it?"

"I just fucked you, didn't I?" asked Teddy.

"That would've been enough to satisfy me a few months ago."

"What changed?" asked Teddy.

"Me."

"I could feel you slipping away," said Teddy.

"Is that why you turned up the heat?"

"Maybe."

"Maybe?" asked Elijah.

"I thought if I pleased you more, you would love me."

"So you wanted to fuck me into loving you?" asked Elijah.

"Basically," said Teddy.

"Unbelievable."

"Most guys would kill to be with someone like me," answered Teddy.

"Well, I'm different," said Elijah.

"How?"

"At first, I thought being with someone like you would make me feel better about myself. If I can get you, I must be beautiful," said Elijah.

"You are. Everyone else sees it. Why can't you?" asked Teddy.

"I'm starting to see it now." Elijah closed his eyes, opened them, and took a breath. "I haven't been totally faithful to you."

"I know. I haven't been totally faithful to you either," said Teddy.

"I know."

"Elijah, you dedicated too much time and energy to your writing to focus on building our relationship. You never had balance in your life. Since you didn't spend time with me, I had to spend time with someone else."

"Why didn't you tell me?"

"Why didn't you listen?" asked Teddy.

"I was afraid."

"Of what?"

"Being happy," said Elijah.

"You can be happy with me. It's not too late to save this relationship. We can work it out."

"A relationship that needs to be worked out is a relationship that doesn't need to be," said Elijah.

"Too much distance," Teddy replied.

"Distance, unfaithfulness, you name it."

"I don't believe this. There was a time when I could pull out my cock, and you would fall right to your knees," said Teddy, with a laugh.

Elijah smiled. "I've changed. My self-esteem is no longer tethered to someone's dick. I can play with my own."

"Wow," said Teddy. "I guess you've made up your mind."

"I guess so."

"I'm sorry," said Teddy

"Nothing to be sorry about. I hope you understand."

"It's okay," Teddy said. "I hate to let you go. You're the first guy I've ever been in a relationship with."

"And probably the last, right?" asked Elijah.

"Yes. Too complicated."

"No, it's not complicated. It's complex," said Elijah.

"What's the difference?" asked Teddy.

"Complexities are inherent. Complications are created."

"Semantics," said Teddy.

Elijah shrugged his shoulders. "For what it's worth, I'll miss you," he said, and meant it.

"I'll miss you too. You were truly my first love, Elijah. I'll never forget you."

Before they went to sleep, Teddy stood there naked, his penis dangling like a participle. When Teddy got in bed, Elijah put his head on Teddy's warm chest, and they fell serenely into a slumber. It was the first time they'd spent the night together. Teddy had just loved all of the worry out of Elijah, and they both felt it.

Elijah woke up first and decided to write, although he wasn't a morning person. The previous night had given him artistic inspiration he wanted to cash in on, so he sat in front of his computer and typed away, shooting occasional glances at Teddy, who was fast asleep with one hairy leg hanging out of the bed and his other hidden underneath the sheets. Elijah stared at him. He felt sorry for Teddy.

Lord, please forgive me for what I'm doing to him, Elijah thought.

Teddy woke up.

"What are you doing?" he asked.

"Just getting a little work done. Go back to sleep."

Elijah sat on the end of the bed and rubbed his hands through Teddy's hair, though Teddy felt none of that since he'd fallen back asleep before Elijah had even gotten up from his computer.

I don't deserve you, Teddy. Then again, I don't deserve much of anything right now, Elijah thought.

The sun eventually came up and woke Teddy, who sprang out of bed like a kid on the first day of school. Elijah laughed.

"Did you sleep all right?" Teddy asked.

"Yes," Elijah answered in a whisper.

"The other guys on the hall won't mind if I use you guys' shower will they?"

"Probably," said Elijah.

"Fuck those bastards. I'll use it anyway."

Laughing silently, Elijah handed Teddy a towel from the closet and watched him walk out. Elijah waited until he could hear the water running from the shower before checking his voice mail. One message was from an actor in *Rainbow Dancer* who wanted to meet for dinner that night. The second message was from Grayson. The sound of his voice sent chills through Elijah's little body.

"Hey, guy. This is Grayson. I was hoping to catch you, but I guess you're not there. I always feel a little silly talking to voice mail. I just wanted to let you know I was thinking about you and I'm okay. I'll be home soon. Later, Little Guy."

I'll be home soon. What's soon? Elijah thought.

The message left more questions than answers as Elijah went back to his computer and checked his e-mail, hoping to find some clues about Grayson's return. He found nothing. The rumble from the plumbing ceased, and Elijah wondered if he could listen to the message again before Teddy came into the room. The door swung open. In came Teddy in a towel. They kissed quickly, and he looked down at Elijah.

"What's wrong now?" asked Teddy.

"Nothing."

"You sure?"

"Yeah, I'm sure," said Elijah.

His state of mind could have been called emptiness, except there was no void. It was more like fullness of the self-hate that came with meaningless sex. But Elijah was more concerned about Teddy, the frat boy who could never teach Elijah self-worth, despite the fact that Teddy had an amazing penis.

Teddy was preoccupied with covering up his remarkable semen

dispenser by putting on the same clothes he had worn the previous day. Elijah didn't notice as he typed away at the computer. The message from Grayson had inspired a new plot twist in the novel he had started in the café, and he wanted to get it down before it left his mind for good. That had happened once, and it was a devastating feeling Elijah didn't want to relive.

He wished he could write himself a new life full of real love. Yes, there would be a little lovemaking here and there, but no more dates or kissing or holding hands in public. The message from Grayson had reminded him of what romance really was, and Teddy wasn't the one to provide that for him. Would anyone have been good enough after Grayson? Elijah would continue to look for romance, or for Grayson, whichever came first. Love wasn't something that came so easily to Elijah. He'd seen it and had toyed with it, but real love was much too far away. Kind of like a rainbow that seemed local—though it was probably across the state line.

PART V

The Funeral

15

The funeral, a large ceremonious affair, had impressed even Abby, who thought she had been to the grandest functions the world could offer. But nothing, absolutely nothing, was as lavish as the funeral of Teddy Worthington, her ex-husband who, even in death, could bring out all of the dignitaries in the Boston area and beyond. Those hundreds of mourners and Abby didn't get to see Teddy since, naturally, the casket had to be closed, considering how thoroughly Abby had cooked his body. But most didn't want to see him anyway, preferring instead to remember him as a vibrant man who had beautiful eyes.

The good, the bad, and the worst raced through Abby's mind as she walked down the aisle of the cathedral, eyes fixed on the wooden casket with gold handles lining the sides.

What have I done? she thought.

Her tears blurred the casket, and the sound of bagpipes made her knees buckle. A man in a kilt played "Amazing Grace," which seemed to drag on forever when presented in the cold, dismal melody of a bagpipe. Hearing the song was too much for her. So, with each chorus she gasped for air, while trying to walk with dignity, but she needed help from Susie, who herself was crying. Abby wasn't the least bit upset about Teddy's death; being in the cathedral was what upset her. They had gotten married there, and she'd forgotten how long the walk to the front of the church had been. The saunter was just as long in a wedding dress, although it seemed to dart by.

But this one lingered, giving her time to remember the decline of the life she had created.

Rebecca Smith's funeral the previous day had been nothing compared to this, and Abby had mistaken her lack of emotion at that event as a precursor to this one, thinking her composure would carry over into the next day like a cold front. But like dry lightning or a funnel cloud dipping toward the ground, despondency came with little or no warning at all. A temporary sadness came over Abby as she realized that her dreams of a perfect life with ideal nuptials were now gone for good—though the marriage itself had died years ago. She had thought her divorce had been her biggest failure, and now she—not Teddy's corpse—was on full display.

To make matters worse, everyone was looking at her. Despite the onlookers and the conjured-up memories, the sorrow was completely gone by the time she took her seat and stared at the casket and Teddy's picture smiling at the crowd from the easel. A sense of triumph came over Abby, replacing the melancholy that was never about Teddy, but about the loss of her much-romanticized self-image. Her feelings definitely had nothing to do with her best friend, the other person she had killed and whose burial ceremony she had just attended.

Rebecca's funeral had been a quaint affair, charmingly so, in a small church in Boston that seemed like it was somewhere in the country away from industrialization and all of the toxicity it brings. It didn't feel like the city Boston had become—a place where people didn't acknowledge each other with as much as a nod and where people were more concerned about the lukewarm coffee in their hands than the well-being of someone standing next to them. There was no molasses speech up here, and instead of wind pushing their chests, there was a breeze that pressed against their backs. Everyone, dressed appropriately in dull hues, seemed to know each other at Rebecca's funeral; and strangers from different parts of the country hugged like they'd known each other all of their lives.

A sense of envy overcame Abby as she questioned who would come to her funeral. Would anyone show up? Since she didn't belong to a church, where would they have it? It amazed her that people there could swap brief stories about Rebecca, showing how she had touched their lives. What troubled Abby even more was that there wasn't a place for her near the front of the church. She had to sit in the back, just beside the young men who worked for the funeral home. The family didn't seem to remember Abby, and those who did pretended to barely know her.

But there wasn't a tinge of guilt in her, even when she watched Rebecca's parents walk out of the church, eyes red and faces distorted. There wasn't even a trace of remorse when the silver box with matching handles was lowered into the ground and a handful of dirt was thrown atop it, while yells of despair came from the mouths of Rebecca's three sisters and her old friends from her college days.

Abby and Rebecca had been childhood friends and had grown up in the same trailer park. Though when they left Tennessee to attend separate schools in Massachusetts, they had completely different outlooks about their background. Abby saw poverty as shameful, something to hide and distance herself from. She drew alliances with wealthy students, emulated their mannerisms and liberal politics, and even tried to mimic their accents. The curls in her hair were replaced with straight hair accented with bows, and her blue jeans were traded in for tennis skirts, silk blouses, and simple shoes. Her large plastic-framed glasses were substituted with a sleek wire-framed pair. In the period of a semester, Abby had reinvented herself as a sophisticated New England woman prone to going to mixers and hanging out with fraternity boys, some of whom she dated. One, Teddy Worthington, was the wealthiest.

She could afford the expensive clothes, the jewelry, and the wire-framed glasses because she worked at the library. Not the one on campus, but the public library. That way Abby could hide the fact that she had to work to buy things. Thanks to a full scholarship, which she hid as well, 100 percent of her paycheck was earmarked for pretending to be a rich girl, and it worked until she began to want more things.

That was when she started to earn most of her money by being a prostitute. Friday nights were peak hours in Boston, and Abby found that out by chance when walking down the street one day and stopping to use a pay phone to call a cab. She stood there thumbing through the phone book when a thirty-six-year-old man with a broad smile came into her life.

"I'll give you a grand if you let me fuck you," he yelled from the window of his car. Abby turned around and gave him the finger. When he asked again, she looked into his eyes and saw seriousness hanging over his smile. The next morning when Abby stumbled out of the hotel room one thousand dollars richer she blamed intoxication. She walked down the same street the following week and stood on the corner to find a less attractive man with a similar offer. With no alcohol in her system, she jumped into his car. He had resembled her father, the time she'd seen him clean-shaven with somewhere classy to go. She hooked at least four times a month during her last three years of college. Selling herself shamed her, but it gave her the money to buy herself a new image.

Everyone was deceived. Even Teddy, who himself recognized old money, had been fooled all the way until graduation day, when he met Abby's mother, who had curly hair and wore a plaid blouse and blue jean shorts. Abby didn't want her family to come to the ceremony because it would expose the truth about her, that she was not raised in the upscale side of Memphis, but in a singlewide trailer.

Her childhood was like empty pews in a cathedral, full of messages with no one to hear them. She didn't even notice the signs she gave off—signs that pointed to a sexual and emotional quest for paternal love that could never be reached—because that part was way above the pews, in the stained-glass window above the crucified Jesus, too far to touch but close enough to see the chips in the glass.

Rebecca also had a bad childhood but chose not to hide it. Abby envied her for being honest. Rebecca never denied her upbringing and, when asked, would proudly say that her father was a garbage man and her mother was a janitor. She didn't mind how some of the students at Wellesley used to look down on her because of her background and for her job cleaning the cafeteria. It wasn't the occupation she'd really wanted, but the pay was enough for her to buy books and occasionally go to a decent restaurant. Her life didn't revolve around the world of fraternities and sororities. She chose to embrace the academic challenges at Wellesley, delving into books instead of alcohol. She graduated at the top of her class, while Abby, who spent so much time trying to fit in, needed more time to get her degree. By the time Abby graduated, Rebecca had already earned a master's in art history and had been working on a PhD. Abby despised her for that, even when starting the blaze that would end Rebecca's life.

Unlike her best friend, Rebecca didn't even take the time to get involved in any serious romance until she was nearly thirty, focusing instead on her career, eventually becoming a tenured professor at Abby's alma mater. This wasn't intentional on Rebecca's part, but Abby cried to herself when finding this out. But she had gotten to the altar before Rebecca and clung to her marriage to make herself feel like she had bested her friend.

So after her nuptials crumbled, so did her relationship with Rebecca. Despite having grown up together and having been best friends, Abby fled the city of Boston to get away from her because, in Abby's warped mind, Rebecca had won the game of life. She was the one who had the PhD; the one whose career wasn't predicated on her husband's connections; the one who was truly an independent, modern woman who didn't need a man. Above all, Rebecca was the woman Teddy had wanted Abby to be.

So when the last prayer was said and her former best friend's body had been lowered into the ground, Abby felt a sense of victory and loss. That explained the way she behaved when walking off the funeral grounds and seeing Rebecca's parents, who were still pretending not to know her. Rather than hug them and cry with them, she did something cold and brittle—like the Bostonian Abby aspired to be, she just passed by them with lukewarm coffee in her hand.

But that was the day before. Now, as soon as she took her seat at Teddy's funeral, tears flowed from her eyes as she stared at the casket, wondering if he died knowing she was his killer. One thing was for sure: Abby thought no one else would ever suspect her since, by her own design, an arsonist named Simon Blanc had been on a rampage in Massachusetts, having burned down nine homes with Molotov cocktails.

Every single person in the cathedral believed Blanc had killed Teddy and Rebecca. When Abby read the newspaper, she was impressed by her perfect double murder and once again doubled over in laughter while reading the article about Blanc, whose whereabouts were still unknown. It was the first time in a long while that she felt accomplished. But the feeling of achievement went away when she read two words: *Molotov cocktails.* "This can't be," Abby said to herself, remembering she had used gasoline. Then, she thought, *I have nothing to worry about. I'm rich. I can buy an alibi.* She laughed again.

But Muriel was not pleased.

When the piper finished "Amazing Grace," Abby turned on the faucet some more, even going as far as letting out a wail that resonated throughout the cathedral, seeming to make the stained glass vibrate and the pictures of the Virgin Mary fall from the wall behind the pulpit.

They bought it.

Teddy's parents, the rest of the Worthington family, Susie, the priest, the bagpipe player, and every mourner…they all bought it.

Those beside Abby consoled her as best they could, passing tissues down the pew and patting her on the back and saying "It's okay" in whispers. Their gullibility amazed her, even as she pseudo-gathered herself and walked up to the lectern to give a eulogy, the priest helping her up the stairs with a steady hand. She didn't make the sartorial mistakes of the previous day. Her outfit was perfect: a black dress with pumps to match, a black pocketbook thrown across her shoulder, black gloves with a silver ring placed on the middle finger of her right hand, and black earrings that were rare diamonds from a boutique in Sweden she had stumbled upon while on one of her European vacations. The dress was cut well below the knee and was hemmed to perfection, giving her room to walk (or traipse, even) but giving no allowance for a strut. To complete the ensemble, she wore a black hat—with a thin suede line trimming the brim and a bow in the front—tilted slightly to one side. But the bow on her hat wasn't red.

As she walked up the thin stairs, guided by the priest, Abby fixed her eyes on a large cross hanging on the wall. It was the centerpiece of the entire cathedral: a gold crucifix that managed to sparkle in the dim light. Everyone who entered had gazed at it before finding a seat. And some who listened to the eulogy looked back and forth at her and the gold cross on the wall.

Abby, stuttering and gasping for breath on purpose, spoke without using notes. "I remember when I met Teddy. It was at Boston College. Teddy was so proud of his alma mater. I'm sure he would want me to mention that in his eulogy. It seemed he loved Boston College more than he loved me."

Everyone laughed before she continued. "He walked up to me as I was going to class and asked if he could carry my books for me.

It seemed like such a juvenile way to approach a college girl, but Teddy found a way to make it sound adult. And I did. I-I gave him my books, and he walked me to class every day after that. That was when we first got to know each other, in the brief ten or so minutes it would take to walk to class. We would exchange little tidbits of information about ourselves—well, as much as we could in that length of time. And after a month of walking to class together, we were in love. That's how we fell in love. Nothing terribly romantic. No fancy tales about how he swept me off my feet at a ball. He didn't need any of that. All he needed was ten minutes of my time. And ten minutes eventually turned into years of marriage. It went by so fast, so quick. Though the marriage didn't last, we loved each other right up until he passed away. And that is enough to keep me going for the rest of my life."

Abby pulled out a tissue and looked down at the casket and said, "I love you, Teddy, wherever you are."

Then she looked up at the ceiling of the cathedral and purposely fell to the floor beside the lectern, crying and crying until the priest helped her up and walked her to the pew. There were a few people who could contain their emotions, but most began to cry as soon as Abby fell to the floor.

She fake-fainted at the burial grounds as well. As they lowered the casket into the ground, she finally composed herself, bowed her head in mock prayer, and made the sign of the cross in the wrong direction. She laughed internally after realizing her mistake. Then Abby slowly walked to the limousine to be chauffeured to the hotel. She had performed brilliantly.

∽♡∼

When nighttime came and the stars shone brilliantly in the sky, memories of Teddy entered her thoughts. When they had bought their first condo, they had danced around in the room while Teddy hummed out of tune. That was before the furniture arrived, so they had enough room to do the waltz they'd learned when they took dance classes just for fun. Teddy and Abby were the youngest people there, so each of them felt they could move and do spins and twirls that would put the elderly to shame. In their new home, both were dancing without the benefit of music, and they tripped over each other's feet and landed on the floor. They laughed until the sky went from Carolina blue to black.

Once the amusement subsided, they had one of the only true discussions they had in their lives. He wrapped her in his arms, making her forget they were on the floor with neither mattress nor pillow. For the first few months of their marriage, they cuddled often. That was the only way they could get to sleep. But more Carolina blue skies came and went, and eventually they were sleeping in different rooms, waking up, not eating breakfast together, and leaving without saying good-bye.

They didn't fall out of love; they simply fell apart. They began to resent one another and eventually hate each other. But they both had wanted to stay married, Teddy for religious reasons and Abby to have a man. She then realized what she had liked most about him: he had always called her his "little girl," something her father had never called her.

But Teddy was gone, and despite her hand in his death, she felt it was part of her plan, set way in advance, back when her father had thrown a bottle at her and her mother had ignored her. There still wasn't a tinge of guilt in her soul for having taken two lives, but there was enough creativity stirring in Abby for her to get some of the paper off the desk in the hotel room and one of the pens bearing the hotel's name. She wrote until she fell asleep in the wooden chair, ignoring the queen-sized bed that had been so comfortable and kind to her the previous night. Her sister, meanwhile, was on an entirely different floor in a lesser room; Abby set it up that way, not wanting to be aggravated by her white trash sister. Susie knew what Abby thought about her and also knew there was nothing white trash about owning one of the most popular restaurants in Memphis.

16

Abby had stolen the hotel pen and twirled it around in her fingers as she sat on the plane. She made attempts to write a short story, but the cramped quarters and the many people around her hindered her thoughts. Susie, who looked surprisingly fresh and alert, glanced back and forth at Abby, occasionally taking sips from the plastic cup of soda in front of her. As soon as Abby let out a sigh and placed the pen down on the pad she had also stolen from the hotel, Susie broke the silence.

"Abby, are you all right?" Susie asked.

"I'm okay."

"You've been quiet for a while now," said Susie.

"Just thinking." Abby looked out the window and saw the wing of the plane hanging over thick clouds.

"Thinking about what?"

"The time we were lying in the grass at home and looking up at the clouds with Mom. Remember?" asked Abby.

"Yeah, I remember. Those were good times, weren't they?"

"Yeah, they were." Abby grabbed Susie's hand and said, "I never thought things would end up quite like this."

"Like what?"

"Mom gone. Me divorced and living alone, careerless."

"You're just upset over Teddy's death. Tragedies always make you think," said Susie.

"You're probably right." Abby let go of her sister's hand as a hint of crimson found its way to her cheeks. Then she said, "I hope so" without knowing what she was hoping for.

"Do you want me to stay with you for a little while? I can postpone my flight."

"No, you don't have to do that. I'd rather be alone anyway," said Abby.

"I understand." Susie glanced at her. "My flight back to Memphis isn't until tonight, so we still have a couple of hours."

"We can go get some coffee or something. I'll show you one of my favorite places to go. It's where I met Spencer."

"Spencer?"

"My boyfriend. At least, that's what I think he is." Abby laughed for no reason.

"The real-estate guy you told me about?"

"He's not a real-estate guy," Abby said.

"What is he?"

"An ex-marine." Abby answered.

"You said he was…"

"I lied," Abby said, while looking down at the tiny houses beneath her, trying to figure out if they were flying over Virginia or North Carolina. "He was discharged. I think he's embarrassed about it." Abby turned toward her sister then looked away and said, "You know, people think they have to be perfect around me, so they never tell the truth until long after they know me." She offered another synthetic laugh. "It must be something I give off." Through the corner of her eye, she could see Susie nodding her head.

"He's starting to open up, though," Abby added.

"What does he look like? Give me details."

"He's tall with a really nice build. And…he's black."

"What?"

"You heard me. He's black." Abby smiled. "And he just turned twenty-four."

"Twenty-four? You little slut," Susie said.

They could hear the man in front of them chuckle.

"I'll tell you the rest later," Abby said.

"No. Tell me now."

"Good Lord, the sex is hot," Abby whispered.

"You let him fuck you?"

"Shhhhhh. Not so loud. People might hear."

"I don't give a shit. Tell me about it, sis. Give me all the details." Susie took a sip from her cup and asked, "Is it true what they say about black men?"

"What?" Abby asked.

"That they have big dicks."

"It's true."

The man in front of them laughed again.

"How big is it?" Susie asked.

"I'm not going there."

"Please tell me. How big is it?" Susie asked again.

"Like a can of hairspray," Abby replied.

"Whoa." A little soda escaped Susie's mouth. She wiped it away with a napkin and placed it underneath the cup and asked, "Will I get the chance to meet this sex god?"

"Maybe one day, just not today," Abby said.

"Bitch."

"Fuck you."

They laughed. So did the man in front of them.

The tiny houses below the plane were in South Carolina. Time flew.

ᏼᎻᏳ

They entered Abby's South Carolina estate, and Susie said,

"Okay, sis, we have a while before I have to go to the airport. Call Spencer so I can meet him."

"Whatever." Abby began lugging her own bags upstairs. "Help me out here. I'm struggling."

"Not until you promise me you'll invite Spencer."

"I tell you what. How about I call and have him meet us at the café? That way we can leave from there, and I'll drop you off at the airport."

"Are you kicking me out?"

Abby responded with a laugh as they lugged her bags up the staircase.

After making it to the bedroom, they sat down on the end of Abby's bed, looking straight ahead.

"Are you sure you're all right about Teddy?" Susie asked.

"Yeah, I'm good." Abby let out a breath. "It's actually like closure of some weird kind. Now I can move on. Knowing he was in Boston without me hurt. It hurt me even more to find out he was moving on with his life."

Abby sighed again. "I thought about him all the time. It would've been nice for me to get a call from him from time to time—or maybe a call from some of my old friends—to let me know they were still thinking about me. But they didn't. Well, they did call at first, but I pushed them away like I did everyone else. And eventually the phone stopped ringing. Even Momma had stopped calling for a while." She glanced at Susie and said, "It's my fault. I guess I can't deal with pressure. But Spencer came along and gave me a little hope. And he really loves me too. At least I think so. Thank God he came into my life."

"I bet he came in your mouth too," Susie said, with a laugh.

"Would you shut up, Susie. I'm trying to be serious here." Abby turned away to hide her smile.

"Yeah, whatever. Let's call him. You know I don't have much time."

"Okay. I hope he answers. He might be painting or something. When he's painting, he doesn't pick up the phone."

"He's a painter? That's hot."

Abby, with the phone to her ear, put her index finger over her mouth and said, "Shhhhhh."

"Hello," Spencer said, with a raspy voice.

"Did I wake you?" Abby asked.

"Yeah, but it's okay."

Susie leaned toward the phone. Abby nudged her and laughed.

"What's so funny?" Spencer asked.

"Nothing. My sister's in town, and I want you to meet her. You up for it?"

"Yeah, I'm down. When?" Spencer asked.

"Like now. We don't have much time before I have to take her to the airport."

"Okay." Spencer cleared his throat and asked, "Where?"

"Dough House."

"Okay. I'll get ready and head over there."

"Hurry," Abby said.

"I will. I love you, baby."

"I love you, too, Spencer."

Susie's mouth flew open, and Abby jabbed her left side with her elbow.

"He has a sexy voice," Susie said.

"I know. That's one of the things I like most about him," Abby said.

"And his dick?"

"And his dick." Abby stood up. "Come on, let's get ready. No need to dress up or anything."

"Well, then why are you spraying on that cheap perfume?" Susie asked.

"The only thing cheap in this room is you."

17

Abby and Susie had been sitting at the table in the Dough House Café for almost twenty minutes. Abby would glance at her watch before looking out the window.

"Don't worry. He's coming."

"I know."

Abby smiled when Spencer pulled his SUV into the parking lot.

"There he is." Abby rose from the table and walked outside to meet him.

"Hey, girl," Spencer said.

"Hey, guy." Abby leaned in and kissed him, hoping her sister was watching. She was glad to see that Spencer was wearing his workout clothes.

As they walked toward the table, Abby almost tripped, focusing more on her sister's reaction to Spencer than on the floor underneath her shoes. Her sister's face was blank at first until he approached and held out a hand.

"Hi," Spencer said, as he pulled the chair out for Abby.

"Hey. Heard a lot about you." Susie looked him up and down from across the table. She gave him license to match her vulgarity and candor when she asked, "So you're the guy who's been boning my little sister?"

"Oh my God. Shut up," Abby said.

"Did you know you were her first black guy?" Susie asked.

"I suspected it," Spencer answered.

"Is she your first white girl?" Susie asked.

"No."

"Really? That surprises me. I assumed you had only dated black women."

"I like black women, but a lot of them are fake," Spencer said.

"How so?" asked Susie.

"The chemicals they put in their hair," Spencer said.

"What's wrong with that?"

"They use so many products to straighten their hair. They're trying to look white."

"I can see that," Abby said. "I never thought about it that way." Then she said to Susie, "I told you he was brutally honest and opinionated even when you first meet him."

"That's my style." Spencer leaned forward in his chair and continued, "I think a lot of black women try to fit into a white standard of beauty. I dated this woman who used to put all of these chemicals in her hair to straighten it. She used to say if she left it in her hair too long, it would make it fall out. If it can make your hair fall out, you shouldn't put it in your hair."

Abby and Susie laughed.

"Is that why you're with a white woman now?" Susie asked.

"Maybe," Spencer said.

"I don't mean to offend you, but you don't seem like the type of guy who likes white women," Susie said, attempting to be provocative.

"Sometimes I don't like white people in general," said Spencer, who seemed surprised at his own bluntness.

"Really?" asked Susie.

"Sometimes, not all the time."

"Good save," Abby said.

"Black people and white people are just different," Spencer continued.

"How?" asked Susie.

"The food we eat, our political views, the way we talk."

"How is the way we talk different?" asked Abby.

"For instance, a white person will say, 'I'm hungry. I need to get some food from the cupboard.'"

"What's wrong with that?" Susie asked.

"It's not a cupboard," Spencer said. "It's a motherfucking cabinet."

They laughed before Abby said, "I say cupboard."

"That's because you're white."

"I say cupboard too," Susie said, with a smile.

"There you go," Spencer said.

The three of them laughed.

After that, they talked over coffee and pastries. Susie and Spencer relegated Abby to the margins, but she didn't mind, since Spencer's arm was around her. In fact, she loved to sit in silence and watch him interact with someone else, because she hadn't seen much of that, save for the times he had worked behind the counter swiping credit cards and handing people cups of coffee.

Noticing that her sister seemed fidgety, Abby looked at her watch and said, "Susie, I think we better get going."

"I think you're right," said Susie, who shook her head from side to side as they got up and walked out of the café.

Spencer followed them.

"I'll see you later, okay?" Abby said to Spencer, hugging herself to fight an imaginary breeze.

"Okay," Spencer said, as he opened the door of the SUV for Abby.

Abby rolled down the window, and Spencer leaned in and kissed her. He looked at her pocketbook, and that was the point when she backed out of the parking space.

"Susie, you seem sad to leave," Abby said.

"I am."

The rest of the car ride was silent, save for the wind seeping through a slightly opened window, making a whistle that both would rather hear than the sound of Susie's questions and Abby's lies. For a minute, it seemed as if Teddy were still alive, until they remembered the casket underneath the surface of Boston. The apparatus that lowered the casket had made the same shrill, except it wasn't nearly as loud, though it was just as dreary.

Abby didn't help her sister with her bags and nodded her head instead of saying good-bye. Then she drove away swiftly. When Abby arrived at home, a few stars were visible in the sky, waiting for their turn to really sparkle in a couple of hours when the black would be behind them. She walked upstairs and unpacked the bags she'd left on the floor, and then she saw a certified check on her dresser. She had gotten it from the bank the day before she'd flown to Boston, and it was made payable to Spencer Gibson. That same day he'd told her how difficult it was to pay his rent, considering he hadn't been working. She asked how much his monthly rent was. She remembered the number, multiplied it by twelve, and told the teller to make the check out for that amount. Abby loved Spencer and lusted for him but still wanted to buy him.

She stood in her bedroom looking at the check, reading and re-reading his name as if it would look different the second time. It struck her how little she really knew about this man. Abby knew his body, had memorized it, but aside from the day she had discovered he was an artist, she had never really had a meaningful conversation with him. After having sex, they could've talked, but the sleepiness was too much to fight back. Sure, he'd told her his life story: the tragedy of growing up with a dead father and an imprisoned mother. But that was the kind of information that really didn't matter; it was merely a summary of a greater life she didn't know. Abby refused to ask. Spencer would have refused to answer.

By the time the black posted behind the stars, she was looking up at the ceiling with the lights turned out, trying to imagine who Spencer really was. She decided then and there to write a story about him, a desperate attempt to fill in the blanks to her liking. She called Spencer to invite him to her house for a late dinner, hoping he would spend the night. He said yes without hesitation.

By the time he arrived, she had already gotten the food from the restaurant: lobster tails and salad. And she had taken champagne from her wine cellar. While Spencer ate, she stared at him—at the way his mouth moved, the muscles in his jaw protruding, the licking of his thick lips to remove the sauce, the glances at her across the table, the pointless smiles he displayed. His movements reminded her why she had given herself to him in the first place. They spoke little, since they both knew what was about to happen next.

They kissed.

The touch of his lips to hers made Abby feel as though she were standing in the airport kissing her soldier goodbye before his fifteen-month tour, but she opened her eyes and saw gaudy furniture, not passengers waiting in line. This wasn't one of those airport kisses, for her unknown soldier would die on the battlefield, never to return again. But not before one last night of lovemaking. Even though there was no love to be made, they could still pretend with the imagination of a child too poor to have playthings. They were a doll and an action figure, holding plastic hands attached to bodies that were hollow, no beating hearts inside their chests.

Not wanting to be the slut her sister had called her, Abby attempted to make idle conversation. But the heat overcame her, so she removed her panties from underneath her skirt, sat on the tabletop, leaned back, and assumed the Pap smear position. Spencer removed his shirt, pulled his pants and underwear down to his thick thighs, and entered her with a penis that was as hard as the table. Abby let him ravish her right then and there, enjoying the feeling of him inside her and relishing the slap of his body against her thighs and the pressure of his scrotum against her. And she loved the way the mushroom-shaped part of his penis felt during the out-strokes, as his coronal ridge hook scraped her vaginal walls. When he put her legs over his shoulders and fondled her nipples while still moving in and out of her, she thought, *I should've told the teller to add more money to the check.*

They walked up to the bedroom, panting and stumbling in the dark, and felt their way to the bed. The sheets were a lot warmer than the table downstairs. Spencer entered her again; it was different this time. They were having sex in a way that signaled the end—like the last time Abby had made love to Teddy before they divorced. They both knew something was different about his stroke, so she wanted to prolong the experience of having companionship in the face of an otherwise lonely existence.

"Have you ever tried anal sex?" Spencer asked.

"No."

"Do you want to?" he asked.

"Okay." Her voice was uncertain.

"Turn over."

After she took his orders, Spencer spread her cheeks and licked her backside before fingering her asshole with his middle and index fingers. He then spit in her crack before slowly working his penis inside her. Abby moaned in pleasurable pain. He began to stroke with thrusts unlike those her vagina had endured. These motions were more passionate and powerful. Spencer himself moaned with every move.

Then he unknowingly said in a whisper, "Man, your ass feels so good."

"What did you call me?" she asked.

"I called you Abby."

She cried as he continued to fuck her. Abby's body went completely numb. She could no longer feel the physical pain of him going in and out of her backside. After a few more strokes, Spencer came. He pulled out and lay down beside her. He looked up at the ceiling and said, "You okay?"

"I need to take a bath," said Abby, as her voice began to crack.

"Me too." He got up and went to the bathroom to draw a bath while she waited in the bed alone. She eventually joined him. And they looked at the nakedness of each other before submerging their bodies in the foam-covered water of the garden tub and staring out the window through curtains that distorted the lights outside.

"This feels good," Abby lied, while leaning her back against his chest and holding his hands.

"Really?"

"Yes."

They stayed in that position until, without another word, they rose from the tub and walked across the floor, leaving wet footprints in the carpet. Abby suddenly realized her exposure, ran to the closet, and came out wearing a robe. She threw a towel at him, but he didn't try to catch it.

Abby stared at Spencer, whose already dark skin became as dark as the night sky. But unlike before, there was nothing savage about that color. She then looked at her own hands, and the paleness began to look dirty and evil as she saw history on them. At that epiphany, Abby wanted to wash her hands—but that wouldn't wash away the whiteness. That was when a sense of guilt brought her to say, "I have something for you."

"What is it?" he asked.

She fished the check from her desk drawer and gave it to him.

"I can't take this."

"Please take it."

"I can't."

"Why?" she asked.

"Because I…"

"Because you don't love me?" she interrupted.

Spencer let out a deep breath that warmed her face. Abby looked at him, standing there, watching water dance its way down his dark skin.

"I understand." She wiped the tears from her eyes. "Take it anyway. It's the least I can do."

"What?" he asked.

"Never mind. Just take it. And spend the night."

Spencer had never given the check back to her but nodded his head anyway and slid it into the pocket of his pants, which were sprawled on the floor. Once he dried, they eased themselves under the sheets and listened to the wind beat the windowpane. Spencer held her the same way he had the first time they had sex.

"You want to explain why?" she asked.

"Why what?"

"You know what I mean." Abby propped herself up with her elbow and regarded his face as best she could in the dim light.

"You want me to explain why I can't be with you?" Spencer asked.

When he spoke, she could feel vibrations coming from his chest that made her tingle. She closed her eyes and responded, "Yes."

"I'm not who you think I am." Spencer turned to gauge her reaction and turned away. "Abby, I tried this before, but it never works. You know, love and relationships and shit like that. I can never be the man everyone wants me to be. I knew that early on in life. That's why I started painting and drawing. It gave me a way to create a perfect world, a life I can really live. I see all these beautiful things I can't have, so I paint them."

Spencer stared at the ceiling. "When I signed up for the Marines, it had nothing to do with fighting for my country. But I felt like I needed to go to show everyone what kind of man I was. I wasn't there as long as some people were, but I paid my dues. I'm a real man. And that's what real men do, you know?"

"Before I got on that plane," he continued, "I had never been outside of South Carolina, and when I looked around, I was in Iraq. It kind of fucks with your head, but you adjust to it as best you can. That's what soldiers do."

He looked away from her as he spoke. "I remember sleeping in overcrowded quarters, getting to know people from all over the country. It was new for me. All I've ever known were the people in my neighborhood. I felt like I was doing something with my life by signing up for the Marines. Being an artist is fine and everything, but that can only get you so far. Don't think I stopped being an artist. That's what's most important to me. You saw the sketches I made when I was over there. When you looked at my work, you saw the shit I was going through." Spencer studied Abby's face before continuing, "You also saw the reason I left."

She remembered thumbing through his sketches and seeing a drawing of someone.

"That's why I can't love you, because…"

"Shhhhhh." Abby put her index finger over his lips and said, "I know, sweetie. I know." She thought of his sketch of the handsome young soldier.

And with the wind still trying to break into the house, they fell asleep. Spencer was still facing the ceiling with his arm around Abby, and she went to sleep with her head on his still-strong chest. She knew then that she couldn't be with Spencer and would never love him.

Abby should've known that she wasn't in love with him. It was just infatuation, an obsessive, sexual curiosity of the unknown. On her unending quest for self-esteem, she'd lost sight of love and was drawn into relationships with two men she thought she was in love with—Teddy Worthington and now Spencer Gibson.

⊙ⅢⅢ⊙

When morning came, Abby sat on the side of the bed and watched Spencer, who was getting dressed. She said, "You take care of yourself, okay?" Then she stood up, covering herself with her robe.

Spencer said, "Okay," then hugged her and whispered, "I'm sorry."

"You have nothing to be sorry about" were the last words Abby would ever speak to him.

Then Spencer walked out of the room, out of the house, and out of her life.

As soon as his SUV faded into the distance, Abby realized that, for the first time, she had watched someone drive down Memory Lane, and Spencer Gibson had become another pothole on the end of her lonely road.

She could have paved over the dust and gravel if she would have looked within herself. She could have filled in the potholes if she had bought a journal and had taken time for self-reflection. If Abby had done those things, this imbalance—this chemical melancholy—could have been treated and managed into artistic and chronicled benefit, because she had the power to mold this sadness into something beautiful. Sure, she had spent many hours writing, but the problem was her inconsistency. Writing was like medication that had to be taken each day, but Abby—bless her heart—was so consumed with outward appearances (her clothes, her jewelry, her weight, her home) that she would go for weeks without a dose.

Her creative license wasn't like those dollhouses in the lighthouse over yonder, because her literary imagination was a toy that would never bore her.

Even her fling with Spencer could have been turned into the focal point of a masterpiece if she would have cashed in on her desolation. But, vis-à-vis artistic inspiration and sexual expression, he was out of her life. That realization brought tears to Abby's eyes as she watched him through the window and waved at the taillights that disappeared in the distance. That was how her relationships always seemed to end, with a man dashing off with her self-worth—severing all ties—and leaving her there, hopeless and lonely. Part of the reason for the tears was her coming to terms with the notion that her life might always be cold.

Like Muriel said, "A warm flow of the waters may never be."

PART VI

Vermillion Red

18

In Baghdad, an American soldier ran, a patch bearing Old Glory on his shoulder. A rifle, loaded to capacity, was in his trembling hands. Everyone else in his platoon was dead, but he looked for them anyway. Everything appeared blurry. The sky melded with the ground. The heat was too much to bear, intensified by seventy pounds of equipment—the guns, the grenades, an unopened first-aid kit, flares, rations packed tightly into a package the size of his hand. He breathed hard before seeing a foreign object. Upon taking a few paces forward, the foreign object revealed itself to be a tree. He sat against it, hoping the sky and the ground would separate. They did not. Lonely, the soldier sat there, took a breath, and clutched his rifle, wondering if it was loaded.

The sky began to separate from the ground. He saw the sand underneath his feet. He looked up and recognized the familiar color of the sky, Carolina blue. Shuffles in the ground, somewhere off to his left. He heard the sound, grabbed his rifle, called out random names of his platoon members. No answer. More shuffles, this time to his right. His hands trembled. The shuffles became louder.

He saw a small object coming toward him very fast.

He saw a long-ago Christmas, opening up a toy pistol—compliments of his father. Memories of blowing out candles on a birthday cake filled him, seven candles but fewer friends at the table. A soccer ball came off his foot and landed in the net; ten weeks later a gray-haired man, his coach, presented him with a trophy. The trophy: a plastic man in a shirt and shorts with a soccer ball underneath his foot. The plate read: Grayson Sinclair Dobson, 9th Grade Player of the Year. *A locker room, he saw a teammate naked. He looked down at himself, naked. They stared. They kissed. He penetrated the guy. Virginity was gone. They never spoke again. A letter came in the mail, he opened it, and he balled up his acceptance letter. It was the only college he'd applied to. He packed. Left home. Didn't look at the house as he left. A boy was asleep on the floor, small and very attractive. His smile, beautiful. Connection. A kiss in the sky, above a rainbow. Hands trembled while writing a letter. Placed letter on bed. Boot camp. Rigorous exercises. Sleeping on a hard bed. The water was so vast and wide, the Atlantic. Two friends died in a helicopter crash. Writing a letter to the love of his life. Sleeping in a tent he pitched himself. Crying himself to sleep, thinking of home, thinking of Elijah. Running through a wooded area, comrades falling to the ground, killed. Looking for them. Realizing they were dead, he shook—not from fear, but from sadness. He was not scared, just exhausted.*

The soldier reached for his gun and ran. The heat wave hit him ten minutes later and forced him to a halt. He panted and leaned forward to rest. More shuffles. He turned around, rifle in hand. He saw something very small traveling fast toward him. It slowed down as it approached him. It was a bullet, small and shiny. It slowed just enough for him to see its imperfections. The imperfect object entered his neck. He fell. Died looking up at the vast sky…Carolina blue, not a rainbow in sight.

⦿ⅢⅢ๑

Noah stood in the hotel room and looked out the window at the vast sky that, on this holy day, was Carolina blue. This was the first weekend he had been away from Elijah since they had been an item.

Noah missed him already and, after answering the phone, flashed a wide smile when hearing Elijah's voice.

"Hey, Noah."

"Hey."

"How's everything going up there?"

"Everything's good," Noah said. "I'm about to go meet my ex-girlfriend."

"Yeah, right."

"You don't want me to?" Noah asked.

"Of course not."

"She called me today. She wants to come over here and have sex with me," Noah said.

"Really?"

"I wonder what she'll do when she gets here," Noah said.

"She better not touch you. I'll get a knife and cut that heifer."

Noah laughed. "So how's everything down there?"

"Good."

Elijah and Noah both realized how mundane the conversation seemed and were too afraid to speak with any degree of sentiment.

"Have you started your tradition yet?" Elijah asked.

"No, not until sundown."

"Sorry," said Elijah, who sounded like a shy student reading aloud in class.

"It's okay. You don't have to feel sorry about anything. I know you're still learning about my religion."

"I just wish I could learn a little faster. I just don't want there to be a disconnect."

"Disconnect? Stop talking like a research paper," Noah said.

"Sorry, sugar."

"You're really cute right now—you know that, don't you?"

Elijah answered with a quick laugh. Then he said, "You're just saying that to get me back in bed."

"Is it working?"

"A little."

"So when I get back, am I going to get to bang you like I did the last time?"

"Shut up," Elijah said.

Noah laughed. "I'm serious."

"So you want some more of my cat?"

"Yeah, I want some." Noah chuckled.

"I might give you some if you stop making fun of me."

"I can't help it. You're an easy target."

"Whatever." Elijah cleared his throat. "When are you coming back?"

"In two days. That's not that long," Noah replied.

"No, it's not, but it'll feel like it, especially since I'm horny right now. How am I going to make it without sex?"

"You're so silly," said Noah. "You'll survive. I'm horny too."

"Really?"

"Yeah, really," said Noah.

"When you get here, are you going to fuck me with your big Jewish cock?"

Noah offered another chuckle. "Yeah, real hard."

"Real hard?"

"Yeah."

Elijah and Noah both started laughing.

"Okay, I'll hold you to that," Elijah said. "I know you'll be thinking about my cat for the next two days."

"I will be." Noah didn't realize he was grabbing himself. "Elijah, I wanted to talk to you about something kind of important."

"What is it?"

"About the other night. When we…"

"What about it?" Elijah interrupted.

"Was I good?"

"Yeah, you were."

"Really?" Noah asked.

"Yeah. I enjoyed everything about it."

"Okay. I've been thinking about it. I wanted to make sure it was, you know, special."

"It was. It was one of the best moments of my life. You were such a gentleman, the way you were trying to make sure I enjoyed it You were more into pleasing me than pleasing yourself. That really meant a lot to me, you know? It still means a lot. It lets me know you care about me on a different level. It was the first time someone really made love to me," Elijah said.

"Thanks."

"I should be the one thanking you." Elijah cleared his throat once more. "Well, I have to go."

"Okay."

"Call me tomorrow if you get some time," Elijah said.

"I will."

"Bye, Noah."

"Bye."

Noah hung up the phone and thought of the sex with Elijah. Noah had done the unthinkable. Rather than remove his penis from Elijah, he had made a seminal deposit into Elijah's rectal account. They were banking on their monogamy, so their sexual currency was not held in *a* trust, but in trust itself. The interest was in each other, and the returns were an orgasm.

Now, standing alone in the hotel room, he was eager to see his investment mature.

19

Later that day, Noah watched the news while rushing to finish his meal: two turkey sandwiches, chips, and juice. He had decided to have an early dinner to avoid eating after sundown, and choosing two sandwiches was his way of filling himself up because he would not consume food again until really late the following day. After eating, he sat on the bed and watched the news, enthralled with stories of suicide bombers in the Middle East, nuclear proliferation in North Korea, and people dying of malaria in Africa.

"Don't they have ways to treat people with malaria?" he said to himself.

Noah, who had removed his clothes, felt a tingle in his genitals as he sat on the bed. He looked down at himself and watched every strand of his pubic hair jump one by one onto the bed. The hairs formed a sphere that bounced around. The ball of Hasidic pubes then grew two legs, then two arms, then a round head. The ball itself narrowed to become the torso. Noah sat there and watched his pubic hair walk toward him in the shape of a stick figure. It resembled a gingerbread man that was made out of his pubic hair.

"Hey, Noah. How are you?" Pube asked.

"I'm doing okay, Pube. How are you?"

"I'm good."

"I haven't seen you in a while. What have you been doing?" Noah asked.

"Keeping your dick warm. What the fuck did you think I was doing?" Pube said.

Noah laughed. "You always were sarcastic. You only show up when you have something important to say. So spill it."

"I can tell you're having those thoughts again," Pube said.

"What thoughts?"

"You know—thoughts of fucking little boys up the ass."

"Wow. How did you know?"

"I can feel your dick get hard when you watch kiddy shows," Pube said.

"Is it that obvious?"

"Yeah. Every time I hear little boys' voices, you get an erection," Pube said.

"So I have a problem?"

"You already know the answer to that shit."

"So what do I do? The thoughts and feelings are getting worse."

"Channel them," Pube said.

"Into what?"

"Do I really need to spell this shit out?" Pube asked.

"Just say it," Noah said.

"You have a gift for creating art. Art that's special."

"And?"

"Channel your sick, fucked-up thoughts into that. Use your fucked-up-edness as a resource to be creative."

"I get it," Noah said.

"Art can keep you from going crazy. Well, not from going crazy but from acting crazy," Pube said.

"I know, but I'll still have these thoughts—these disgusting thoughts."

"You might not be able to control your thoughts, but you sure as hell can control your actions. So instead of your thoughts being shoved up a thirteen-year-old's ass, put some paint on your dick and rub it on a canvas."

Noah laughed.

Pube continued, "Everyone has demons. But people call them different things. Some people call them skeletons in their closet. Others call them ghosts. You've identified your ghost, and that's the biggest step in controlling it. You've been confronting your ghost all along. You just didn't know it."

"Really?"

"Let me ask you a question."

"Shoot."

"If a ghost—your ghost—appears, do you run from it? Or do you confront it?" asked Pube.

"You confront it."

"Why?" Pube asked.

"Because it will intensify if you try to run from it."

"Exactly. You don't want to be the weak-minded person who sees the ghost and runs to the bed and tries to hide under the sheets. Hiding under the sheets won't protect you from a ghost. Because the ghost is inside you. You can't run from yourself. You have to get the ghost out of your system with art, with talking, with exercise. With things that are deep and meaningful—not with superficial things. Those who hide lose sight of who they are. They become insecure and shallow. They chase things that are not worth chasing. They do dirty things to people because they hate themselves. They push people away and end up living a life of misery and loneliness. All because they are afraid to look at the past and figure out what made them the way they are. Sheets are made to keep you warm, not to keep you cold."

"I understand."

"I know you do," Pube said. "I've seen you paint your way out of acting on your thoughts, and it's an amazing thing."

"Do you think it will work?"

"It's worked so far, right?"

"Right," Noah said.

"So keep it up. I'm really proud of you."

"Thanks," Noah replied.

"You're welcome." Pube held up his left hand and said, "One more thing."

"What?"

"That Elijah kid, he's the real deal."

"I know," Noah said.

"I can tell you love him."

"Really?"

"Yeah. You fuck him differently," Pube said. "I've had a front-row seat for every fuck session you've had in your life—all one million of them."

"Whatever," Noah said, with a laugh.

"With him your strokes are different. He can be your canvas."

"What?" Noah asked.

"It was a metaphor, you dumb fuck. What I mean is, he can help you control yourself. It's obvious you love him, and he obviously loves you. So be with him. At the risk of sounding corny, it'll bring you happiness. And the happier you are, the less fucked up you'll be. That's a life lesson most people never get. Your life will be much better with him."

"Think so?"

"Know so," Pube said.

"My life really would be better with him," Noah said, though he was really talking to himself. Then he added, "Don't get me wrong. He's not perfect."

"No one is," Pube said.

"He's irresponsible with money. He made about twenty thousand dollars from his play, and he's already talking about spending it on some vintage car."

"How much of it?"

"Almost all of it. He thinks he has more money than he really has.

He doesn't understand the concept of money. When he got his signing bonus, the first thing he did was buy clothes. He blew through it in one day. At least that's what he told me."

"Wow."

"I know." Noah shook his head and continued, "Then the theater company called to tell him they wouldn't renew his contract, and he was surprised. Did he really think his play would be that big of a hit? Did he really think he would make enough money from the play to retire? It's just crazy. You would think that would've stopped him from spending. But he's still talking about getting the car."

"You have to teach him," Pube said.

"Teach him what? Teach him not to buy a vintage car, only to graduate from college and live with his mom? Who does that? He could save or even invest some of that money to start a good life for himself."

"He's younger than you."

"Not by much. Hell, when I was his age, I saved. I didn't even have a credit card."

"Everyone's not the same," Pube said.

"When I try to tell him, he gets agitated."

"What did you tell him?" Pube asked.

"I told him if you have to use credit to buy something, you can't afford it," Noah answered.

"But he's not using credit. He's using money from the play, right?"

"Some of it is from the play. Some of it is credit."

"Are his spending habits a deal breaker?" Pube asked.

"No. I think it can be corrected if I show him," Noah said.

"Good. So just go with that. You have your issues too," Pube said.

"Yeah. We just went over that, remember?"

"Is this really about him, or is it about you?"

"Part of it is about me," Noah said.

"What part?"

"I'm bisexual, and I think that might be a problem."

"Are you still attracted to girls?" Pube asked.

"Of course. I still think about them sometimes when I masturbate."

"When is the last time you fucked a girl?"

"About a week before I met Elijah. You should know."

"I remember now. It was two of them, and you fucked them both back-to-back. It was hot."

Noah laughed.

"So what about *after* you met Elijah?" Pube asked.

"The attraction went away."

"The attraction to girls?" Pube asked.

"My attraction to everyone except him."

"Then you're not just bisexual," Pube said.

"What else am I?"

"In love."

"I understand." Noah's voice was laced with welcomed resignation. "So what do I do?"

"You fight for him. Make him yours forever."

"Mine forever? How?" Noah asked.

"I'll let you figure that one out," Pube answered.

"Okay."

"Well, I have to get going," Pube said.

"See you later," Noah replied.

"Just remember—never hide under the sheets."

"I won't," Noah said.

Then Pube formed a ball that bounced its way back to Noah's genitals. Each strand of pubic hair found its follicle. The sensation made Noah laugh before he rose from the bed and made his way to the bathroom. He started the faucet and tested the water with the tips of his fingers; then he plugged the drain with the touch of a silver knob. Noah stepped into the water and sat down, so tall he had to bend his knees to fit. He closed his eyes as the water rose above his heels and smiled when it rose higher to tickle his scrotum.

Less than an hour later, Noah got up and let drops of water run down his body. He stood there—cool, free, naked—and admired the length and thickness of his Hebrew pride. He believed his penis was intelligently designed, an appropriate thought given that sundown marked Yom Kippur. Noah Cohen was relaxed after taking a long, cleansing bath in warm water that had felt more living than alive.

Before going to sleep that night, he called Elijah and left a message on his voice mail: "Elijah, I was thinking about you. Just wanted to talk to you before going to bed. You must be asleep already. I—I love you Elijah," said Noah, who, after hanging up the phone, regretted having stuttered.

I should've said it in person, he thought, while flinging the sheets, getting in bed, and covering his body up to his waist. He slept peacefully all night, except to wake up briefly and turn his pillow over to rest his head on the cooler side.

෮෨෩෪෨ඹ

When morning came, Noah showered and looked at himself in the mirror, appreciating the stubble on his face and the faint mustache under his nose. After finally getting dressed, he walked out of the hotel and frowned when the air hit his face. He then took his bicycle from his SUV and pedaled it eastward, stopping when reaching a structure that stood tall behind a group of people. Many of the men had dark hair—textured like lamb's wool—and skin that resembled a light shade of bronze.

The building looked exactly as he remembered it. It seemed as if ten years of weather had had no effect on its stone exterior.

No one will remember me, he thought, while positioning his bicycle where dozens of others were.

"Shalom," said a twenty-year-old guy who navigated his ten-speed between two bicycles.

"Shalom," Noah responded, as he locked his bike.

"I'm Alan."

"Nice to meet you. I'm Noah."

They shook hands, and Alan, the rabbi's son, made his way up the staircase. Noah looked back at his bike for good measure and followed suit. He found himself standing in line at the top of the staircase, waiting to shake the rabbi's hand before entering the building.

"Hi. I'm Noah."

"Nice to meet you, Noah. I'm Rabbi Rosen," the man responded with a smile that was hidden by a mustache and beard. Alan, who himself had signs of an emerging beard, was standing beside him, also flashing a smile.

Noah walked through the doorway into the synagogue and focused on getting used to an unfamiliar environment. The room was warm, a result of the sharp contrast outside or possibly because the space was thin, giving it a confined feel despite its length. Ten minutes later, Rabbi Rosen was at the podium, scanning the crowd as he began to speak in a voice that was at once authoritative and cordial.

During the middle of the service, he spoke words Noah would never forget: "There are some traditions," Rabbi Rosen said, "that many people don't keep alive. Even those who consider themselves orthodox let important rituals slip through the cracks. I want to remind you of an important tradition called a mikvah."

The members sat with studious gazes hanging on their faces as the rabbi talked about living water and the symbolism of bathing in natural water. Noah rubbed the sides of his face as Rabbi Rosen described the ritual of washing the hands and face, and Noah turned the corners of his mouth upward while allowing tears to form. The tears blurred his sight of the rabbi's yarmulke.

Sitting there, watching the rabbi step away from the microphone, Noah had a revelation: There was no such thing as the covenant between God and Jewish people, a covenant that had been used to explain Jewish triumph. Rather, it was the traditions—the sense of community and self-reliance in the face of opposition—that made them who they were, a brave and intelligent people who valued social progress over wealth and treasured education more than religious indoctrination.

At that epiphany, Noah's eyes produced water that was more living than alive. The release of emotion cleansed him like only a traditional bath can, washing him in spiritual places that, at one time, had been dirtied by orthodoxy.

Before Rabbi Rosen sat down, Noah rubbed the hair on the sides of his face again and beamed. He displayed a similar smile on his way back to the hotel because he saw something that enhanced the still-young day: two eleven-year-old boys were standing by Noah's SUV, using their fingers to write into the fog on the windows of his automobile. Before this day, that vehicle had been his most prized possession.

Noah didn't mind because he loved prepubescent boys, and these two were exactly the type that raised his sex drive. He noticed they were each wearing crucifixes. And he found himself getting an erection at the thought of what he knew was under their clothing. Smooth, hairless bodies that were virgin in every way, waiting to be touched by a grown man like him. As he approached them on his bicycle, they scattered and ran across the street laughing as they passed by the cathedral they attended. Though the boys had showed no deference for the church, Noah hoped and assumed they were Catholic, which, in his reasoning, meant they wouldn't mind being fondled.

Instead of going after them like he wanted to, he did what he always did when confronted with this urge: sketch erotic pictures of prepubescent boys to get the thoughts of pederasty off his mind. Out of respect for the special day it was, he would wait until the following afternoon.

⚬⚬⚬

When he made it back to his apartment in North Carolina, Noah finished sketching a picture of nude Catholic boys to impede his frequent thoughts of their soft, pinkish young lips touching him below the waist. After that, his urges to be with those boys were gone, permanently conquered with graphite and a sheet of paper. Just after he put away his drawing materials, Elijah called.

"Hello," Noah answered.

"Hey, Noah. How are you doing?" Elijah asked.

"All right. How'd your paper go?" Noah replied.

"Good, I guess. It'll be enough for me to graduate."

Noah laughed and said, "Well, that's good enough."

"I called you because I need you to take me somewhere."

"Where?"

"Somewhere down in the country. Like an hour from here."

"For what?" Noah asked.

"I'm going to buy the car I told you about. I looked on the Internet and saw a Mustang for sale, a '65. It's the car I've always wanted, but I already told you that." Elijah paused to catch his breath. "I just hope it's still there."

Noah didn't say anything.

"You there?" Elijah asked.

"I'm here," Noah said.

"So will you take me?"

"Okay," said Noah, who had decided not to fight this battle. "When do you want to go?"

"Whenever you're ready," Elijah said.

"I can come now."

"Okay."

When Noah arrived at the dorm, he trailed someone into the entrance because he didn't have a key and surprised Elijah by entering his room without knocking.

"Hey," said Noah, who was smiling broadly, his chubby cheeks still red from the weather.

"Hey, sugar. Give me some Jewishness."

That was Noah's cue to kiss him.

"Is that all the Jewishness I'm going to get?" Elijah asked.

"You want some more?"

"Yes."

Noah kissed him again.

"Let me finish getting ready." Elijah pulled a shirt over his head. "Didn't expect you to get here so fast," he said, his voice muffled underneath the shirt.

"Take your time. I don't feel like going right now anyway," said Noah.

"You don't?"

"No, Elijah. I want to make love. Right now." Noah grabbed himself and smiled broadly.

"Maybe I'm not in the mood for lovemaking. Maybe I'm in the mood to get fucked."

"Get fucked?" asked Noah, who patted Elijah on the backside.

"Yeah. Hot, sweaty sex," said Elijah, who was putting in an earring, leaning his head to the side and looking in the mirror.

"That sounds like a good idea to me. We can do that. What else do you want to do?" asked Noah, with another pat on Elijah's backside.

"I want you to give me a Jewish martini," Elijah responded.

"What's a Jewish martini?" Noah asked.

"It's when you give a Jew a blowjob, and he cums in your mouth."

"You're silly," said Noah with a laugh. Then he asked, "Where did you get that from?"

"I made it up."

"Why do you call it a Jewish martini?"

"I have this theory that Jewish cum tastes like vermouth."

"You are silly," was the only response Noah could muster as he laughed until his face turned colors. He watched Elijah put an earring in the other ear. Glad to be with him, Noah was overcome with joy. He was as happy as a candy-bearing pedophile on Halloween.

20

While riding in Noah's jeep, they said little to each other, but as always, they didn't really need to speak. Occasionally, Noah would reach over and hold Elijah's soft hand as he guided the steering wheel. These were the times when Elijah's mind would wander to the profound space of his consciousness. He wondered how the land came to be what it was, with cars going down the road and people holding manufactured cups and walking down sidewalks that were poured with manmade concrete. He had never pondered such things when he'd been with Teddy. But now, while holding Noah's hand, Elijah thought of the music coming from the stereo and wondered how an MP3 could make sound emanate from car speakers. And he reflected on the miracle he'd witnessed in his room: the time when he sat in front of his computer and pushed a letter on the keyboard, and that same letter, because of a magical spell called binary code, appeared on the monitor, which itself was enchanting.

Noah's hands did that to him—sent him to the far reaches of the mind, the space where you wonder about synthetic miracles, like being able to eat shrimp and lobster when visiting a place like Kansas, a state that is a long way from the sea.

But Elijah's reflections were interrupted when Noah abruptly slowed the car down to let a woman cross the street. Noah said, "She could've looked both ways before crossing the road. I guess she didn't pay attention in elementary school."

Elijah frowned when looking at the woman and said, "She's definitely a lesbian."

"What makes you say that?"

"Because I see a five o'clock shadow."

Noah laughed.

"Here comes another one," Elijah said.

"You think she's a lesbian too?"

"Yeah. Can't you tell?"

"No, I can't," said Noah.

"If you look closely, you can see the imprint of a strap-on cock."

Noah laughed again as he accelerated before abruptly stopping again. "What the hell is going on? People just walk across the street without looking both ways," he said.

"You're the one who looks both ways because you're bisexual," Elijah said.

"Go to hell," said Noah, with a grin. Then he said, "I should've run him over."

"No, you shouldn't have, because he was hot."

"You're such a snow queen."

"Why? Because I'm only attracted to white guys?" Elijah asked.

"That's what a snow queen is—a black guy who only dates white guys," Noah said.

"I know that already."

"Well, that makes you a snow queen."

"No, I'm not, because I'm dating you now," Elijah replied.

"I'm white."

"Yeah, but you're Jewish, so I'm not a snow queen."

"I don't understand. I'm still white."

"But you're Jewish, so I don't qualify as a snow queen because of the Hebrew loophole."

"The Hebrew loophole?" Noah asked.

"Yeah. If a black guy dates a Jew, he's not a snow queen."

"Okay." Noah shrugged his shoulders and smiled. "Where did you get that from?"

"I made it up."

"You made it up?" Noah asked.

"Yeah."

"First Jewish martini, now Hebrew loophole." Noah accelerated and continued driving to the shop.

∽✺∾

The people at the shop looked on with discerning faces when Elijah and Noah got out of the car, walking shoulder to shoulder. Through the window, they could see Elijah's earrings sparkling in the sunlight, a clue to them that he wasn't the kind of guy they were used to dealing with.

This place was a motorcycle shop that also sold fully restored used cars. It was old on the outside, boasting a sign just above the door reading COME ON IN, in crooked handwriting. To the right of the sign was a sticker of a confederate flag, just above the NO SMOKING sign everyone ignored. No one in the room was under thirty, and they all had facial hair—not Noah's kind of facial hair but a dirty variation, making each of them appear about five years older than they really were.

There were signs in some grocery stores that read SHIRT AND SHOES REQUIRED. Those signs were made specifically for the type of people in this shop.

"Can I help y'all boys?" a man asked.

"I'm looking for the '65 Mustang," Elijah responded, leaning his shoulder into Noah for comfort. It was awfully chilly in the room, due in part to the contrast with the mugginess outside but also owed to the new window unit installed there the previous week.

And in some measure, the chill also came from the cold stares of the six men in the back room who had seen Elijah and Noah get out of the car. And though Elijah couldn't have seen them through what amounted to a tinted window, he still felt the crisp frost on the back of his neck.

"The Stang's out back," the man said, pretending to read a magazine. He never looked at Elijah when speaking, though he had watched him and Noah get out of the jeep and walk much closer than most men he'd known.

"May I take a look at it?" Noah asked, protecting Elijah again.

The man, who seemed annoyed for no valid reason, put the magazine down on the counter, picked his cigarette out of the ashtray, and walked out the backdoor without speaking. Once at the car, the guy lifted the hood to show off the sparkling parts that were put in the engine with the hopes of it one day being entered in a car show.

"Which one of y'all boys is wanting to buy it?"

"Me," Elijah said.

The man snickered, throwing his cigarette to the ground, making sure it landed just in front of Elijah's feet.

Elijah understood.

"It's going to cost you sixteen thousand dollars. Sorry, buddy," the man said, walking back into the smoky room. Elijah and Noah followed.

By then other men were sitting at tables just behind the cash register, which bore credit-card logos on the front, just above a plastic container full of pennies.

"I want it," Elijah said.

"Told you, it'll cost you sixteen thousand dollars. We don't do loans. If you want to buy the car, you pay every dime of it right now. It's the only way I operate." He looked at the men behind him for approval. "Sorry, buddy," the guy said, as the men behind him laughed.

"You said sixteen thousand dollars?" Elijah asked.

"Yep."

The men laughed again.

Elijah pulled out his bank card, placed it on the counter, and said, "I didn't expect it to be so cheap."

Disappointed in Elijah's actions and in himself for not stopping the transaction, Noah shook his head from side to side as the men behind the counter stopped laughing. A red flush of embarrassment stole over their faces as the salesman handed the keys to Elijah.

⚭

Elijah would graduate in a few weeks, and it would be a long time before he ever saw the campus again. Most seniors stayed for the week of graduation to drink and party and spend their last days on campus together with people whom they'd gone into adulthood with. Elijah had no reason to stay for that. He wasn't the drinking type, and even if he were, he had no one to drink with. Teddy had stopped calling long ago, and Elijah had resigned from the *New Age Letter* without notice, though none was needed. Despite opening the mailbox religiously, no letters from Grayson had arrived. His e-mail inbox was the same.

So what reason was there to stay in this hellhole containing thousands and thousands of people who had made him feel lonely?

When he turned in his room key, his hands shook, knowing full well the solitude and the cool air of an empty room wouldn't be available at home in South Carolina, where the air was a little less fresh and the rooms were a little less empty. And where his family, the mass of people who'd caused him the most harm, would be.

When he reached the state line, the urge to turn around put a knot in his stomach. Three hours up the interstate, he thought of the social opportunities he'd squandered by leaving and of all the mistakes he'd made at the place where Teddy was just then knocking on his door, attempting to say one last goodbye before they each put on a cap and gown and marched.

But Elijah didn't look back for long. He drove in the first major purchase he'd made: a 1965 Mustang convertible. Every chance he got, he'd put the top down to let the wind blow in his face. The car was more than a means of transportation for Elijah. It represented freedom of expression, like poetry or short stories on wheels, telling a story with each twist and turn. It was the first time he never cared what people thought. And because he wasn't yet comfortable with solitude, with sitting in an empty room accompanied by his own thoughts, Elijah Redwater needed to cruise down a road. All the while, he left sadness in the trunk of the car to deal with the bumps and rattle of the muffler, while he sat in front, controlling how the car moved and dictating how fast the wind would blow with the gentle press of a pedal.

When opening the door to his mother's home, Elijah didn't leave his bags in the foyer this time, gladly toting his suitcases and laundry baskets upstairs to his room, which took several trips. This time, it was easier to go to that desolate room and look out the window. Though there was no wealth on his part, what he thought was financial security made him feel less dependent on the approval of his family. If they made an offhand comment, he could easily get on the Internet and book a flight to San Francisco or Key West or Chicago, where he could put on a pair of distressed jeans, throw his messenger bag over his shoulder, and walk through Boystown without the judging heat of a South Carolina spring. In short, adulthood had entered the house and helped him lug those bags up to his old room.

Hours later, the sound of keys rattling was followed by his mother saying, "Elijah, come down here and help me bring this shit in the house. Just because you're graduating next Sunday don't mean you too good to get these groceries."

That was the greeting of a mother who hadn't seen her young-est son in almost three months and hadn't talked to him in two. After *Rainbow Dancer*, the conversations had been sparse, sometimes heated, and always filled with references to the most famous book in the world. And after a while, the rainbow spirit took over him, and he put it into his brown leather bag and didn't let her worry him. And that bothered his mother. It angered her to hear the shrug of shoulders in her son's voice when she read verses of the Bible aimed at removing that rainbow spirit from his messenger bag.

"Elijah, come your ass down here and get this shit."

Elijah cried at the past, at the times when he would look out this window, which hadn't been broken since he'd been born. The same glass had been in place since he'd been alive and had given him his only view into the vast world once thought to be the size of South Carolina. Now he'd seen so much more. The windows on campus were smaller than this one, but he could see more out of them because there were no oaks and elms blocking his view and filtering social progressivism out of his consciousness, forcing him to fake an interest in football or to buy hip-hop albums whose lyrics, like the design of a broken puzzle, were not discernible. His mind had been a board of scattered pieces that had been placed in every opening but the socially liberal one where he'd been all along. Elijah was now surer of himself because a handsome Hasidic prince had fucked some self-worth into him.

"Thank you, Grayson…wherever you are," Elijah said to himself, and when the breath from the words hit the windowsill, it rained from his face because he should've been thanking Noah, because Noah, not Grayson, had given him love.

"Okay, Momma. I'm coming."

"It's about time. I been calling you for the past five minutes. You didn't hear me calling you?"

"Yeah, I heard you," Elijah said.

"Were you in the bathroom?"

"No, I was trying to ignore you." Elijah walked out of the house, got into his Mustang, and drove away.

While driving, Elijah thought of the countless times his parents had shown favoritism toward their other sons. He recalled how his parents taunted and disrespected him with their use of the words *faggot* and *punk*. Back when he was nine years old, his father whipped him because the car had run out of gas. His father beat him to release stress and to try to beat the femininity out of Elijah while his mother silently watched. They always blamed Elijah and persecuted him for things he didn't do, so he had always felt like a Jewish child: a child marginalized in a Christian world in which boys played with toy trucks and girls played with dolls, a world in which thin-nosed, masculine gentile men ruled.

But now, as he drove away in his own car with a full tank of gas, Elijah didn't make the connection, failing to realize why he and Noah had understood each other so well. Instead, he looked in the rearview mirror while waiting at the stoplight, thinking about the dolls he used to hide under his bed when he was a girlish boy.

CRUUS

The local library had been a safe haven for him while growing up. After he'd finally gotten his driver's license, that was where Elijah spent most of his time, reading old books, surfing the Internet, and writing. Often he'd go way to the back of the top floor, where the biographies were, since people rarely went there, save for a few college students or librarians who, by the time he was a high school senior, would walk right past him since they were so used to seeing him there. After he'd gone off to college, they wondered why that chair in the back of the library was so empty.

Elijah thought about what it was like back in his dorm room the last time he'd seen Teddy, just before Teddy had left. When Elijah had looked him square in the face, it was as though Teddy's face was paler—uglier. And Teddy's hair looked blonder and stringier and, in turn, devilish and dirty. Those thoughts troubled Elijah as he sat in the parking lot of the local library, so he got out of his car and threw his messenger bag across his right shoulder.

It smelled like a hint of smoke had layered the air in the building, though smoking had never been allowed. Perhaps it was a mere hallucination, or maybe it was the stuffiness of entering a place that was so much smaller than the library at college. Whatever the case, guided by his tunnel vision, Elijah traipsed up the staircase and met the revolting smell of cleaning solution emanating from a yellow bucket just in front of the men's restroom. Odors like that frightened him for reasons he'd never articulate to others. He thought the smell of cleaning solution would enter his nose and make him high, killing off the brain cells that were responsible for his creativity. He thought inhaling fumes of any kind would magically murder his creative license. That was why the temptation of marijuana had never really been a temptation at all.

Now, the smoky odor in the library didn't seem so bad as he walked and walked until the smell of cleaning solution became fainter and fainter, or until he'd gotten used to it. It was the former, but he didn't know it. When sitting down, he looked above his head at the sign that read BIOGRAPHY in a jerry-rigging of laminated construction paper. Unlike the signs in the college libraries, this one hung crooked, suspended by pieces of yarn. He moved to a table where it wasn't so visible, where the contrast between home and college life wasn't so striking.

Elijah turned on his laptop to review his old files: essays, short stories, notes. Looking at a laptop wasn't nearly as poetic as going through old papers stashed in the corners of a closet he hadn't been in for years. Nor was going over computer files as sad as staring at old pictures of his inauthentic self during his days in junior high.

"Hey, Elijah." The woman who said this was heavyset. Her blond hair should have been gray by now, but thanks to relentless applications of dye, no one noticed anything, not even the gray at the temples that, if it were on a man, she herself would consider distinguished. Her face, soft and flushed, filled out in a way that made her look younger.

"Hey, Missus P."

"Haven't seen you in here in a long while." Missus P. looked upward as if to search her brain for what to say next. "I knew you'd gone off to school. How's it going up there?"

There was a smile forming at the corners of Elijah's mouth, but a hand quickly covered it since, in his mind, a college degree was no big deal for someone like him. Then he said, "Graduation is this weekend."

"Well, my goodness. Time sure does fly. Well, congratulations," said Missus P., as an extra shade of flush entered her cheeks.

"Thank you," he said.

"Well, I have to get back to work. Seems like I got a million books to reshelf."

"All right."

"You take care, young man," she said, walking away holding a biography in her hand.

"You too, Missus P."

She remembered him. *They probably won't remember me back at the college library,* Elijah thought. He again looked up at the sign that read BIOGRAPHY, and it began to look much more adult, as if it had come of age right in front of him, going from a wide-eyed pack of construction paper to a prepubescent poster to a jaded old sign directing people to a section of the library where they could read about the lives of hundreds of people who made the world spin a little differently on its axis.

Looking at his computer as if it were brand new, Elijah saw a file named *Muriel*. He opened it to find a short story he'd written to keep himself company the day he found out Grayson wouldn't be around to hold him like a little doll and cuddle him into a dream world. His original plan was to turn it into a novel, but he had abandoned it for *Rainbow Dancer*. Double-clicking on the icon, he smiled at the thought of reading his old words:

Muriel
A Short Story by
Elijah Redwater

In a lighthouse just off the coast of South Carolina, a little ghost girl stands in the window, looking over the island...waiting for someone to rescue her. She's been there for decades now, watching the waters of the Atlantic become cooler with the coming of new seasons. Once, she was more than a white light in a little gown with a bow. She lived and breathed and herself was able to sway back and forth like the currents of the water before her, sometimes placing her little feet in the saltwater and laughing as the fish tickled her ankles. It's been a while since laughter came from her mouth, because on the occasions when her lips puckered to form a word, the only thing that came out was "Help." But separated by the currents and the loud wish-washing of waves, no one could hear her, and the few who thought they'd seen her turned around in their boats and sped off toward the sand, too afraid to speak a word of it to anyone, thinking it would free the poor little girl without a friend in the world; and by freeing her, they assumed, she would follow them everywhere. That was something no one wanted—a little girl made of white light following them. Why would someone want that? She understood, though understanding did nothing to soften the hurt of being the keeper of a lighthouse visited by no one. If there were no people there, at least she could find a toy, something to keep her company until someone dared to come to the island and open the door and walk the dizzying walk up the spiral staircase leading to a ghost trapped by the inability to grow up. Trapped by her need to break the planks of the floor and make a dollhouse only to stash it away and make another one with planks from the other side of the floor. By now the floor underneath her was gone, so a toy she could no longer make. A toy she could no longer play with and call a companion in the absence of a real one who lived and breathed and sometimes placed her little feet in the saltwater, laughing as the fish tickled her ankles.

One day in autumn, so the story goes, a stranger entered her room and entered her, taking innocence and leaving without a trace. The man, tall and bold, would move away, running from what no one could possibly run from, never to be heard from again. His absence didn't stop the nightmares, nor did they stop the chill that would overcome her body when the floor made footstep noises and the door squeaked on its rusty hinges. At night she would hide to stop the monster from coming into the room and retaking her innocence, but it was always the voice of her mother or father, friendly, familiar, kind and, above all, comforting. Only then would she sleep until the stars fell away into the sunlight. Only then would the monster seem make-believe, like the families she now talks to in those dollhouses, lining the top floor of the lighthouse to resemble a neighborhood of townhouses with one wall torn out so the furniture could be seen from the outside.

One night, the night before becoming the youngest light-keeper on the coast, the footstep noises and the squeaking door were too much to bear, loud and frightening with a voice telling her, "Your parents can't protect you this time either." So before the door could open to reveal what it would reveal, the little girl ran toward the open window and tried to fly away...and that's what happened...she flew away.

With blood stains on her gown, the last thing she saw was her mother, three stories up, standing in the window weeping while trying to scream. At that moment, the child left her real body on the ground, floated above the water to the island, opened the door, and made that hover to the top of the lighthouse where—after years and years—she would learn to occupy her time breaking up the floor, using the wooden planks to craft dollhouses, and having make-believe friends like only a little girl can. Never, never, did she open the door. And after all these years, after the innocence was returned and she became a child of folklore, the hinges of her door would remain silent. Silent, silent, would remain the hinges of the door on the top floor of the lighthouse, for no one would visit.

21

Elijah left the library. Using his computer to retrace his footsteps had forced him to face good things about his life; it made him look at Noah differently. All of the love poems he'd written reminded him of Noah. And every time his little index finger had double-clicked the mouse to open a file, Noah Cohen entered his thoughts before the words of the file became clear—and that was all Elijah needed to know. Finally understanding his love for his Jewish prince, he decided he would run to Noah the way a Christian child runs down the staircase on Christmas morning.

When Elijah arrived back at home, he checked the mailbox and found a letter from Grayson. Upon seeing Grayson's handwriting, he smiled and went back to his car to open it, hoping his soldier could somehow hug him from Iraq.

Dear Elijah,

If you receive this letter, it means I'm dead. I told one of my buddies to keep it and mail it to you in case I don't make it. Hopefully, this letter will free you emotionally, because you can stop waiting for me and find someone to love you. Just don't forget about me. Enlisting was one of the biggest mistakes of my life. As liberal as I am about religion, I still bought into American propaganda. We're killing people over here, innocent people. We've invaded their land for what? To take their oil and install a US-friendly government that's not even functioning. Whatever patriotism I had is gone, because I know that all of the army commercials and the movies that portray heroic soldiers have fooled us into believing that there's something noble about picking up a gun. It's wrong to kill innocent people, but when you put on a military uniform and murder someone, it's suddenly okay.

Nothing could be more immoral than this invasion. Our planes have dropped bombs on babies who had nothing to do with the terrorist attacks on the United States. In fact, no one in this country had anything to do with it. We have this false notion that people who look Arab and practice Islam are evil. And now I have taken part in this racist propaganda, and if there's a hell, I should go—along with the soldiers I've witnessed who have gang-raped and killed people for sport. But the government covers that up.

I'm ashamed to say I died in vain, and many of my comrades—thousands of them—have died in vain as well. I wish I had known beforehand that having the most powerful military doesn't mean having an all-powerful military. I listened to the President tell the world about weapons of mass destruction in Iraq, knowing full well that he was pushing an agenda that had more to do with oil and showing the world how big his dick was. There were no WMD and he knew that, but the country was too afraid to question him. He took advantage of the emotions that were still lingering from September 11th and knew that overly emotional Americans couldn't question him because we were all scared. And scared people are not smart people.

I'm sorry to go on this rant against my own country, but I know I can tell you this because you'll understand. Please

enjoy life, and don't waste it. And don't waste your life crying about me. I love you enough to tell you to find someone
to love you and do something I never got the chance to:
make love to you.

I love you, Little Guy,
Grayson

P.S. Wear the dog tags I gave you. Wherever I am, I'll know
you're wearing them.

Elijah dropped the letter and cried longer than he ever had. After
collecting himself, he picked up the correspondence and read it two
more times, hoping to find answers that would relieve the pain. He
found nothing but confirmation that Grayson had expired.

⌀⍣⍣⍣⍜

Later that day, while lying on his bed, Elijah wondered what dog
tags Grayson was referring to. He began to cry again, and his head
started to ache as much as his heart. He got up, went to the bathroom, and washed his face in warm water in an attempt to conceal
the anguish. But this wasn't living water, because this situation was
far from spiritually cleansing. It was dying water that washed him
on the outside but did nothing to purify his weakened soul. Elijah
stared at the reflection of his clean face and realized his efforts had
not been in vain. He had composed himself enough—at least ex-
ternally—to face his mother. No longer thinking of Grayson, but
recalling the lack of love in his childhood, he looked in the mirror
again before going downstairs to the kitchen.

"I'll help you cook, Momma," he said.

"Okay."

Elijah had a blank stare.

"What's wrong, boy?" his mother asked.

"You always loved them more than me."

"Boy, what are you talking about? I love all of my kids the same."

"No, you don't," Elijah said.

"You're talking crazy. You told me you wanted to come in here and help me cook."

"I am helping you."

"Well, snap those string beans right. You're snapping them lopsided," she said.

"Yes, ma'am."

"Here, let me do it. You need to start mashing this dough. And don't mess up."

"I'm twenty-two years old, Momma. I think I can handle kneading dough."

"Kneading? I didn't say nothing about kneading. I said 'mash.' Stop using those white-folks words. You went up there to that fancy North Carolina school and forgot you were black. No matter where you go, you'll always be a country-ass nigga from Rock Hill, South Carolina."

"Whatever, Momma."

"Speak up, so I can hear you. Your voice is so soft. You'll never get a girlfriend talking like that."

"Enough, Momma."

"Enough of what? I'm telling the truth. A respectable girl don't want a man with a sissy voice. You need to change it, so you can get a wife. Then I'll finally have some grandkids."

"I won't have any kids, Momma. That's not the kind of life I want."

"That better be the kind of life you want. You're supposed to procreate. That's in the Bible."

"Jesus never procreated, and you don't have a problem with him," Elijah said.

"Boy, don't you badmouth the Savior in my house. I raised you better than that."

"I'm not trying to be disrespectful. I'm simply saying I don't believe in that stuff."

"It's called Christianity," she said.

"I know what it's called. I just think it's…"

"Boy, shut up and start splitting up them biscuits. Here, get a cup and turn it upside down and mash it into the dough."

"Okay," Elijah said.

"See there? You made a perfect circle. You don't need all those fancy gadgets to make a circle in dough."

"I understand."

"You need to eat plenty of them biscuits to put some meat on your bones. You're too skinny," she said.

"This is my natural frame, Momma. I've always been small."

"Well, small looks too weak. You're made up like a white woman."

"I'm not built like a white woman," Elijah said.

"You sure didn't get my hips. I got collard green and fatback hips. I used to be small too, you know?"

"I know. Do you mind talking about something else?"

"Like what?" she asked.

"Like my summer plans."

"What plans you got?"

"I'm moving to Boston with a friend," Elijah said.

"A friend from that North Carolina school? Who is she?"

"He."

"You're going to Boston with a man? Oh, Lord. I don't like the way that look. What are the people at church going to think?" she asked.

"The people at church probably don't even know what Boston is, because it's not mentioned in Exodus."

"Stop sassing."

"Yes, ma'am."

"You can tell the people at church you going to Boston, but you better not tell them you going with a boy," she said.

"Why?"

"Because black folks talk."

"Whatever you say, Momma."

"I want you to meet Mrs. Pickett's daughter. She's pretty and light-skinned with good hair."

"Light skin doesn't equal beauty," Elijah said.

"That's not what I meant."

"And there's no such thing as good hair," Elijah added.

"Let me finish telling you what she look like."

"Not that I care, but okay, go ahead."

"She got that straight hair, the kind without the naps you can't comb out. And she don't have that ugly kind of nose that spreads across her face."

"Momma, you're confused."

"I'm not confused. "

"Yes, you…"

"Do you want to meet her or not?" she interrupted.

"No."

"Why not?" she asked.

"Because…"

"Make another circle in that dough."

"I was saying…"

"Just pull that piece from the rest of the dough and put it in this skillet," she interrupted.

"You need to get a baking sheet, Momma."

"I don't need a baking sheet."

"You're right, Momma. The Bible says you don't need to cook the right way."

"Boy, you better stop playing with the Lord. And you better stop getting smart with me," she said.

"What do I turn the oven on?"

"Stove."

"Okay, stove," Elijah said.

"I already turned it on. Just put the skillet in there."

"Yes, ma'am."

"I don't know what you're doing in here anyway. A man isn't supposed to enjoy cooking. That's women stuff. You been that way since you were little. All the boys were outside playing while you were in the kitchen with the women. Embarrassed me and your daddy. We couldn't figure out what was wrong with you."

"You know what it is, Momma. It's…"

"Here, take the rest of these beans and snap them."

"I was about to say…"

"Snap them beans, you hear?" she interrupted.

"I was never what you wanted me to be."

"You were always reading and studying, trying your best to be white."

"Studying has nothing to do with race, Momma."

"You should've been studying the Bible. Teaches you about life and relationships."

"Dad read the Bible, and he still cheated. So it didn't give him good relationship advice."

"That was the devil. It wasn't your daddy," she said.

"So it's the devil's fault? Dad's not to blame for his own actions?"

"Boy, finish snapping them string beans while the biscuits cook."

"Okay," Elijah said.

"You're snapping the string beans wrong."

"This isn't the right way?"

"No. Give them back to me. You can make the tea. You can't mess up tea. Lord, I should've called my oldest son to help me."

"The one who can give you grandkids?"

"Don't get smart. You can give me grandkids too. Keep talking back. I'll knock you into the middle of next week."

"Good. At least I'll miss church this Sunday," Elijah said.

"You're getting too grown."

"I am grown."

"Not in my house."

"Momma, you got a lot to learn. There are more places to go than church. You should get out more."

"Get out and do what?" she asked.

"Start living."

"I am living."

"I mean, experience new things and stop living in a bubble. There's a lot out there. And if you got out more, your views would change," Elijah said.

"You're talking nonsense. You been influenced by too much of that sinful TV."

"Sinful TV?" Elijah asked.

"Yes, sinful TV. All these people getting kilt."

"People get killed because they believe what you believe. That's why there are so many wars in the world. The Middle East wouldn't be such a horrible place if people gave up religion," Elijah said.

"Don't blame this on God. I wasn't even talking about the Middle East. You're going off on a tangerine."

"A tangent, Momma."

"Boy, don't correct me."

"Sorry," Elijah said.

"Anyway, I was talking about rap videos with songs about killing and selling drugs. And girls walking around with they thighs out, showing men they goods. It's a shame is what it is. It's the devil."

"The devil?" Elijah asked.

"That's right. He's the one making these girls show themselves to every man they meet."

"It has much more to do with self-esteem, Momma."

"For once, you're right. They parents didn't give them enough love, so they grow up and start looking for it. And they look with they thighs and not with they hearts."

"I didn't have enough love in my home," Elijah said.

"Yes, you did. I did the best I could."

"You did for your other sons, not me."

"Check on those biscuits. They should be browning by now."

"What is it, Momma?"

"What is what?"

"What is it about me you hate so much?" Elijah asked.

"Turn the stove down a little bit. You don't want the biscuits to draw up and get tight."

"Are you listening?" Elijah asked.

"You know, my momma used to make some good biscuits. She would slap a little molasses on them. She was the best cook in the family."

"What about Grandpa? Did he cook?" Elijah asked.

"No. Too busy chasing women. Messed up a good house. My momma turned on us when she found out about his ways. Started yelling and screaming at us for no reason. It's a shame for a woman to turn on her kids because of things they can't help."

"It must be a cycle."

"What's a cycle?" she asked.

"The way you make biscuits. You probably cook the way Grandma did."

"I sure do. I can mash up some dough just the way she did."

"And ignore all your problems," Elijah said.

"That's right. Nothing better than a good time in the kitchen to get your mind off troubles."

"I understand, Momma."

"You ain't talking about biscuits, are you? I know you, boy. You speak in riddles. Don't compare me to my momma. I raised y'all with love and never hurt none of you. Ain't that right? Wasn't I a good mother?"

"Momma, you should turn the stove down a little, so the biscuits won't burn."

Someone knocked on the front door of the house.

"I'll get it," Elijah said.

When he opened the door, there was a soldier standing there— handsome, dressed in army fatigues, with a padded helmet pulled down over his eyes.

"Hey, Elijah," the soldier said.

"Hi," Elijah responded, thinking he must be an army recruiter trying to increase his numbers. He thought the man would take one look at Elijah's small body, jump back in his jeep, and look for a more manly man.

"Do you want to talk for a while? I'm not a recruiter."

"Okay." Elijah smiled.

The first bit of emotion the soldier displayed came from seeing Elijah's smile.

"Come with me." The soldier made a quick motion for him to follow.

Elijah had never been in an army jeep before and sat quietly as the man turned down the street and drove, going nowhere in particular.

"What do you think about the military?" the soldier asked.

"Never really gave it much thought." Elijah felt the man was lying about not being a recruiter, so he formed a bunch of liberal, antiwar rhetoric in his head, just in case.

"Well, I guess what I was trying to ask is, what do you think about people who go to the military?"

"I used to think the military was for stupid people who weren't smart enough to go to college, but that changed a few years ago." Elijah's candor surprised even himself.

"Really? What changed your opinion?" the soldier asked.

"My roommate, Grayson. He was one of the smartest people I've ever known, and he decided to enlist."

The soldier smiled, showing teeth for the first time.

Elijah's voice was cloaked in sadness. "I figured if the military was good enough for him, it must be worth something. Grayson was probably the best thing that ever happened to the military."

The smile on the soldier's face suddenly faded, and he made an abrupt U-turn, making it apparent they were going back to Elijah's house.

"It's really dangerous out there, you know. In Iraq and all," the soldier said.

"I know. That's why Grayson is dead." Tears fell from Elijah's eyes.

"Well, what I mean to say is, you don't have to wait for him. Don't spend the rest of your life waiting for him to come back. You'll end up all by yourself. You don't deserve to be lonely for the rest of your life. So when love comes along, don't push it away. Go for it, and go all out. Don't wait around for Grayson. You'll see him one day, sooner than you think."

Crying and leaning over to touch the soldier's hand, Elijah understood, knowing the hand would feel familiar.

The soldier pulled the jeep into the driveway, and Elijah got out without speaking.

"Well, you take care of yourself, Little Guy."

"All right. You do the same." Elijah's voice cracked.

The soldier removed a chain that was around his neck and put it around Elijah's, the clanging of the metal resonating like symbols from a marching band. Elijah clutched the dog tags that were attached to the chain as if the wind could blow them away. The two men looked at one another, wanting to kiss.

"Bye," was the only word Elijah could muster.

Then the soldier just nodded his head and drove away, away, away as Elijah sat down on the ground and buried his face in his hands. Meanwhile, his mother was looking out the window, trying to figure out how a jeep could drive itself away. But she figured her eyes were tired and went back to cooking, seasoning away the taste of truth. For a moment there was sympathy for who her child really was, a boy lonely and determined to be understood. But before the wind could make the leaves rustle louder, the compassion was gone, bent on an opinion formed before Elijah was even born. Besides, preparing the meal was more important.

Miles and miles away, just in the front yard, her child was there, despondent and alone, being ignored like the TV dinners in the freezer.

Could it be that I'm meant to move on from this place? Elijah thought, and then he answered his own question when Noah's image formed in his mind. But he decided he'd call Noah later—in the morning, after mourning. All Elijah could do then was clutch the dog tags around his neck and look for the tire tracks of a jeep that, unlike his mother had thought, didn't drive itself away.

That's when he pulled the container of pixie dust out of his pocket.

"Phillip the Fairy, I'm counting on you," Elijah said. Then he poured the dust onto the ground, and it flew into the air, floating around like glitter. It formed the outline of two pink triangles, and Elijah saw his own countenance in one but couldn't make out the face in the other. The two triangles slowly came together and formed a Star of David that sparkled like the reflection of moonlight in a brook.

"Jesus," he said.

But like the other times in his life, Jesus didn't answer. Elijah didn't need a response from a man whose centuries-old body had long turned to dust—just like the grains of pixie that floated in the air. Besides, the blood of another Jewish man would heal him, blood that wasn't just any color. It was vermillion red, and there was nothing holy about it.

PART VII

Beautifully Jewish

22

It had been two weeks since the funeral—two weeks since Abby had seen the little ghost who wore the little gown with a bow—and she had feelings of disgust when standing in front of the mirror, because a murderer now stared back at her. A lonely woman stared back at her. An insecure woman stared back at her.

A wealthy woman stared back at her.

Today, Abby was in the attic, going through old boxes that contained her wedding dress, photos, and her early writings. She'd spent the entire day up there in the warmest room in the house. Abby pulled a piece of paper from a box and unfolded it to reveal a poem she had written in college. She looked at the first lines and smiled.

"I'll read this later," she whispered.

She rummaged through the box some more and found a broken picture frame and looked through its cracked glass to see a photograph of herself as a child, standing between her mother and father, holding their hands. Abby was at the age at which she didn't understand the importance of smiling for a camera. So her face was that of an unhappy youth standing between two relatives who themselves bore stone faces.

Abby cried when seeing what she was wearing in the photograph: a pink dress trimmed in white lace, white gloves to match, and a red bow whose ribbons fell all the way to the hem of the dress. She was so focused on the clothing, it took her ten minutes to notice what was in the background: a dollhouse that stood nearly as tall as she, with wooden planks that were falling from the structure. The paint on the dollhouse had seen better days, as had the roof, which itself was losing its color, going from shiny black to charcoal gray.

Before taking the time to look at the photograph of the lighthouse on the wall above the dollhouse, she screamed, threw the picture on the floor, and ran downstairs. She couldn't tell the ghost to get away this time. It was the first instance in all these years that Abby wanted the ghost to return to convince her that she herself wasn't the problem, to make her curl up in the bed and cover herself with the sheets, and to erase herself from the photograph and rid her mind of that ghastly apparel, red bow and all.

When Abby made it to the kitchen, she sat in a wooden chair, panting and crying until realizing the slip of paper was still in her hand. She sighed at the sight of it, hoping it would take her mind off the photograph, but just the opposite happened as she read the poem aloud:

> It rains on the Atlantic, though full is the sea.
> The leaves fall in autumn, though strong is the tree.
> The skies become our dreams; childish it seems.
> Feeling the blue splendor will never be.
> When the oceans are dry and the clouds hesitate,
> The sun will rise with a constant fate.
> Yesterday sings what tomorrow brings…
> A moonlit world brightened far too late.
> Fierce are the cold currents of a northern sea.
> The silence of a glance could set them free.
> Tempting is this place that has no face…
> A warm flow of the waters may never be.

That was when Abby fell to the floor—toppling the chair—and cried with a sense of loneliness, as though she were a wounded child in an empty field. Someone entering the house and seeing her would have grasped the palpable sense of parental desertion, and the sight would hit them like only the strangest image can, as if they had seen an abandoned tricycle covered in snow. An image like that would baffle anyone, raising countless questions.

Just then, she heard loud knocks on her door and a constant ringing of the doorbell.

"I knew Spencer would come back," Abby said to herself, as she rubbed her hands through her hair in preparation.

"Open up! It's the police!"

Abby smiled and walked upstairs.

"Open up! We have a warrant!"

A policeman looked at the locksmith and said, "Do your thing, kid."

"What if she has a gun?"

"Just crack the lock, son. I've been an officer long enough to know she's not the type to go down in a shoot-out. But just in case, keep your guns drawn, boys."

The locksmith said, "I understand, sir. It'll take at least twenty minutes for this one."

"Well, you better get started," the police officer replied.

Upstairs, Abby was changing into her most expensive evening gown. It was a long and shiny silver number with silk fabric that gathered at her feet like a puddle. She put on a pair of black stockings and sat at her vanity. She reached for her makeup, slowly adding foundation and a touch of rouge to her face. She then put on sparkly red lipstick and softened it by pressing her lips into a piece of tissue. Abby put on mascara—her right eyelashes first, then her left. She then searched a drawer and produced a comb and pulled it slowly though her hair.

"Perfection," she whispered, as she rose from the chair.

She heard loud thumps, and as the front door flew open, Abby went to her jewelry box and put on a platinum necklace with a yellow diamond hanging from it, and then put on yellow teardrop diamond earrings. She walked to her closet, found a large black hat, and placed it on her head, so that it tilted to her right.

"Check the kitchen," a man said.

Abby put on a watch, some heels, and a black mink coat. After picking up a silver patent-leather handbag, she finished her ensemble with a pair of oversized sunglasses. As the police officers gathered at the bottom of the stairs, she slowly walked out of the bedroom and stood at the top of the spiral staircase.

"May I interest you boys in a glass of champagne?"

The policemen, guns in hand, looked at each other and waited in silence as Abby slowly walked down the stairs.

"Guns? Really?" she said, with a quick laugh. "Blue-collar people are so cute."

"Put your hands behind your head!"

Abby continued walking slowly down the stairs. When she reached the bottom, the police officers surrounded her.

"Ms. Worthington, you are under arrest for arson and for the murder of Theodore Worthington and Rebecca Smith."

Another officer said, "You have the right to remain silent…"

"The right?" Abby interrupted. "Wealthy people don't have rights. We have privilege."

The officer continued reading the Miranda warning while another policeman handcuffed her.

Abby offered a tight-lipped laugh. "This is ridiculous," she said, as they escorted her outside. She looked at the police cars in her driveway and said, "Thanks for bringing my caravan, gentlemen. Nice touch."

As one of the officers began to push her into the back of the police car, Abby said, "Be careful how you handle this mink coat. I guess they didn't teach you high fashion at the police academy."

That was when Muriel, even at such a tender, young age, knew there was no hope, and she screamed in her lighthouse. But Abby would never acknowledge the crying child within her, the almost infant who had been trying to heal since her days living in Memphis. Raised by a father who didn't care and a mother who didn't love, the little ghost girl had plenty of fuel to burn Abby's soul. Even still, Abby didn't learn. Taking heed meant holding a mirror to herself and standing there—completely natural—without the disguise of makeup or the cloak of expensive clothes. Abby Brooks—just Abby Brooks—was a person she had not been raised to love, which was why the little ghost girl would be stranded forever, playing with toys she made herself, carefully crafted to deal with self-loathing, desperation, and the imprisoning fear of judgment.

"I tried to tell you to go back," said Muriel.

"What are you talking about? Go back where?" asked Abby.

"I tried to tell you to go back and get the silver brooch. It fell from the top of your dress when you burned the beach house. But you kept yelling at me. I was just trying to help."

"My name is engraved on it," Abby said, with a sense of resignation.

Poor Muriel would have to haunt for a lifetime, crying herself to life—while Abby cried herself to death—in a lonely lighthouse off the coast of South Carolina.

And it was all Abby's fault.

The police officers had been listening but could only hear Abby, not the little ghost girl. As the police car slowly pulled out of the driveway, Abby whispered, "Shame on me for forgetting my cashmere gloves."

23

"Why won't you let me buy those cashmere gloves I saw at the mall?" Elijah asked.

"Stop being a bitch," Noah said, as he smiled and kissed Elijah on the cheek.

"I'm not being a bitch."

"Yes, you are."

"I just need to do a little shopping."

"We're on a budget, remember?"

"I know. You remind me every day," Elijah said, as he leaned into Noah's chest and thought about the trust he had put in him, the man who now had so much control over his life. But he was comfortable in Noah's care.

It had been two and a half years since they graduated, Noah earning a PhD and Elijah bachelor's degrees in French and creative writing. Graduation had been the first time Elijah got the chance to meet Noah's family, and he left with a good impression. Noah didn't get the same feeling when meeting Elijah's family, but that had been expected, given the horror stories Elijah had told him. But college life seemed far away despite what the calendar told them.

Life was different now. Noah was content. And Elijah was too, despite his complete dependence on Noah. There was a point when Elijah used to mock people whose lives depended on someone else for emotional and financial support, but he had become one of those people. There was something freeing about staying home and having a man earn the bulk of the household income; it made him feel like the woman he had always wanted to be. Noah understood that and let Elijah be Elijah; in fact, it made Noah feel more like a man, not that he had been an insecure person in the first place. So he also depended on Elijah, his spouse. They were married now; Elijah Redwater had become Elijah Redwater Cohen. Noah knew he would be in charge of both of their lives when Elijah agreed to take his last name.

Now, in the kitchen of their condo in Boston, Elijah, having honed his culinary skills in the two years they had been living together, was preparing dinner for Noah, who had secured an associate professorship in the Department of Political Science at Brandeis University. Elijah assumed he had gotten the job through his father's connections, but chose to keep that conjecture to himself.

They always ate dinner together, though not always at the table. Tonight they were sitting on bar stools around the island in the kitchen. Their arms touched as they ate.

"How's the food?" Elijah asked.

"It's good. Your food is always good."

"It's a new recipe I got from television."

"You are so gay," Noah said.

"And that's why you love me."

Noah kissed him on the cheek.

"We've been married now for over a month," Elijah said.

"Time is just flying by," Noah replied.

"It is. I think about our wedding every day."

"Me too, but it'll probably wear off after a while."

"You're probably right." Elijah cut a piece of the filet and put it in his mouth. "Our wedding was beautiful, though—the flowers, the lavender vests, the music. Too bad we had to rent out a bed and breakfast since no one would let us use a church. But it was good, all the same."

"Yeah," Noah said, poking the salad with his fork. "I'm still surprised your mother came up."

"Me too. I guess not talking to her for over a year helped things along."

"I told you she would come around."

"She did, a little bit. I still don't think she's fully okay with everything. I can tell," Elijah said.

"It'll get better."

"I hope so." Elijah knew exactly what he was hoping for but didn't really mind if it never came to fruition.

"Elijah, you always talk about your mom and your brothers, but I never hear you talk about your dad. What was he like?"

"I've known you all this time, we're married, and you're finally asking about my father?"

Noah laughed and said, "Well, yeah. I know he died of a heart attack when you were in the eighth grade. Was he a good dad?"

"No. He was never home. The few times he was at home, all he did was drink and smoke marijuana with his friends. He was a grown man who refused to grow up. He thought partying was more important than spending time with his family. The times I remember most are when he would cuss me out and whip me for no apparent reason. He could never keep a job for more than a few years, and when he got a decent paycheck, he would blow it on foolish things just to have a good time."

"I didn't know he was that bad," Noah said.

"Yeah, he was bad up until the day he died. I know it's not my place to say this, but I know he's burning in hell."

"The good thing is he's not around to hurt you anymore."

"You're right. It all ended the day I walked in the house and saw him lying on the floor suffering from a heart attack. I was almost fifteen when it happened," Elijah said. He left out the part where his father was still alive and asking Elijah to call an ambulance. He also failed to mention the part where he left his father for dead and walked out of the house, smiling as he shut the front door. Then he said, "I don't really care about him or anyone else in my family. It may sound odd to you, but it's true."

As if he thought Noah somehow knew about how he had ignored his dying father, Elijah asked, "Do you think I'm a bad person?"

Noah didn't respond, nor did Elijah press him for an answer. They just sat there in silence until they finished their meal.

Elijah sneezed.

"Are you okay?" Noah asked.

"I'm okay. Hope I'm not coming down with a cold. I think it's just my allergies."

"I got some cold medicine in my briefcase. They're orange-flavored pills, so they don't taste that bad," Noah said.

"I hope you don't have cock-flavored pills. I don't want to OD."

Noah laughed. "Seriously, do you need them?"

"No, I'm not sick. It's just allergies."

"Okay. So that means I can make out with you and not catch anything?" Noah leaned in to kiss him before he could respond. "You want to do that kinky thing we did the other night?"

"What kinky thing?" Elijah asked.

"The thing I did to you with the vacuum cleaner attachment."

"That was painful."

"But you liked it, didn't you?"

"Yeah," Elijah said.

"You were screaming like hell," Noah said. "So can I try it on you again?"

"Yeah, but don't turn the vacuum cleaner on until I get comfortable."

"Okay," said Noah, whose penis was rock hard.

Elijah then gathered the dishes and washed them as Noah, sitting at the counter, watched Elijah's right elbow move back and forth with the scrubbing of the plates. Seeing Elijah in the kitchen, with yellow gloves on his little hands, turned Noah on, but he would wait to fulfill any of the carnal desires he had at that moment.

They had a dishwasher, but Elijah refused to use it when his husband was home.

"Why are you walking like that?" Noah asked.

"My cat is still sore."

"From what?" Noah asked.

"Last night."

"Right," Noah said, with a smile.

"Last night you fucked me so hard I was screaming dirty words in Hebrew," Elijah said.

Noah laughed, paused for a few seconds, and asked, "How long do you think we're going to stay here?"

"I don't know. I like this place." Elijah put a dish in the drying rack.

"I don't know either," Noah said. "Took us long enough to renovate the place. I feel like we have to stay here for at least a couple of years because of all the work we did fixing it up. This place was a dump."

"But I told you we could fix it."

"Yeah, you did. Thank God for Dad's money."

"I was scared he would think I was spending too much," Elijah said.

"He didn't mind at all."

"You're lying."

"No, I'm not," Noah said.

"Yes, you are."

"Okay, maybe a little."

Elijah looked over his shoulder and saw Noah's huge grin, set between two chubby cheeks.

"I knew it. I knew I was a hassle," Elijah said.

"You're not a hassle. You're just high maintenance," Noah replied.

Elijah laughed. "I guess that's better than being a hassle."

"You're a hassle sometimes."

"Whatever. Give me an example."

"Well, when we moved into this place, you complained the entire time. I'm the one who moved all of the boxes into the house."

"You're the man in this relationship. That's what you're supposed to do. Besides I had just had a manicure, and I wasn't about to schlep all our stuff in here," said Elijah.

"You weren't about to what?" Noah asked.

"Schlep all our stuff in here."

"As each day goes by, you're becoming more and more of a Jew," Noah said, with a chuckle.

"What are you talking about?"

"Never mind." Noah smiled before calling Elijah's name.

"What?"

"Let's go fuck on the couch," Noah said.

"Okay," said Elijah, who began walking to the living room.

"Wait right there. I have to get something. I'll be right back." Noah's face boasted a playful grin.

What Elijah thought he knew about the descendants of Israel had gone away little by little every time Noah had sex with him. With the power of his penis, Noah fucked Elijah so hard it changed Elijah's mind about who murdered Jesus.

Minutes later, just outside their front door, the old man across the hall was leaving his condo and could hear a mechanical humming sound coming from Noah and Elijah's place.

The old man said, "Those young men are always vacuuming."

Later that evening, without sex on their minds and with the vacuum cleaner cooling off in the corner, they found themselves cuddling on the couch, watching the local news, Elijah's back to Noah's chest, Noah's arms around Elijah.

"Why are you so quiet?" Noah asked.

"I was just thinking."

"About what?"

"Us," Elijah said.

"What about us?" Noah couldn't help but chuckle.

"Do you think this will last?"

"What? Our relationship?" asked Noah.

"Yeah."

"Of course I do. Why do you ask? Are you having second thoughts?"

"A little."

Noah sighed. "What is it?"

"I just think everything is a little too good, you know. And life's not supposed to be like this."

"Says who?" Noah asked.

"Me."

"And why do you think that way?"

"I don't know. I just do. I've never seen a good relationship last. And the ones that do are a façade," Elijah said.

"Was it a façade when we laughed until we fell asleep last night?"

"No."

"How about when I held you the other night, and we fell asleep on the floor. Was that a façade?"

"No," Elijah answered.

"The lovemaking?"

"No."

"Well, it looks like we're okay. Right?"

Elijah didn't respond.

"Right?" Noah repeated.

"Right," said Elijah. "At least I hope you're right."

"You hope?"

"Yeah." Elijah sighed. "It's just that I'm afraid of you cheating on me. That's one of my fears."

"I'll never cheat on you."

"You better not. I wouldn't have anything to do with you if you did," Elijah said.

"What, you'll cut me off completely?"

"Yep. And I'll kick you out," Elijah said.

"Kick me out of my own house?"

"Yep," Elijah said.

"So we wouldn't talk about what happened?"

"The only thing we would talk about is how you can get your shit."

Noah laughed. "So you would really throw me out if I cheated on you?"

"Either that, or I'd cut your dick off."

"You'd cut off my cock?"

"Damn right," Elijah said.

"What would you do with it?"

"Keep it," Elijah said.

"Keep it?"

"Yeah, it's the only part of you I like."

Noah laughed again.

They remained silent for almost ten minutes before Noah spoke. "You know, Elijah. I've always heard people say they want to grow old together. Now I know what it means."

"You can grow old by yourself. I'll always be young and beautiful," Elijah said.

"Elijah, I'm being serious."

"I'm sorry. Go ahead. Finish what you were saying, sugar."

"Well, you've ruined the mood now," said Noah. "I'm glad we're together is all."

"Me too." Elijah wanted to giggle at the sentimentality. After years of knowing Noah, he still found comfort in his warmth. "You want to know something?" Elijah asked.

"What?"

"I hope I die young."

"You hope you die young? Why the hell would you say something like that?" Noah sat up on the couch, breaking the cuddle.

"Never mind," said Elijah, who sat up as well.

"Never mind? You can't say something like that and then say never mind."

"I didn't really mean that," Elijah said, before adding a quick chuckle. "But bad things can happen."

Noah turned to make out Elijah's facial expression, but the room's darkness hindered his efforts.

Sensing Noah's concern, Elijah said, "I hope I die with my pants down. That way when you find my dead body, you can fuck me one last time before the rigor mortis sets in."

Noah laughed like a silly cartoon character.

Elijah looked at Noah. "Then I'll scare the hell out of you because when you get ready to cum, I'm going to resurrect."

The cartoonish cackle sounded off again.

Hopefully we'll pass away together, Elijah thought, as his husband's laughter died down.

Minutes later, he said, "I know I just ate, but I'm still kind of hungry."

"There are some chips in the cupboard," Noah said.

"Cupboard," Elijah repeated, with a laugh.

"What's so funny?" asked Noah.

"White people."

"What does that mean?"

"Nothing, sugar," Elijah said, with a grin.

"Whatever." Noah waved his hand as if he were shooing away a fly. Then he whispered Elijah's name.

"What?"

"You're not a bad person," Noah said.

⁂

That night, just after bathing together, they hugged each other, standing in the bedroom beside the four-poster bed Elijah had picked out from an antique store two weeks before. The only light they had to guide them came from the bathroom door, which was slightly cracked. The moon and the streetlights were of no use to them, since the blinds were closed. The light that could have seeped through the blinds met with resistance from the curtains.

"What are you doing?" Elijah asked.

Noah responded by continuing a slow dance that Elijah thought was silly and cute at the same time. Elijah looked at the water on his husband's body and the chain that hung around Noah's neck, bearing a Star of David that was shining despite the dim lighting.

"Cut it out."

"You don't like the way I dance?" Noah asked.

"You have zero coordination and zero rhythm." Elijah smiled as he caught his towel before it fell from his waist.

"Take it off completely," Noah said, taking slow steps toward his spouse, with one corner of his mouth curled upward.

Elijah recognized Noah's look: the squinting of the eyes, the clenching of the jaws, the licking of the lips.

"I'm not in the mood for that."

"Yes, you are." Noah kissed him on the neck, the tender part that made Elijah giggle and raise his shoulders toward his ears.

Before they could remember to turn off the bathroom lights, their towels were on the floor, and they were in bed. Elijah lay still, facing up, until Noah's lips made Elijah's back curl and his chest inch toward the ceiling. Noah found the two most tender parts of Elijah's chest, causing him to hum softly and rub his hand through Noah's long, curly hair, which was still moist from the bath.

"Noah," Elijah said as his back curled upward. It arched again as he called out his husband's name once more. Then he closed his eyes and said, "Daddy, you feel so good."

Noah answered with his tongue, gently sliding it from nipple to nipple, nibbling each one until that dark hand touched his hair, until hearing the word *Daddy* in musical repetition, until he could no longer control the urge to explore other areas of his spouse's body. He kissed Elijah downward, stopping at the navel and kissing until Elijah called his name, a call prompting him to continue. He stayed there as Elijah moved around and wrinkled the sheets with each sensation. Noah understood and remained there a while longer until he moved downward more and more and more and kissed his feet, working his way up the ankles to the inner thigh. That was when Elijah's hums turned into shouts. Noah held one thigh and licked the other, breathing deeply to savor Elijah's fragrance.

He switched to the other thigh and was met with more shouts. Eyes closed and still inhaling, Noah tasted more of his spouse's inner thigh, slowly and methodically, as if it would be painful to move at a faster pace. That was what Elijah wanted, time taken, as he fondled his own nipples, as Noah's strong hands raised Elijah's little legs in the air. The back of his legs felt cold compared to the warmth of being pressed on the sheets, but there was no shock, since Elijah knew what was about to happen next. He continued to fondle his own nipples, closing his eyes, only to open them and let out another shout as Noah moistened him between the cheeks with an up and down motion of his tongue. Elijah felt his husband's nose and tongue moving up and down, and he begged for more, screamed for more.

A warm feeling started at the point where Noah's tongue touched, and the sensation spread throughout Elijah's body and poured from his vocal cords in a soprano. After hitting the last note, Elijah could tell his husband loved his voice, because Noah applauded not with his hands, but with the tip of his tongue. When Noah put Elijah's legs back to the sheets, Elijah closed his eyes to feel the kissing that started at his feet before working its way up his right leg then to the navel then between the nipples and then toward the tender part of the neck. The sensation stopped there, and it felt cold and warm at the same time until he felt his left ear being nibbled. That was when he began to pant and moan at once. It seemed as though this was Noah's cue to finally touch his lips to Elijah's.

Noah's lips were soft, making Elijah recall the first time they'd kissed years before. This time was better because this place—their place—gave them room to sing with passion and time to sing with patience and comfort to sing with ease. Elijah forgot how to open his eyes when he felt Noah's tongue touch his, maintaining the same gentility that was introduced to his feet and inner thigh and navel and nipples and that tender part of the neck that made his shoulders curl toward his ears and his chest toward the ceiling. Feeling Noah's facial hair sent a tingle through him, as if he were being kissed all over. Noah's chest hair rubbed Elijah's nipples to bring forth another shout, except Noah's lips covered Elijah's, turning the shout into a moan that seemed to give Noah another cue.

He watched Noah prop himself up from the bed and gaze down. Elijah looked up at him, then closed his eyes. Noah opened them with a kiss, and Elijah saw the Star of David swing back and forth from Noah's chain. He positioned himself between Elijah's legs, prying them open with a snakelike motion of his long body. Instinctively, Elijah spread his knees apart and put his hands on his husband's hairy stomach to brace himself and guide Noah's entry. But the hands on the stomach never worked, because it seemed as though Noah always overpowered Elijah's little hands, and this time would be no different. Elijah understood that positioning his hands near Noah's navel was in vain, but his fear always made them go upward to feel the curly hair that went from Noah's navel and led all the way to the part of Noah's body that was about to make Elijah moan.

"Are you okay?" Noah asked.

"Yes, sir," Elijah said, though he wasn't okay, nor did he want to be. There was something desirable about having the man he loved lie on top of him and overpower him. He didn't need to be forced, since being dominated was already his desire. Noah knew as much but chose to release his carnal desires anyway by manhandling his weak little spouse. It made Elijah love Noah that much more.

"Don't hurt me, Noah."

"I can't guarantee it won't hurt, but I'll try to be gentle."

"You promise?"

"Yes, I promise," Noah answered, in a whisper.

Elijah screamed when he felt Noah penetrate him. It hurt like hell but pleasured like heaven.

"Are you okay?" Noah asked.

"Yes, sir."

Then Elijah felt the in and out of Noah and the pressure of his husband on top of him, as Noah found a rhythm he had never exhibited before. Elijah closed his weeping eyes each time he was filled with Noah, who wiped the tears away as they rolled gently down the sides of Elijah's face. Noah's touch, combined with the pressure of his body and his newfound rhythm, made Elijah feel better than he'd ever felt before. A tingling warmth emerged in the area where Noah stroked the deepest, and it spread throughout Elijah's feminine area and then throughout his boyish area and then throughout his entire body. After the sensation ran across his nipples and traversed the tender part of his neck, his mouth opened, and he sang a high-pitched note. He opened his eyes and saw Noah smile and tremble and let out a note of his own, except Noah's note was deep and strong and accompanied with shakes of his body. He cried again as Noah wiped more tears away from the sides of his soft face.

Then Elijah spoke. "It was the Romans who murdered Him."

"What?" asked Noah, still stroking.

Elijah responded with an intense moan that Noah appreciated like Old Testament scripture.

"I love you, Elijah." Noah made the Star of David stop swinging.

"I love you too."

Noah quickly removed his penis and placed his body above his open-mouthed spouse. And that was the point when Elijah finally had a Jewish martini—a sexual, interreligious communion.

After the Judeo-Christian anal service, Elijah felt Noah grab him and bring him to his chest. They remained cuddled in that position, with Noah looking up at the ceiling and Elijah lying on his husband's chest. Elijah looked at the Star of David, shining through the darkness. Without speaking another word, he began to fall asleep in his husband's warm arms, listening to the rhythm of Noah's heartbeat and thinking, *It really does taste like vermouth.*

But this type of cuddle wasn't enough for Noah, whose penis was still erect, so he turned Elijah on his side as he himself did the same, putting his chest against Elijah's back. Then he put his penis back into Elijah's moist rectum and heard his spouse groan from a sharp pain that quickly subsided. He then put his arm around Elijah, and they both fell asleep just like that, with Noah's still-erect penis in Elijah.

Having Noah inside him made Elijah sleep better. Noah's penis was like a pacifier that was shoved in the wrong hole.

♒

The next morning, his husband's shuffling and outward stroke awoke Elijah as Noah removed the penile pacifier from his black child and got out of bed. Elijah wanted to cry for his daddy to come back and father him as he watched Noah stand in front of the toilet and relieve himself. Elijah then heard the sound of water spewing from the showerhead and continued sitting up in bed. He thought about Grayson for the first time in a while but didn't get sad. With Noah, there was no need for levitation and rainbows and sugar in the hands.

The authenticity in his life made him ignore the family that had shunned him. Walking into a restaurant full of staring eyes didn't bother him as much anymore; the shaking of the hands and the sweating of his forehead gave way to an embracing of his girlishness, the quality he had desperately tried to conceal ever since he was a toddler who received matchbox cars and train sets and bottle rockets even though he had always wanted dolls and dollhouses and glitter. The past, he knew, couldn't be changed, but when he heard the squeak of the shower knobs followed by the hush of water, Elijah knew he was no longer that frightened girl anymore. He was a different girl now, one who was protected by Noah.

He put on his briefs and snatched one of Noah's button-down shirts from across a chair in the bedroom and decided that would be his outfit for the morning. Side by side, they stood in front of the sink brushing their teeth and gargling with mouthwash; they didn't say a word. When Noah left the bathroom, Elijah cupped his hands underneath the running faucet and brought water to his face and dried it with Noah's towel.

"Why are you putting on a suit?" Elijah asked.

"I have an important meeting today."

"With who?"

"The president of the college," Noah answered.

"Is something wrong?"

"Don't think so. I think it might be good news."

"Okay," Elijah said, and didn't press him further except to kiss him on the cheek and say, "Let me know how it goes."

"Why wouldn't I?" Noah kissed him back.

Then Elijah ambled away.

"Why are you walking like that?" Noah asked.

"I'm in pain."

"From what?"

"After the way you fucked me last night, I think I need hip replacement."

Noah laughed and said, "I'm sorry. Do you want me to get you some painkillers from the bathroom?"

"Yeah, but I won't take the pills orally. I'll stick them in my cat and let them dissolve. Maybe they'll work better that way."

Noah smiled. "Do you really need them?"

"No, I'm okay," Elijah said.

Noah then walked to the bed and put his lips to his spouse's forehead. "Elijah, I have to go."

"Okay, sugar," said Elijah, who watched him walk away. Then he said, "Noah."

"What?"

"I just wanted to thank you."

"Thank me for what?" Noah asked.

"Last night."

"What about last night?" Noah asked.

"Never mind."

"Go ahead. Tell me," Noah said.

"I wanted to thank you for cumming in my mouth."

"You're welcome," said Noah. "That's how much I love you."

"Really?"

"Yeah." Noah went back to the bathroom to relieve himself again.

Elijah watched while appreciating the sound.

"You could've bathed more thoroughly. I still smell like shit," Pube said.

"Shut up," Noah replied.

"Are you talking to your dick?" Elijah asked.

"Of course not," Noah said.

"It looked like you were."

"Do me a favor," Noah said.

"What?" Elijah asked.

"Remind me to shave my cock."

"No problem," Elijah said.

"I have to go."

"Okay. Bye, sugar."

"Bye," Noah said, as he picked up his briefcase and went to work.

As he always did, Elijah went to the window and peered out until he saw Noah's SUV go down the road. When Noah turned the corner and disappeared behind another building, he buttoned up Noah's shirt, which was much too big for Elijah, and made himself breakfast: a glass of orange juice and an omelet stuffed with ham and cheese with a little salt, pepper, and garlic sprinkled on top. Many of his mornings for the past month had been like this, but he didn't complain. The previous night had confirmed how the rest of his life would be, and he was content with what the future could bring. He hoped it would bring more of the lovemaking he'd had the night before. As he sat at the table, his mind—inspired by the sex—produced an idea. He thought of the sweet taste of Noah's Semitic semen. One day, he would ask Noah to masturbate and ejaculate on a piece of dark paper, and after Noah's semen dried, Elijah would laminate the sheet of paper, only to frame it and hang it on the wall. They would laugh when guests visited and complimented what they believed was abstract art.

The thought of that made Elijah yearn for another Jewish martini. He had never been much of a drinker, but he had become addicted to Israeli vermouth.

"We need some more orange juice," he said to himself, while cleaning up the mess he had made in the kitchen.

⌇⌇⌇

Later that day, just after hanging up the phone from Noah's usual lunchtime call, Elijah put on some clothes while thinking about the way his husband had felt inside him the night before. Wanting to smell like Noah, he didn't take a shower before heading to the grocery store.

The breeze coming in from the Atlantic made him fold his arms and walk briskly. He waved at those who looked at him and didn't think much of those who didn't, save for a woman sitting alone on a park bench. Rocking back and forth, she neither made eye contact nor waved; all she did was look at the building, as if to make sure it was still there. Elijah continued his brisk walk.

He thought about how warm it must be back in South Carolina. *They're probably walking around without jackets*, he thought to himself. *I'm glad I'm up here in this miserable cold.* He unfolded his arms, went into the grocery store, and, with Noah's credit card, bought more than orange juice: bread, iced tea, his husband's favorite brand of beer, cookie mix, the newspaper, and a magazine about interior design. That was about all he was willing to carry home without the benefit of their jeep or Mustang. Elijah asked the bagger for a paper bag instead of plastic.

"You have a nice day," the cashier said, while handing him the receipt.

"You too, sir," Elijah replied.

The paper bag blocked the breeze from hitting Elijah's left side as he retraced his footsteps. Minutes later, he approached the green park bench, and the woman was still there, rocking back and forth for reasons not apparent to Elijah. While approaching, he looked at her and was convinced she wasn't homeless after all. She was wearing a string of pearls around her neck, just above an ascot, tucked underneath a cashmere coat that had seen better days. Her black leather shoes were scuffed at the tips, but they still matched the leather gloves, which looked blacker, juxtaposed with off-white cashmere. Her shoes and gloves matched the purse she held to her side. She should've been wearing a hat to cover her hair, which had also seen better days, as it lay scattered atop her head like a borrowed wig. At least her makeup was flawless—the rouge that highlighted her cheeks, her crimson lipstick, her foundation so perfect it didn't look like foundation at all.

"How are you doing, young man?" Abby asked.

"I'm doing fine. How are you?" Elijah stopped walking just in front of her scuffed shoes.

"Wish I could tell you I'm just fine, but life hasn't given me a reason to say that."

"Sorry," was the only word Elijah could think to say as he positioned his bag on his other side.

Just as he began to walk away, she stopped him with this: "My husband and I used to live in that building right there."

"Really?" Elijah asked.

"Yes." Abby put her right hand to the side of her face, looked at the building, and said, "It's a beautiful place, isn't it?"

"Yes, it is. My husband and I love it," Elijah answered.

At that moment she looked up and resumed her inclination to rock back and forth.

"That's nice" was the only thing she said while placing her purse on her other side.

"It's pretty cold out here. You should go indoors where it's warm," Elijah said.

"I'm fine right here."

"Okay. Well, I have to get going. It was nice meeting you."

She didn't respond until Elijah started to walk away. "Young man."

"Yes?"

"I'm sure your husband is a good man. Keep him close," Abby said.

"I will." Elijah thought he saw a tear trickle down the side of her face, a tear that quickly turned to ice.

She glanced at the two men standing near the sidewalk.

Elijah looked as well and wondered who they were but didn't ask, not realizing they were police escorts who were monitoring her every move. Although her passport had been confiscated, they followed her to make sure she didn't flee the country. Still very wealthy, Abby had hired lawyers who negotiated a change of venue and her release on the condition that she had police escorts she was required to pay for with her own money. Abby herself realized she would be found guilty of double murder and arson the next day. Her lawyers had already prepared her, so she knew she would spend the rest of her life in a prison that was a far cry from the plantation house she had recently sold. But Abby took delight in knowing she would be the wealthiest woman in the penitentiary.

Elijah glanced at the spot on the bench beside her and thought he briefly saw a translucent red bow adorning what appeared to be a little girl. He took a step back and said, "Well, I have to go now. It was nice meeting you, Muriel."

"What did you say?" asked Abby, leaning forward.

"I said it was nice meeting you, ma'am."

"Oh, thought you said something else."

"Have a good day," Elijah said.

"Same to you," said Abby, as she watched him walk away.

If only Abby had decided against running up the stairs and hiding in bed that long-ago day in South Carolina, her sheets would have kept her warm instead of cold.

⚇

Later that evening, Elijah awoke with a shiver when Noah entered and startled him. Elijah had prepared dinner: baked chicken, corn, macaroni and cheese, and yeast rolls—but it had become cold before Noah had gotten the chance to eat it.

"Sorry I'm so late," said Noah.

Elijah looked at the tie hanging from Noah's neck and said, "I forgot about your meeting."

Noah flashed a big smile.

"What are you smiling for?"

"I got tenure."

"Already?"

"Yeah," Noah said.

Elijah went to his husband to be embraced. "I guess we need to celebrate."

"Let's celebrate the way we did last night." Noah kissed his spouse on the forehead.

"Do you want me to heat your food up?" Elijah asked.

"Yeah."

Noah sat at the head of the table, peering into the kitchen at Elijah, who was putting a plate of food in the microwave. After the *ding,* Elijah removed the plate and brought it to him.

"Thanks," Noah said.

Later that night, Elijah was the one saying thanks to Noah, who was massaging his back as Elijah lay on the floor in the bedroom.

"You remember when we first moved here and didn't have much furniture?" Elijah asked.

"Yeah, we've come a long way, haven't we?"

"Yes, we have," Elijah said.

"We have a nice condo together, the sex is hot…"

Elijah laughed and added, "And now your career has taken off."

"Yours will too." Noah placed his hands on Elijah's bottom. "I'll see one of your books on a shelf one day."

"You think so?" Elijah asked.

"I know so."

Elijah rolled over on his back, put his hands behind his head, looked up at the ceiling, and said, "You know what?"

"What?"

"I don't really want that anymore."

"You don't want any of your books published?" Noah asked.

"Not really. If it happens, it happens." Elijah's voice was filled with certainty. "I just want to be a writer, and I can do that right here."

"I guess you're right."

Elijah picked himself up from the floor and walked to the window. Noah sat down in a chair beside the bed. Elijah looked out and saw the woman; she was still rocking back and forth on the park bench. The people who passed by her didn't even look in her direction.

"Poor woman," Elijah said.

"Who?" Noah asked, getting up to stand behind him. He wrapped his arms around Elijah and put his lips to the side of Elijah's face. "I wonder what's wrong with her," he said.

"I've been wondering the same thing all day," Elijah replied.

"What?" Noah asked.

"Never mind," Elijah said, as he closed the blinds to make the woman disappear. "I wrote this poem while you were at work today. You want to hear it?"

"Yeah," Noah said, reassuming his position on the chair and watching Elijah fumble through a notebook.

"Okay, here it is," Elijah said.

Noah patted himself on the thighs. "Don't read it over there. Come sit on Daddy's lap."

Elijah did exactly as he was told.

"What is it called?" Noah asked.

"I don't have a title yet, but it'll come to me eventually."

"Okay. Read it."

When he felt Noah's arms wrap around his waist, Elijah knew he would see the Star of David swing back and forth that night, an experience that would be beautifully Jewish. And when he felt Noah kiss him on the cheek, Elijah Redwater Cohen leaned back into his husband's strong chest and read:

> The changing of fate opens a new gate,
> And something special is forgotten once more.
> Thoughts' constantly changing and minds' rearranging—
> Bring a masterpiece more precious than before.
> The emotion rages as the artwork ages,
> And the life of the canvas is repeatedly torn.
> Boredom intervened; the canvas is cleaned.
> A splendid work of art is quickly reborn.
> There is little fear as the death comes near,
> And soon the portrait shall fade into space.
> Taken at a glance, the art will enhance,
> And moments later, it will boast a new face.
> Resting on bare glass that cracks slowly whereas—
> A sturdy canvas is not bound to break.
> Pessimism is conceiving; optimism is disbelieving.

A remarkable reputation is repeatedly at stake.
The portrait's brilliance gives itself resilience,
And it always seems to keep its original form.
Words unspoken leave the silence unbroken,
And the level of respect sinks beyond the norm.
Standing with compassion while holding a new fashion,
Its future becomes a mere fraction of its past.
Its value is leaking—although still not speaking,
It tells how the paint vainly longs to last.
Human malevolence overpowers artistic benevolence—
Causing the beauty of the art to render everyone blind.
Death is on the way; there is nowhere else to stay.
Another place on the wall is truly difficult to find.
Once cherished like a child, the love has become mild,
And the painting will soon lack its wondrous joy.
It will find less healing with a mindless feeling,
For it is momentarily adored…Like a Child's New Toy.

www.ingramcontent.com/pod-product-compliance
Lightning Source LLC
Chambersburg PA
CBHW070221030726
47505CB00006B/1754